THE LATE
DOCTOR SAVAGE

THE LATE
DOCTOR SAVAGE

The Frank May Chronicles

Lawrence Friedman

A QP Mystery

QP BOOKS
New Orleans, Louisiana

THE LATE DOCTOR SAVAGE
The Frank May Chronicles

A QP Mystery, published in 2016 by QP Books.

QUID PRO, LLC
5860 Citrus Blvd., Suite D-101
New Orleans, Louisiana 70123
www.qpbooks.com

ISBN 978-1-61027-366-4 (paperback)
ISBN 978-1-61027-367-1 (eBook)

Publisher's Cataloging-in-Publication

Friedman, Lawrence.
    The Late Doctor Savage / Lawrence Friedman.
        p. cm.
    Series: *The Frank May Chronicles* (#10)
    ISBN 978-1-61027-366-4 (pbk.)

1. Lawyers—California—Fiction. 2. San Mateo (Cal.)—Fiction. 3. May, Frank (Fictitious character)—Fiction. I. Friedman, Lawrence. II. Title. III. Series.
PS357.F729 2016   813.'2'7251—dc22
                                                          20165414731
                                                                  CIP

for Leah, Jane, Amy, Sarah,
David, Lucy, and Irene

THE LATE
DOCTOR SAVAGE

1

I was enjoying a quiet evening at home. It was a cool, refreshing evening. We specialize in that kind of evening, here in northern California. I was watching a television program when my wife Celia showed me an item in the *San Mateo Daily*; and that item dragged me, unwillingly, into an affair that I would have gladly avoided.

It was, as I said, just a normal middle-class evening. The girls (my two teenaged daughters) were away at the house of some friend. They were working, they said, on a project for their high school history class. This was quite possibly a lie; but like many parents, I had long ago given up the struggle for effective control. So long as they don't get pregnant, or expelled from school, or arrested for shoplifting, I let them do most of what they want. They get decent grades, on the whole. We never got ominous calls from the principal. Sometimes, the two girls even got along with each other. So I have no real complaints.

My name is Frank May. I'm in my 40's—the exact age doesn't matter, does it?—and I'm a member of the California bar. A lawyer, in other words. I have my own practice. I'm what's called a solo practitioner, which means I have no partners. There's a firm called Baker & McKenzie that consists of 3,000 or so lawyers. That seems absolutely appalling to me. It evokes this fantasy of mine: I'm a member of this firm, I go to a cocktail party, and I meet this guy; I tell him I'm a lawyer, and I ask him, what do you do for a living? And he says, "Jerk, I'm your partner."

That's would never be my problem. I have no partners at all, let alone thousands.

When one of the kings of Saudi Arabia died, he left behind 70 sons (according to the obituary in the newspaper). Daughters were apparently not worth mentioning. I can imagine some sort of affair where this young man goes up to the King, and says hello, and when the King says, "Who are you?" The man answers, "I'm your son, I'm number 63."

Saudi Arabia has nothing whatsoever to do with this narrative. Except that my story does concern a father, who, although he had only one child, a daughter, might have passed her on the street, and have no idea who she was. But more on that later.

As I said, I'm a lawyer. I have an office in San Mateo, California. San Mateo is a suburb of San Francisco. It's some miles south of San Francisco, down the peninsula. I have a general practice. Of course, a "general practice" doesn't mean I do everything. I don't do criminal law. I don't do patents. And I dislike divorces, though I have handled a few. Mainly I do estate work: wills, trusts, estate planning, probate—work of that nature. It's an important field of law—less glamorous than litigation or representing Google in China or doing entertainment law and meeting the stars; but it impacts the lives of millions of people. Mostly people with money, to be sure.

The whole field is based on one simple, basic premise, from which everything else follows: you can't take it with you. That being the case, something has to be done with your worldly goods. If you have money, and family, it's best to make a plan before you die. I help people do that. If you don't have family, it's even more important.

Anyway, that evening, I was watching television, half asleep. The local public station was on. It was quite a boring night: first, because it was pledge night, which the station really needs but is essentially intolerable; second, because the show that the pleas for money interrupted was about somebody's travels through the Balkans, including Albania and Kosovo. I have trouble working up an interest in the Balkans, especially

Albania and Kosovo. They are not on my list of places to visit before I die. The feeling might be mutual, as far as I know.

Celia was reading the *San Mateo Daily,* one of those free local newspapers that land on our driveway once a week. I suppose it has to be free, otherwise nobody would read it. It is, however, extremely valuable if you are looking for a used car, or are interested in who won the high school soccer game. I fall into neither category. "Frank," she said, "don't you have a client named Savage? I think you mentioned her. A young woman."

"I do. Ashley Savage. Don't tell me she's in the newspaper."

"No, not an Ashley Savage. Somebody named Langley Savage."

The name rang a bell but only vaguely. I thought I had heard it somewhere before. But I said, "I don't think I know anybody named Langley Savage. What did he do?"

"He didn't do anything. He was a victim. Somebody killed him. Shot him to death. In Palo Alto. He was in a hotel room."

"People don't get killed in Palo Alto," I said. "They've got an ordinance forbidding it. It's a very upscale community. Steve Jobs lived there. It's infested with people who start companies, and there's also a sprinkling of Chinese millionaires."

"Don't be obnoxious, Frank. Anyway, I'm relieved to hear you don't know this Langley Savage. You seem to get tangled up in one murder after another. I'm beginning to wonder."

"Wonder away," I said. I looked back at the television screen. The pledge break was over. The traveler in the Balkans had just crossed the frontier into Croatia.

"He was registered under a different name," Celia said. "That's odd, isn't it? The paper said there were 'suspicious circumstances.'"

"I should think it's suspicious in itself, if you're shot dead in Palo Alto," I said.

"It says that an investigation is going on, but no arrests have been made. And, oh yes, it says he was a doctor."

"A doctor?" I began to be slightly alarmed. Ashley Savage, my client, had told me her father was a doctor. She also told me she had never seen the man. Ashley had come to me about a month before this with a very strange tale, and a very strange problem; but I'll get to that shortly.

"Yes, a doctor," Celia said. "It doesn't say what kind of doctor, though."

I had a sinking feeling in the pit of my stomach. How many doctors named Savage could there be? Yes, more than one I suppose. Yet my gut was telling me that *this* Dr. Savage was Ashley's father. And I had this awful fear that, whether I wanted to or not, I was in danger of getting involved, against my better judgment. Assuming I have a better judgment.

Celia is extremely acute. She reads me like a book. "Frank," she said, "I can see from your face that this man has some connection with your client."

It would be wrong to say I cannot tell a lie. I can. But only certain lies. "Celia dear," I said, "I'm not sure, but I do think this might be my client's father."

She put down the paper and gave me a stern and serious look.

"Frank," she said. "Promise me you'll stay out of it. Promise me."

I promised. But this was a promise I was almost certain to break ... and of course I did.

2

But let me go back a step. I remember the first time I saw Ashley Savage. It was a gloomy December day, hints of rain in the air, and big puffs of blackish clouds in the sky. The days are short in December, and the dark closes in early. Celia and I had been talking of some sort of mini-vacation. She teaches high school and classes were over. We talked about heading south for more sunshine.

Still, I never turn down a new client, if that client seems promising. Ashley Savage called me on the phone, out of the blue. "Mr. May?" she said, "you don't know me. My name is Ashley Savage. I have a problem, well, a legal problem; it's a bit difficult to explain. It has to do with a trust fund. You were recommended to me. I'd like to come see you, as soon as possible."

"No problem. When would you like to come?"

"Thursday. The day after tomorrow."

We set a time. I asked her who had recommended me. "A woman I know. We go bird-watching together. Her name is Doris Mobius."

"Oh, yes. Of course. I know Doris."

"She said you do estate work, estate planning, wills—that kind of thing."

"I do. And you have a problem you said. Something about a trust."

"It's a long story," she said. "I had better tell you in person."

She came promptly at 3:00 on Thursday afternoon. I remember that session vividly. She was a woman in her late 20's, I would say. She was a striking figure, with long dark hair, a thin face, but attractive features. She seemed to smile only rarely. She seemed sensible, business-like. Serious. She had a habit of running her fingers through her hair. I'm not very good at judging people by their looks—Celia is much better—but somehow I had an impression of a strong but lonely woman, self-sufficient but unsatisfied. Or maybe this is just something I intuited after I heard her story. Quite an unusual story, to be sure.

She said, "I have a problem.... I'm the beneficiary of a trust. It's quite a lot of money ... but, well, there's an issue."

"An issue?"

"If you suddenly came into money," she said, "and you told people, they'd congratulate you. If you won the lottery, for instance. But this is different. It's all very peculiar."

"I'm listening. And I'm used to peculiar."

She paused then began. "I'm afraid I have to give you some of the background. I work at Stanford University, by the way. I'm in the development office, you know, that's a fancy word for fundraising. I do major gifts. Anyway that's not particularly important. I'm 28; I grew up around here. My mother and stepfather, they live in Portola Valley. I never met my biological father. My birth parents were never married, but my mother, well, she was ashamed of this, you know, people talk; and she lived in a small town in eastern California, it was something of a scandal, and she was young; her family was very religious; and the guy, my father, the guy who got her pregnant, he wanted her to have an abortion, but she wouldn't, and he washed his hands of the whole thing. I guess he said to her, well, that's your decision, count me out. So she moved out of that town, came to the Bay Area, had the child, which was me, got a job, and claimed to be a widow. Not that anybody cares about that sort of thing today, whether your parents were married or not, but in her day, her town, and in her family, it made a difference. It was a scandal. Anyway, she thought so."

"And after you were born, your father, did he ... well, take any interest in you?"

"Apparently, he just didn't care. He didn't want a child. He made that very clear to my mother at the outset. As I told you, he more or less said you can have your damn baby, but I won't lift a finger to help—and my mother, she had to agree. He had family in the town, prominent people, I suppose they spoiled him. He was an only child, and his father owned half the town, although I heard that he went broke later on. I never knew any of them, any of that clan. My father, at the time he got my mother pregnant, he was a medical student in San Francisco. He came back to the town on holidays, and ... I honestly don't know how they got together, he and my mother. I guess he felt the whole business was a youthful mistake, maybe they were at a party, maybe he was drinking, I can't imagine my mother drinking, but she was young then. Doesn't matter. When she wouldn't get an abortion, that did it for him. I guess he would have paid for an abortion, but she wouldn't do it. I think I told you her family was religious. My father was, I suppose, a pretty ruthless person. Mother never talked about him. She pretended to be a widow, as I said, so she took his name: Savage. Pretty appropriate name. For him, anyway. That's why I'm Ashley Savage."

"And you never saw him?"

"Never. Mother married a guy, later on, named Joe Woods. He was older than she was, divorced, an insurance broker. I never liked him particularly, to tell you the truth, and I never really thought of him as a real father. He never adopted me, either. Maybe the feeling was mutual. Don't get me wrong. He was a decent man, in his own way, he made a good living, and he got along with mother. I don't think they really loved each other, but what do I know? I was treated well, to the outside world they looked like good parents; but they weren't. Oh, nobody beat me or yelled at me, but they didn't really want me. I don't want to say I was like Cinderella with her stepsisters, it wasn't like that. They treated me OK; but there was no warmth. At least that's the way it felt to me. To my mother, I was a constant reminder of her sins. She had become some sort of born-again fanatic. And my stepfather, well, to him I was like a foster child, nothing more than that, not really part of the family. I mean, that's the way it felt to me. Anyway, he died a couple of years ago. Stomach cancer. It was pretty gruesome. Oh, yes, I also have a half-sister and a half-brother. But they're much younger than I am, and I never felt close to them. They were the favorites. I was the outsider."

"You live with your mother?"

"No, I don't. I have an apartment. Mother and I are such different people. We don't quarrel but we just aren't close. I guess I was always something of a loner. I felt I never fit in, like I told you. Well, I grew up; we all do, don't we? I was pretty much of a handful when I was an adolescent, but that's all over now. I went to college. San Francisco State. I wanted to go to Stanford, but I didn't have the grades. I wanted to be independent. I wanted to be on my own. I was looking for something, and I never found it. It was like, something was missing. You must be wondering, why am I telling you all this, why am I getting so personal, but ... well, it's because of my father."

"He came back into the picture?"

"Maybe. Remember, I never had any contact with him. And mother never talked about him. I mean, it seems ridiculous, but she's still thinking this was a scandal. Of course, now, who cares? In San Francisco these days, anything goes. Having children without getting married, that's the norm, not the exception. Somehow my mother never caught on. Anyway: my father. I guess somehow I knew he was practicing medicine somewhere in the Bay Area, but we never met. And of course I had no notion that my father had any interest in *me*; and that was fine. He was nothing to me. As I said, I never met him. And no contact. Until last year."

"Last year. What happened then?"

"I got the strangest message. It was from an attorney in San Francisco, Gideon Grambling. Do you know him?"

"Actually, I do." In fact, I can't stand Grambling. He was the kind of lawyer I loathe—arrogant, self-centered, and, I'm afraid, somewhat manipulative. But he has a good reputation, and has very wealthy clients. My dealings with him have always been unpleasant, but there was no need to mention this to Ashley.

"He called me, and he told me that he had some information that would be extremely important to me; that somebody had set up a trust fund on my behalf, and that he was the co-trustee, and the trust fund was quite substantial. I said, I don't understand, I don't know anything about trusts, I'm not even sure what they are; and what do you mean when you say, 'substantial.' He seemed really pompous...."

"That's Gideon," I said.

"Anyway, he said, well, the principal is invested in marketable securities, excellent securities, he said, and the value fluctuates, of course, with the market, and so it isn't possible to give you an exact figure, as if I didn't know that, but at today's quotes (he said) I would estimate that the principal amounts to approximately $8,000,000. Then he went on and on about quarterly payments of the income, and his best estimate of what that income might be, and so on. And I barely heard what hc was saying, I was so shocked and surprised, and there he was, spewing these lawyer phrases, jargon, and he seemed totally unaware of how a person would react to this kind of news. I mean, millions of dollars dropped down out of heaven. And I even wondered if this was some kind of practical joke, so I said, look, what is this all about, I don't believe a word you're saying, but he said, oh, it's true, and I can provide you with documentation; and in any event, you will begin receiving the payments shortly."

She went on: "I kept saying, there must be some mistake, are you sure you have the right person? But there was no mistake, he said, you are Ashley Savage, are you not, at such and such an address, and he even knew my social security number. But where does this money come from, I asked him. He refused point-blank to tell me who set this trust up, or to provide me with a copy ... though he said, at some point, I might provide you with a 'redacted' copy: that's the word he used, 'redacted.' He said the 'settlor,' the man who established this trust—well, at least I knew it was a man—wishes to remain anonymous. The trustee, the manager of this thing, well, that's

Grambling himself, he said, along with some bank in San Jose. And then he went on and on again, how the payments are going to go on for the rest of my life, and when I die, the trust ends and my children inherit, if I have any, and if there are no children, the money goes to a bunch of charities. And he mentioned them, but I don't even remember what they were, I was so confused. I couldn't really believe any of this. I know, there are people who win the lottery, but I never bought a lottery ticket in my life. And here I've won the lottery, in a way. At least that's what he told me. He also said that it would be best if I said nothing about this to my family. Well, I've done that. It's not something I want to advertise. Not at this point. So I haven't told anybody about this. Not even mother. Especially not mother."

"Why especially not your mother?"

"Because the money must come from my father. I mean, who else? And he's the one who set the trust up. You'll hear the rest of the story, and it'll be clear to you. Grambling added that the donor also wishes you to have a gift, a very valuable gift, and it will be delivered to you in a day or two. Then I did receive a package. I opened it up, and it was a beautiful doll.... Porcelain, with blonde hair, and shiny eyes."

"A doll?"

"Yes.... A doll. Grambling said it was valuable, and I checked on it, I asked somebody who knows about these things, an antique dealer who sells old dolls, and he said, yes, it was an antique and worth a lot of money. I called Grambling and I said, look, put yourself in my place, all this is just too mysterious. Where does this money come from? And he hemmed and hawed, and said he was not at liberty, and so on. But I knew where it came from. I just knew. And then my hunch was confirmed. It was my father. Just as I suspected."

"Confirmed? He spoke to you?"

"No. Not then, anyway. But here's what happened: I got a call from somebody named Christopher Risley, and he asked is this Ashley Savage, and I said yes. And is your father a doctor named Langley Savage? I said, why are you asking? He said, well, is he or isn't he? And I said, actually he is. But my father and mother are divorced—well, that was a little white lie—I told him, I'm not in contact with my father, I wouldn't know him if I met him on the street. And this guy said, please don't lie to me. So I said, I'm not in the habit of lying, and who are you anyway? Why should I talk to you? And he said, well, you'll hear from my lawyer soon enough, and then you'll know. I mean, he was quite nasty."

"And *did* you hear from his lawyer?"

"Oh yes, I did. It turns out, Mr. May...."

"Please call me Frank."

"It turns out, Frank, that not only did I suddenly become the beneficiary of a trust worth eight million dollars, I also became the defendant, or the potential defendant, in a lawsuit. Over the same eight million dollars. I suppose if I lose the suit, it would be a case of easy come, easy go."

"But what is this lawsuit about?"

"It's about my father. He's sort of a fugitive from justice. Maybe not literally. But this man, this Christopher Risley, he and his family are making some serious accusations against my father. Very serious. Like: he stole this money. The eight million and who knows what else. Stole it from the Risley family."

"How did that happen?" I asked.

"I think this might explain things," she said, and she handed me a folder. Inside were several newspaper clippings. "Read these," she said.

The first was an obituary of a woman named Hortense Risley, who died at the age of 99, in the South Bay Hospital in San Jose, California, about a year before this. Hortense Risley, according to the story, had been an enormously wealthy woman. She was the only child of Simon Risley, the "titanium king," whose mineral holdings, real estate, and other investments were valued, when he died, at several hundred million—and that had been in 1975. He was a widower, and he left his entire estate to his only child, his daughter Hortense. According to the article, Hortense had been a very shy and reclusive woman, brought up very strictly, and educated in Catholic schools. At the age of 40, against the wishes of her father, she married a scoundrel named Claus, who claimed to be a member of European aristocracy but was in fact an American swindler. She had a son with Claus but quickly became disillusioned with him, since he was unsavory, unfaithful, and abusive. Simon Risley paid him a substantial amount of money to get him out of Hortense's life. Hortense got a divorce. Claus died—in prison—in 1995. Hortense took back her maiden name and insisted on using the name Risley for her son as well (in fact, she named him Simon Risley II). Simon, alas, apparently took after his father; he was thrown out of several colleges and died fairly young, of complications from diabetes, made worse by drugs and alcohol. He left behind four children, and a wife (his fifth).

All this was in the clipping, which ran to two pages. Normally, I am a faithful reader of newspapers, and especially the obituaries, since, after all, the affairs of dead people are my bread and butter. Somehow I had missed this particular obituary. I might have been on vacation. Anyway, Hortense, particularly after her father died and her son shortly afterwards, became something of a recluse. She owned condos in London, New York, and Paris, but she never went near any of these; she lived in the Big Sur area, where she owned a sprawling estate. She never entertained guests or even had visitors. Then, at the age of 84, she was admitted to the hospital in San Jose. She complained about terrible pains in her legs, and a rash on her face, which she was convinced was some sort of horrible and fatal kind of cancer. Apparently, the hospital had a kind of super-suite for very rich patients; once Hortense was ensconced in this suite, she never left. For fifteen years, in fact. The pains in her legs went away under the ministrations of a podiatrist, Peter Christoff; and the facial rash responded to treatment as well. She was, in fact, quite healthy for a woman of her age—and she lived to be 99, after all. Still, Hortense had decided that the hospital was where she wanted to live. She had the money to make sure people did what she wanted. She stayed in that suite until she died. During those years, she had virtually no visitors. Indeed, most of the time she refused to see visitors, even her grandchildren.

Hospitals, of course, do not normally function as luxury hotels. But then again, patients are rarely as rich as Hortense Risley. Rich and generous. She was quite lavish in her gifts to the hospital, and to the hospital personnel. She contributed millions to the hospital. The only string she attached to the gifts was that her gifts should be totally anonymous. She was also— and this is more controversial—amazingly generous to the staff that cared for her. Three people in particular: Dr. Langley Savage, her chief physician; Dr. Peter Christoff, the podiatrist, who came every day and massaged her feet; and Matilda Barbash, her personal nurse. She surrounded herself with her doll collection and dozens of stuffed animals. Not only did she never leave the hospital, she never left the suite she lived in. She watched television and played gin rummy with the nurse. Her physical health remained quite good until the last five or so years of her life, when she began to go downhill. At the end, she was seriously demented. This, as is often the case, was something that developed slowly. But in the last years she recognized almost nobody, became incontinent, and was essentially bedridden.

Now she was dead. The newspaper said nothing about a will, whether she had one, and if there was a will, what its provisions were. But the newspaper account did mention a lawsuit. Christopher Risley, her oldest grandchild, had filed suit on behalf of the family against Dr. Savage, Dr. Christoff, nurse Barbash, and the hospital itself, alleging they had plundered Hortense's estate of millions and millions of dollars in assets. The family's lawyer, Wentworth Fain, a partner in a fancy San Francisco firm, made a statement to the effect that the grandchildren had an "iron-clad case." Of course, he was expected to say that. He was quoted as follows: "Dr. Savage induced this old, frail woman to grant him power of attorney. He then took control of her vast income, cashing her dividend checks, buying and selling stocks, and transferring huge sums to accounts in the Cayman Islands. Dr. Christoff and nurse Barbash shared in this plunder. They were at least accessories, and they also profited, in exchange for their silence and complicity." There were no details about the claims against the hospital.

"Quite a story," I said.

"But you see my problem, Frank," she said. "I need your advice. What should I do about all this? Suppose this money does come from my father, which seems pretty certain. It might be stolen money, or illegal money, I don't know what. And now they're going to sue me."

"I wouldn't worry too much about the lawsuit," I said. "I don't see how this Christopher Risley has any claim against you. It's against the trust, the trustees, or whoever is managing it. That's not you. And you haven't gotten a penny of the money yet."

"But what if I do get money? Grambling said I would."

"Here's what I'd do. If you get a check, put the money in a bank account. A special account. Open up an account and call it 'trust money,' or whatever you want to call it, but keep it strictly separate from the rest of your money. And don't spend a dime of it unless there's some sort of dire emergency. Meanwhile, we'll wait and see what happens."

"And what do you think is going to happen, Frank? What are we waiting to see?"

"We're waiting to see how the lawsuit turns out. If the money doesn't belong to your father, he's going to have to give it back. But maybe not all of it. Look: Gideon Grambling is a pretty cautious guy.... He must have looked into this, and he decided it was worth the risk. After all, it's not a risk for him. The risk is for your father."

She nodded. She seemed relieved.

"It's only temporary," I said. "But ... this way, you're protected. So long as you don't spend the money."

When she left, I leaned back in my chair and thought about the situation. It was certainly unusual. And somewhat sordid. I had never met Dr. Langley Savage (and never would), but he seemed like something less than a model citizen. Did I really want to get involved in this mess?

And: would I make any money out of it? I'm not mercenary, but I have a mortgage and a family; the practice of law is the source of my income, it's the way I put food on the table. It's hard enough to collect fees from some of my clients. If the trust turned out to be legal, Ashley might well be a valuable client. A trust beneficiary, with some eight million dollars in her trust would be, normally speaking, an excellent client. Normally speaking. But this was far from normal. Ashley Savage's affairs might turn into a colossal headache, with very little in the way of fees at the end of it.

And this was even before Dr. Langley Savage met his end: before he was found dead in a hotel room, with a bullet in his brain, lying on the bed with a beautiful antique doll on either side of his body.

3

When I read about the murder in the newspaper—or, rather, when Celia saw the news and passed it on to me—I thought: not again. Why do these things happen to me? Or to my clients? It has to be some sort of statistical freak. I mean, Adam Finkel, the guy who teaches math at Celia's school, the guy with the terrible complexion, is an expert on probability; and he once tried to explain to me the laws of probability. "Suppose you toss a coin," he said, "and it comes up tails ten times in a row. What's the chance the next toss will come up tails?"

"Pretty high," I said, "because there's something wrong with the coin."

That wasn't the right answer of course. I felt like asking Adam what the chances are that several clients in a row either get murdered, or murder somebody, or become entangled in a murder. But I held my tongue.

The next day I called Ashley at her work number. "Terrible thing, about your father," I said.

She said. "It's an awful shock, Frank. But you have to remember, I never saw him in my life. Now I never will. He's dead. Does this complicate things, I mean, him being dead?"

"I think so," I said.

"I said I never saw him. But I spoke to him once on the phone."

"You did?"

"It was after our conversation.... Frank, I have to come see you again. I need to tell you about what happened ... and I'm going to need more advice."

When she arrived, she seemed upset. I offered her coffee, but she refused. "Frank," she said, "I don't know what to do. The man never paid any attention to me from the day I was born, and then suddenly he butts into my life; and then just as suddenly, he's dead."

"You said he called you."

"He did. He said he wanted to see me. He said he was staying in a hotel, in Palo Alto, for the time being at least, and would I come see him. He gave me the room number, even. He said, 'I'm at the Intercontinental Hotel, in Palo Alto. I'm registered under the name of S. Langley. I'm in Room 706.'"

"And what did you say?"

"I said, frankly, I don't want to see you. And I don't want your money. I'm doing OK, I said, I've got a life, I've got a job; and anyway, this is supposedly stolen money. He said, it's not stolen. I know what you think, don't believe all the stuff in the newspapers. That old lady gave me the money. She gave me power of attorney. She didn't need the money, she was filthy rich. And I took care of her. She got value for the money, believe me. I said, I don't care; and anyway, why, after all these years, did you decide you had a daughter? You never paid any attention to me, so why now ... why give me money? He said that's why I want to see you. I want to explain it to you. I know I haven't been a good father. I said, well, that's an understatement. You haven't been a father at all. He said, I know that, and I want to make amends."

"And did you agree to go see him?"

"No," she said. "I told him I wouldn't. He seemed disappointed, but he said he could respect my decision. Maybe later on. And when I put down the phone, I felt, well, a little disappointed with myself. Had I done the right thing? Anyway, I had a breakfast meeting, in Palo Alto, at the Intercontinental. This was later on. The date is significant, as you'll see. Well, I had the meeting, the usual boring stuff; and after it was over, and I said goodbye, I thought, well, here I am in downtown Palo Alto, at the very hotel my father is staying at. And I looked around the room, the breakfast room, and I thought, for all I know, he's here and I don't even recognize him. I said to myself, I don't feel like going right back to the office; maybe it's fate or something like that. I knew his room number after all. So I went up to the room, and I knocked on the door. This was some time in the morning. Pretty early, but I honestly don't remember the exact time."

"And what happened?"

"Nothing. Nobody answered. Well, I thought, he isn't in. Nothing surprising about that. But you see, my attitude had changed. Somewhat. I felt frustrated. Disappointed. So I thought, should I leave him a note? I went back and forth in my mind about that. And in the end, I decided to do it. So I went to the desk, and I said, I'd like to leave a note for Mr. Langley, in room so-and-so. And the clerk said, would you like me to call him? He's in his room. And I said, no, he isn't, I knocked on the door, and nobody answered. And the clerk said, oh, well, I haven't seen him this morning, but this is a big hotel, and I don't recognize most of the guests, so I suppose he went out, and naturally I wouldn't notice. Which is true, of course. It's a big hotel, like I said. I must say though that the clerk, I don't know his name, the receptionist, a young guy, seemed keenly aware of my father. But maybe I'm just imagining this."

"Did you leave the note?"

"No, I didn't. I changed my mind. I thought, a note, that won't mean anything. So I just went away."

"You said the date was significant."

"Yes. Because it was the day he died. Because I think he was already dead. I think that's why he didn't answer when I knocked on the door."

"Oh my God, Ashley. That must be a creepy feeling."

"Yes. It's very creepy. And the police ... well, somehow they found out I was his daughter, and I had to answer all sorts of questions. I told them my story. About the hotel, and how I knocked on his door, and so on. I don't know if they were suspicious. It was an awful experience."

"I'm sure it was."

"Oh yes; and by the way, I got the first installment of money—it was over $30,000.... And I did what you told me to do; I opened an account, at Wells Fargo, and I called it, 'Ashley Savage Trust Account.' But what I want to know is, does this change things? I mean, my father being dead."

"Well, in a way it does," I said. "I don't suppose you know if your father left a will, or what his assets were. I think I'll have to have a talk with Grambling. I'll let you know what I find out."

"On top of everything else," she said, "I had to finally talk to my mother. We haven't been getting along, I think I told you that. I told her about the trust, and I said, but the money was probably stolen, and I'd have to give it back. And I told her he tried to reach me, and that he was dead. She was very upset with me, which I think is quite unfair. But that's mother. I wish I could have a normal family. I don't like talking about it, but I never felt anybody loved me. Certainly not my mother and father, or my stepfather. And my half-sister is a total brat."

I expressed my sympathy. In my business, I come in contact with a lot of dysfunctional families. Brothers and sisters who hate each other. Ex-wives and ex-husbands whose love has curdled into blind, insensate hatred. Family members who squabbles over wills, money, property, somebody's diamond ring, even who gets the dog or the cat. I've seen it all. I did feel sorry for Ashley, even though I found it hard to warm up to her. Maybe that's not fair. I hardly knew her. But she did seem somewhat cold. Remote. Hard to connect to.

I could see nothing much ahead but headaches, for both of us. I knew I would have to deal with Gideon Grambling, which is something I really didn't want to do. If you knew Gideon, you'd agree with me.

4

At any rate, I did call Gideon the very next day. The receptionist told me he was "in conference." Gideon was always in conference when I called. I suppose if one of his multi-millionaire clients called, the conference would vanish into smoke.

I could have pushed things, but I wasn't in the mood. I did reach him a day later, and I said that we had to talk about the affairs of Langley Savage and my client, Ashley Savage. He said he was extremely busy. I don't doubt that he was busy. Gideon has built himself a very cozy practice. I find him insufferable, but I suppose some clients don't mind insufferable people, for example, people who are themselves insufferable. "I represent some of the most notable people in San Francisco," he told me once.

"High-tech people?" I asked.

He said something sneering about Silicon Valley billionaires who made their money at the age of 25. I'm sure this was sour grapes; no way would Gideon, or anybody else, turn down some Google or Facebook zillionaire who wanted to do business. Gideon apparently had no such clients, so he talked incessantly about "old money" and the "fine families that have been here since the Gold Rush." Of course, families that had been around since the Gold Rush were the descendants of robber barons, Australian convicts, and other low-lifes. But the passage of time launders money extremely effectively. At least it does for Gideon.

To Gideon, I am nothing but a humble suburban lawyer, perhaps a cut above the woman who mops his floors, but he did deign to make room for me on his busy schedule, and I agreed to make the trek to San Francisco to meet him for lunch. Even though rush hour was theoretically over, Highway 101, which snakes up the peninsula along the bay side, was clogged with traffic; this is not a rare event, even in the middle of the day. That day, however, was worse than usual: some sort of accident slowed traffic to a crawl, or even less than a crawl. I thought about the hundreds of people sitting in their cars fuming with rage. But where on earth were all of them going? At least they were not scheduled to have lunch with Gideon Grambling.

Gideon was a man in his 40's. He was always meticulously dressed; and his hair had touches of silver, which struck me somehow as artificial. I can't ever recall seeing him smile. Gideon had chosen an extremely expensive restaurant, The Golden Calf, which specialized in "healthy local food." I was fifteen minutes late, and he was visibly annoyed. "Time is money for me, Frank," he said. "I can't afford to dawdle."

He could afford, however, to spend some of his valuable time talking about his diet. "I'm avoiding carbohydrates," he said. "They're poison. My doctor assures me of that." Personally, I never met a carbohydrate I didn't love: rice, bread, pasta, potatoes. Gideon ordered a glass of red wine, "It has antioxidants," he said. He then had something for lunch which seemed to be mostly kale and arugula, foods currently favored by people who basically hate to eat.

"Look, Gideon," I said. "As you know, Ashley Savage is my client. And Langley Savage was your client. Tell me about him."

"Yes, he was my client," Gideon said. "For a time, anyway. But he was a very private person. And his affairs, as you must realize, they're strictly confidential."

"Come off it, Gideon," I said. "The man is dead. Murdered. You can't hide behind that confidentiality stuff."

"Well, Frank," he said, in a sour tone of voice. "I realize that his death, uh, alters the perspective one might have. Did you know, I was supposed to see him the day he died? And that I actually went to that wretched hotel he died in? I had to drive all the way down to Palo Alto, as a matter of fact, which I bitterly resented. Still, it was necessary. And I didn't get to see him. Because he was already dead, though I didn't know that, of course. It's strange that his daughter is your client. I have to say, what is it with you, Frank? Last time I was involved with you, my client was also murdered; it was a similar experience: I had an appointment, I went to see my client, and guess what, he was dead."

"Maybe I killed them," I said.

"I don't appreciate the sarcasm. Anyway, Dr. Savage had made this arrangement a day or so earlier; I don't recall the details. I actually had to cancel a couple of appointments; and Palo Alto, where this wretched man was staying, is a good thirty-five miles from here. I resented this, but Savage said he could not get away, and it was important, he had an important document for me. Well, can't you fax it, I said. He said, no, he wanted to give me the original, and so on. I could have refused, but I did want to see him in person. I was, to be frank, going to suggest, uh, a change in our relationship. In any event, I charge for traveling time, and I thought: he'll have to pay for those wasted hours. He gave me his room number, and he said, just come up to my room, I'll be waiting for you."

"And you didn't see him?"

"When I knocked on the door, nobody answered. I tell you, I was extremely perturbed. Those wasted hours! Of course, I said to myself, he'll have to pay; and I would certainly not keep him as a client. At any rate, how was I to know that he was dead? Incidentally, nobody knows that I was there that day. Apparently our wonderful police officers have no idea. But then they never do. I'm happy to leave it that way, of course. I certainly don't want to get involved."

"I can understand that," I said.

"I do have something of a moral dilemma. I think I may have seen the person who killed Savage."

"Really? Who was that?"

"I have no idea who he is, or what his name is. This is what happened. Savage's room was on the seventh floor, but when I got into the elevator, I suppose my mind was somewhere else: I was thinking about the affairs of one of my clients, an extremely wealthy man from one of the great families, you know, and he plans to set up a charitable foundation; in any event, I went up to the eighth floor, I must have pushed the wrong button. Irritating. But I decided, rather than take the elevator, they're incredibly slow in that hotel, I would just walk down the one flight of stairs. So I started down, and there, in the stairwell, outside the seventh floor, and totally blocking my way, a young man was sprawled on the stairs, sobbing and wailing and carrying on. Oh Lord, I felt, who is this creature? It was extremely annoying, of course, what on earth was he doing there? And I said, do you mind, I have to go past. And he got up, and said sorry in a kind of sobbing voice. A young man, blond hair, no idea what he was doing there. And he started walking down the stairs, still sobbing, and wiping his eyes with a handkerchief. Now, it might just be a coincidence, but when I found out that Savage was dead ... well, I remembered this strange person, in the stairwell."

"Gideon," I said, "you really must report this. To the police."

"Please don't tell me what to do. I'll decide for myself."

He lapsed into a kind of sullen silence. I ordered dessert. "Gideon," I said, "can I ask you some questions? For starters, the late Dr. Savage: are you going to handle his estate? Did he have money? And did he have a will?"

"Oh, yes, he had a will. He executed the will at the same time he executed the trust. A rather odd will, but then everything he did was odd. He named me as executor, and he left half of his money to be poured into the trust for his daughter Ashley. For the other half, he created a new trust. Ashley was also the beneficiary of that trust, but he reserved the right, during his lifetime, to make changes in the designation of beneficiaries."

"That's quite unusual—in a will," I said.

"I know that, Frank. Please. Don't talk to me as if I didn't know anything. It's standard in a living trust, but in a testamentary trust, no. I reminded him about that, of course. I said if anything happened to him, he would no longer be able to make any changes. One can always change a will, or make a codicil. I asked him what he had in mind. And why he wasn't willing to do it right now, whatever it was. But he refused to say."

"You're the executor, so you must be handling the estate."

"I'd rather not go into that. I am sorry I ever met the man. I don't like to be involved in these sordid affairs. My other clients would certainly think it was strange if I suddenly got mixed up in this sort of business. And everyone and his cousin is suing Langley Savage. No thank you. This is not my normal line of work."

I ignored his complaints and asked, "Did he ... leave a size-able estate? Ashley, you remember, is my client."

"A sizeable estate? That depends. I am really not at liberty to say."

"Oh, come on, Gideon. Please don't play games. Did he or didn't he have money?'

I eventually found out what I wanted to know, although it was like pulling teeth. What the Savage estate depended on was, in part, dependent on what the managers of the Hortense Risley estate did or tried to do. "Everything is tied up in litigation," Gideon said. I wondered if she had left money to the late Dr. Langley Savage. If you believe the stories in the newspapers, Langley Savage had gotten a great deal of Hortense Risley's property from her while she was still alive. By hook or by crook. The lawyers for Hortense's estate would certainly try to get back every penny of Langley Savage's ill-gotten gains.

The bill for my fish and salad was downright extortionate, and so was the parking fee I had to pay. Gideon may charge people for his time, but I could not pass the costs of this lunch on to Ashley Savage. Nor could I pass on the aggravation, first, of dealing with Gideon Grambling, and second, of dealing with Highway 101. It was just as bad going as coming, clogged once more with cars, cars, cars, each one encasing a driver cursing the fate that landed him inside this hopeless tangle of auto-mobiles. I got back in as sour a mood as I can remember.

5

I didn't think of Gideon Grambling as a risk taker, but the estate of Langley Savage was a very risky proposition. If Dr. Savage really was an heir to part of the Risley fortune, that would make Ashley Savage seriously rich. But the estate was a very iffy proposition. *Very* iffy. I did not yet have the facts about Hortense's will, but she probably was over 90 when she made it out, and she was living in a hospital, tended to by two doctors and a nurse. And if she left them her money, and cut off her grandchildren, then the will would be on very shaky grounds. I could have written the lawyer's brief myself: arguing that the will was a worthless piece of paper, on the grounds of undue influence, and lack of testamentary capacity. Or, in lay language, the woman was mentally incompetent and the beneficiaries had taken advantage of her, overpowering her feeble brain and diverting the money to themselves. Moreover, it was a so-called "unnatural" will. This is legalese for a will that shuts out the family and leaves the money to "strangers."

Actually, I know a lot of families where there would be nothing "unnatural" about cutting out a bunch of greedy, worthless relatives and leaving money to charity, the Red Cross, a neighbor, a friend, or anybody else. A woman as rich as Hortense, in my experience, must have set up some sort of trust for the grandchildren and, as I later found out, she had in fact done so. This might or might not affect a court's judgment about a will that left these grandchildren out—if there was such a will.

And then there was Langley's will. Ashley was no doubt an

heiress; but would there be anything left in the estate after the vultures picked it over?

I had lunch the next day with Ashley, and I told her about my meeting with Grambling, and as much as I knew about the situation. "You might be in for a lot more money," I said, "under Hortense Risley's will. I mean, not directly. But she may have left money to your father; and you're his heir, as far as I know. Then there's your father's will. Grambling refused to give me details, but it'll all come out, and very soon; if you're an heir, you'll be notified; and you'll get a copy. So far it's just guesswork. I don't know who's going to be handling all this. Grambling clearly wants out. Ashley, I'm afraid, we just have to be patient, and not do anything rash. Your father's estate and the estate of Hortense Risley, they'll be tied up in litigation for years, unless I miss my bet."

She said, "Frank, I like money as much as the next person; but I have to wonder, is any of this worth it? I mean, these Risleys with their lawsuits—I don't need that. Not to mention the fact that now my mother is all upset; when I told her the story, it stirred up bad memories. I have to tell you, in all honesty, I have very little sympathy with her. But that's neither here nor there. And the Risley family is bugging me. First this Christopher Risley, and now somebody called Bobby Risley. I gather he's another one of the grandchildren."

"I suppose. I read somewhere there were four of them. You heard from this Bobby Risley?"

"A phone call. He said, I'm Bobby Risley, and I have something important to say to you. I said, well, what is it and who are you? I was tempted to hang up, but I didn't. He told me he was one of the grandchildren of Hortense Risley. But that's not important, he said. What's important is, I want to see you, want to meet you, talk to you. I said, well, I don't want to see *you*. I know you're suing me. And he said, no, no, it's not that, I'd never sue you, Ashley. I said, but you *are* suing me. He said, no, that's my brother Christopher, he's the one, I don't want to sue you. I said, well, that's good news; but why are you calling me?"

"And what did he say?"

"He said, because I really want to meet you. It's terribly

important to me. I said, why? And he said, well, there are four of us, four grandchildren, and we had a meeting, with our lawyer, awful man, and he told us Dr. Savage was dead, and that he was your father. That's true, isn't it? And I said yes. And he said I want to tell you how sorry I am. I said, save your breath, I never knew the man. And he said, I understand, my own father is dead, and he was a terrible person, but a father is a father, and he went on and on about parents, and the loss of parents, and how terrible it is. I told him again, I had no emotional connection whatsoever with my father, and I didn't have time for whatever it was he was calling me about. And then I heard these funny noises, like sobs on the phone. And I said, Mr. Risley? And he said, in a choked voice, call me Bobby. And I said, are you alright? What's the matter? And he said, nothing, pay no attention. But he went on sobbing. I mean, it's possible the man is mentally ill. Have you had any contact with him, Frank?"

"None at all."

"Anyway, after a while, he stopped sobbing, and he said, Ashley, please listen to me. My brother, Christopher, he talked to your father's lawyer, Grumble is his name or something like that, I said, it's Grambling; he said, well, whatever, anyway, this lawyer was all nasty and close-mouthed, but he did say, Dr. Savage had a daughter, and Christopher found out that your father set up a trust for you, he was asking questions about assets or whatever, and this Grumble had to tell him, your father had done this, and Christopher was so upset about it, and he's going to sue and stuff. But that's not me, Ashley. Something about your name, it appealed to me. I checked you out on Facebook, and I saw your picture, and I'm desperate to meet you. Can I make an appointment?"

"An appointment?"

"Weird. As if I was a dentist or something. So I said no, of course not. Your family is suing me, isn't that enough? I don't need to talk to you. You had better talk to my lawyer, Frank May. And then he said absolutely the strangest thing of all. He said, no, I need to see you, Ashley. Not your lawyer, you. Ashley, I'm in love with you."

"In love with you?"

"Those were his words. His very words. I told him he was crazy, and I hung up."

"You did the right thing, Ashley. He sounds unbalanced. Just ignore him. If he calls again, maybe you should do something. I mean, call the police. But you don't have to deal with him. And that was the right thing to do, to tell him, don't pester you; if he has any actual reason to be interested in you, I can take care of it."

Not that I wanted to see Bobby Risley, but lawyers are meant to take the heat sometimes. At any rate, Ashley left and I went home to my family. It was just Celia and me that evening. The girls were off somewhere, as usual; they were working on something for Advanced Placement English. At least they said so. They would be at Heather's house, they said. Possibly this was even true. I suppose if we called up Heather, she would vouch for them. But what would be the point?

I was in no mood to precipitate a family crisis. I welcomed the idea of a quiet evening at home. I brought Celia up to date on the Risley and Savage affair. When I told her about Bobby's phone call, she said: "Frank, did she mention your name?"

"Yes, she did. She said, if he had any business or anything, he should take it up with me."

"Watch out," she said, "this guy will show up at your office."

"Celia, don't be ridiculous," I said. But she turned out to be right, as usual.

6

When I arrived at the office the next morning—a bit later than usual—I saw a young man standing outside my office door. He was in his 20's, I would say. He was short, had dark blond hair, greenish eyes, and a round face, almost moon-shaped. He was dressed in blue jeans, and a plaid shirt. He had a small pug nose; but on the whole, I would say he was good-looking, in a kind of baby-faced way. I had no doubt that this was Bobby Risley.

As soon as he saw me, he said, "Frank May?"

"Yes?"

He took hold of my arm; his lips were quivering. "Please. I need to talk to you."

Celia says I'm a terrible judge of character. But even those of us who are terrible judges of character do judge character all the time. We have to. Bobby seemed mildly unhinged, certainly highly emotional; but there was something about him that struck me as completely harmless. Child-like, I think. I took him into the office. He sat down on the chair across from my desk. He was trembling.

"Mr. May ... you're Ashley Savage's lawyer, aren't you?"

"Yes, I am."

"My name is Bobby Risley," he said. "I ... I knew her father. He was my grandmother's doctor."

"Mr. Risley," I said. "This is highly irregular. Do you know that? You're suing my client...."

"No, no, Mr. May; I'm not suing your client. And call me

Bobby. And I'm not suing anybody. My brother is, not me."

"In that case," I said, "I don't see what we have to talk about."

"Oh, but you don't understand," he said, bursting into tears. "I've fallen in love. With your client. With Ashley."

"But Bobby," I said, "you've never met her, isn't that right?"

"No, I haven't." But then he blurted out his story, in emotional gasps, between sobs, about how his grandmother was dead, and there were all these lawyers, and they talked about Dr. Savage, and how Dr. Savage had a daughter, Ashley, and even the name, somehow, it spoke to him, he had a feeling, an intuition, he wondered, why does the very name make me feel this way, and then he saw her picture on Facebook, and read things, things she wrote, she was a kindred spirit, kind of a lonely life, and that was him, too; and when he saw the picture, something happened, it was like lightning striking him, believe me, Mr. May (he said), you think I'm crazy, but I was never more serious in my life, it was the picture, it was those eyes. She seemed ... melancholy.... "I was haunted by those eyes," he said. "I felt: she needs me. And I need her. Mr. May, you have to let me meet her. She says she doesn't want to, but it's because of Christopher and his damn lawsuit. I would never sue her, never never never. I'm in love with her."

More tears. I said, "Bobby, I'm sorry, but she doesn't want to meet you. You can understand why; I mean, you called her up, and said you were in love with her. Bobby, what would you think, if you were in her position?"

"Oh, I know, I know. I'm stupid about these things. I don't know how to talk to women. Cassandra told me that. She's my sister. I'm divorced, did you know that? I had a terrible marriage. I made an awful mistake. I've got a son, a little boy, I love him madly, he's been the only thing I've ever loved, really, well, I guess I love Cassandra, I talk too much, I know that. My life is a total disaster. I did love my grandmother. Hildegarde, she was my wife, she hates me now, she's trying to do terrible things to me—I'm just not good with women, never have been. But Ashley, she's different. I know she is. Mr. May, can you do something for me? I'm desperate."

"Bobby," I said, "this is utterly ridiculous. Get a grip on yourself."

"Could you at least talk to her? I ... I wrote her a letter. Can you deliver it to her?"

"Bobby," I said, "I'm not a mailman. Honestly, I don't think she wants your letter. I hope you understand."

He looked as if the tears were about to start flowing again. "Please," he said. "Look: I'll show you the letter. You'll see what it says." He opened a plain white envelope and took out a sheet of paper. Nice stationery, with the words Bobby Risley embossed at the top, in gold lettering. The letter was handwritten:

"Dear Ashley," it said. "I know this is something you didn't expect, and I don't blame you for being skeptical. But I mean this from the bottom of my heart: I love you, and I want to get to know you. I went to a psychic, Madame Zarathustra she called herself. Not that I believe in it. I really don't. But she predicted this. She said love was going to come into my life, and very soon. So I was primed for something. I don't think she can really see the future. But I think she can read *people*, and she looked into my heart and saw that I was ready. And I *was* ready. Something about your name, when I heard it, I felt, something is different about this woman. Even the name. Ashley. It sounded beautiful to me. So soft and gentle. And then I saw your picture. I knew then, that we were meant for each other. I know my brother Christopher is suing you. I won't do that. And I'll try to convince my sisters, too. My grandmother had tons of money, there's lots of it left for us. I want to marry you. Please. I beg of you. Maybe you think this is crazy. But it's not. It's fate, it's karma. Maybe you believe in karma. I have the feeling you're a very spiritual person."

It was signed, Bobby Risley; and he enclosed a small snapshot of himself, smiling a kind of cherubic smile.

I liked the idea that Bobby Risley was backing out of the lawsuit. That part was good. Whether he could persuade the other grandchildren was another question. And I was sure Ashley wanted no part of any of the Risleys, especially Bobby, who seemed, well, a bit unstable.

"Bobby," I said, "it's a lovely letter. But I'm not going to deliver it to my client. I don't think that would be right."

"Please! If it came through you, I think she'd pay attention."

"Bobby," I said. "Try the United States post office. Not me."

He started to say something; but he saw that I was serious. I handed back the letter to him, and I smiled. I had no desire to antagonize him. Or, more likely, to start him crying again. I handed him a tissue, just in case.

Sobbing, he left my office. And that, I thought, is the last of it.

Which turned out not to be true.

7

I felt I had a duty to tell Ashley about this meeting. I called her at the office, but there was no response. I sent her an email, and got word that she had gone to a conference of Development Officers, taking place in Omaha, and would be back in four days. I felt what I had to say was better in person than by email, so I waited. In fact, I waited a whole week, because I was extremely busy with other clients. One of my clients, the Armenian restaurant owner, had tax troubles and troubles with his third wife. The fourth wife, his former receptionist, was pregnant; it was his baby, and he wanted to amend his will to take care of this as yet unborn child.

"Herant," I said, "how come all these women get pregnant? On second thought, don't tell me. I don't want to know."

At any rate, I finally got around to making the call to Ashley Savage, bright and early one morning. "I have something to tell you, Ashley," I said. "I think I should have told you sooner, but, somehow I didn't get around to it. I had this visit, in my office, with a young man...."

"Bobby Risley," she said.

"Oh, you know," I said.

"He sent me a letter, Frank."

"You can just ignore it, Ashley."

But her voice on the phone was hesitant. "Well," she said. "I know that. I could have ignored it. But I didn't."

"Didn't what?"

"Ignore the letter. Frank, I have to talk to you.... Can you have lunch with me today?"

As it happens, I couldn't; I was having lunch with my Armenian client. "Is this urgent, Ashley?"

She seemed to hesitate. But then she said: "No. It can wait."

In fact the next few days were very busy ones for me; and for Ashley, too, as it turned out. Finally, almost a week later, we fixed a date for lunch.

Before our lunch date, on a Friday—I think it was Friday, sometimes it's hard to remember—on my way to the office, I was more or less lost in thought when I heard someone call my name. I looked up, and there, across the street, was Zelda Valdez. I had first met Zelda when I got entangled in another of these puzzling murder cases. My dentist's receptionist, Maggie Swift, had been killed in the dentist's office. It's a long story, but that's when I first met Zelda.

Zelda was a very tall and skinny woman, about six feet tall, with coal-black hair, a somewhat pointy chin, and a pointy nose. I'm afraid she looked a little bit like one of the bad witches in *The Wizard of Oz*. Zelda was a writer: she wrote romance novels and, unlike the bad witches, she was a rather appealing person. At any rate, I liked her a lot.

She had been married to Milo, an avant-garde composer. Milo had been a patient of my dentist, the one whose receptionist was killed. I gave Zelda a hug, and asked her: "How's Milo?"

"Oh, Frank, we're not married any more. His ex-wife Zoe, the fat one, well, she had bariatric surgery, and she's now thin as a rail; and Milo's gone back to her. Anyway, she's pregnant."

"I'm sorry, Zelda. You two seemed like a good couple."

"It's OK. It was time to move on. For both of us. Really. But I'm glad to see you, Frank. In fact I was on my way to your office."

"You were, Zelda? But why? Legal business?"

"Not exactly. Do you have time for coffee? I want to talk to you. I want to help you out, if I can."

"You want to help me, Zelda? What, are you a member of the bar now?"

"No, of course not, Frank. I know you're joking. You're so clever. That's one of the things I admire about you. No, it's not law. I want to help you with the case you're working on."

"Zelda, I'm not working on any case."

"Oh, Frank, you're so modest.... It's the Dr. Savage case, isn't it? I meet, it's utterly fascinating. This strange man, this doctor, maybe he stole millions from an old lady; and then somebody executes him, so dramatic, he's dead in a hotel room, and two beautiful dolls, I mean actual dolls, not women, one on each side. It's enthralling. And then when I found out that you were involved, I just had to talk to you about it. I want to help."

"Zelda, honest to God, I'm not working on this. Or anything. Except law stuff, that is. And how on earth did you learn all these things? From the newspaper?"

"Oh no, Frank. It was like this: I met this guy, Bobby Risley, in my yoga class.... I got to talking to him.... He's a dear soul, but he has big problems. Emotional problems. He feels the yoga is helping him, by the way; and I believe it. It helps people. It's done wonders for me. Cured my writer's block. He's also doing something about anger management. I was attracted to him the minute I saw him, something about him, he's cute as a button, and I thought maybe he and I could get together. But, well, he was terribly sweet, but it was clear, he wasn't interested in me that way. I'm too tall for him, Frank, I think that's the issue. Milo loved tall women, but most men want somebody shorter than they are. That's Bobby's problem, I think. He's quite short. One of his problems anyway. But he's a dear soul."

"And he told you I was 'involved' as you put it? Zelda," I said. "Yes, I'm 'involved.' But not in the murder. I have a role, but it's strictly legal, nothing to do with finding out who killed the guy. What on earth did Bobby Risley tell you?"

"He told me so many things. We talked and talked, after yoga. He told me his whole life story. Did you know, he was married once? A total disaster; but he has a child. He was sitting there in front of me, and he told me his troubles, and he was crying like a baby. I said, Bobby, be a man. Face up to your problems and conquer them; that's the thing to do. I do like him, though."

"Zelda," I said, "forget the whole thing. I've met Bobby. I'm representing Ashley Savage, and she and Bobby are on opposite sides, although it's complicated. And, listen to me, Zelda: I'm a lawyer, remember? I'm not a detective. And I am not, repeat not, working on the case of Dr. Savage. I know about these rumors, they're always pursuing me. But they're not true."

"Oh, Frank," she said. "You're so modest. I know you're involved, you just won't admit it. Bobby mentioned you."

I could see that my protests, my denials, were not going anywhere. Sometimes it's impossible to convince people about something, even though you're telling the truth. The more I denied that I was secretly working on a case, the more they think I am. They say to themselves: he has to deny it; that's part of the game. So I gave up, basically. I let her think maybe I was working on the case, but in an undercover way.

"I respect that, Frank," she said. "And I know, you can't hire me, or use me officially, or anything like that. But I'm going to work on the case myself. I need something to do. I was having this writer's block problem. The yoga helped, it really did. But still, I'm at a crossroads. I'm through with romance novels and vampires, they're so yesterday. I tried zombies, but it just didn't work. It just wasn't me. Then I thought, maybe something with a lot of sex, like that book about shades of grey or whatever it was called. It just didn't happen. It's not that easy to do soft-core porn, and the field is so crowded. I thought I'd write a detective novel. If I did, I could base my hero on you, Frank."

"Oh, Zelda, please don't do that," I said.

"I know, I know, you're worried that I'll reveal too much.... Don't worry, Frank, nobody will know it's you. But when I write, I have to have a picture in mind, an image, you know, what somebody looks like. My best novel, the novel about the pirate, Horatio, who falls in love with a Carmelite nun, Sister Santa Cruz, and abducts her onto his ship in the Caribbean, I don't know if you read it; well, when I wrote about the pirate, I saw in front of me the face of my cousin Pedro, who's a carpenter; he's good-looking, in a funny sort of way, his nose is a little crooked, and he has a nasty scar, but somehow that makes him attractive. By the way, he does wonderful work. He did my kitchen cabinets. Pedro has five kids, and he's never even been married. And the nun, well, she looks just like my gynecologist, Dr. Greeley. A beautiful woman, a little bit humorless, but do you want a gynecologist who makes jokes while she's examining you?"

"I wouldn't know," I said. "I don't have a gynecologist."

I suppose the nearest thing is the check-up for men, when the doctor sticks in his finger and examines your prostate. I have a woman doctor now, after my regular doctor retired. I expect her to be absolutely stone-faced at this point in the physical exam.

"Oh, Frank," Zelda said, "I just love talking to you. You're so clever. But anyway, that's what I'm going to do: when I write about my detective, he's going to look just like you. I call him Max Drone. Those are both good names, strong names. One syllable each. And he's going to use your techniques."

"Zelda, I don't have any techniques. For estate planning, yes; for solving crimes, no."

"He'll look like you, Frank; but he won't be like you, don't worry. You're a modest man, I admire that. Max Drone won't be modest. He'll be a braggart. I started writing already, but I'm a bit stuck at the moment. Oh, it'll pass. Can I report to you, from time to time? About my progress? And can we share notes?"

"Sure, Zelda," I said. "If I have anything to share."

She gave me a hug, and left. I felt tired, all of a sudden. Why does everybody think I'm some sort of Sherlock Holmes? But it was no use fighting it.

8

I had agreed to meet Ashley in Palo Alto, which was more convenient for her; and I didn't mind. I had plenty of free time that day, which was (as I said) a Friday. Parking is an issue in Palo Alto, believe it or not; University Avenue is full of restaurants, and the street is swarming with yuppies, people in designer blue jeans who work for high-tech companies. A few of them are billionaires, and the rest dream of becoming billionaires. They seem to come permanently hooked up to electronic devices. Things are attached to their ears, and they listen, as if they were in the Secret Service, guarding the President. The attachments almost seem like a fixture of their bodies. Maybe if you pulled the plug, so to speak, they would disappear into the cloud, whatever that is.

I met Ashley in one of the upscale cafes, *The Robber Baron*, which served meals in one section and coffee and pastries in another. The sandwiches and salads were said to be good. The usual geeks were sitting around the coffee-and-pastry section, as always, glued to their laptops. Ashley seemed breathless and excited. "Frank, my life has changed. For the good," she said. She ordered a turkey sandwich, with cranberry sauce, on a sourdough roll, and when it came, she bit into it and said, "This is absolutely delicious."

This *was* a different Ashley, more ebullient. Happier, it seemed. I thought to myself: Is she some kind of mildly bipolar person? But then again, we all have moods. Could it really be the sandwich? Turkey is not usually as life-enhancing as, say, a hot fudge sundae, but human beings are so different from each other. Celia, for example, absolutely loves Brussels sprouts. And kale, of course. And arugula.

"I have to tell you what happened," she said, after finishing the sandwich and ordering a fruit tart for dessert—another sign of euphoria. She even asked to have ice cream on top of the tart.

"What happened?"

"I got that letter. From Bobby Risley. And ... I know I should have torn it up, ignored it, done absolutely nothing. But ... there was something about it. Something that spoke to me. I just had a certain feeling. Like, what do I have to lose? So, I responded."

"You responded?"

"He had given me a phone number. His cell phone. I called the number. I said, look, maybe I'm making a huge mistake, but OK, let's meet, let's have coffee. I thought, middle of the afternoon, what's the risk. So we did meet. At Starbucks, on El Camino. And ... Frank, I found him awfully appealing. Not at all what I expected. He's like a little teddy bear. No, that's not right. Not exactly a teddy bear. But ... I can't explain it. He just seemed so earnest, and so sweet. I don't know what came over me. I felt like hugging him. He talked and talked. Told me his whole life story, or anyway a lot of it. A miserable, loveless childhood. He did love his grandmother, used to go see her, but then she became demented, and she didn't even recognize him, toward the end. He had tears in his eyes. I looked at him, and a big tear, an enormous tear, ran down his check. Somehow I felt: This is a kindred spirit."

"A kindred spirit, Ashley? How is that?"

"I've always felt lonely. Unloved, Frank. My father, re-member, ditched me. My mother always resented me. My stepfather, well, he never showed any affection. He never hugged or kissed me. Don't get me wrong; he was fair, honest, I never lacked for anything. But I never felt that this was my family. I felt like a boarder, somebody who gets a room and pays rent. And Bobby, his parents were divorced, his father was some miserable wretch. No one paid any attention to Bobby. His half-brother and half-sister, they didn't figure in his life.

His own sister, Cassandra, he loved her, but she was the only one. Their mother never wanted them around. Married young, never really wanted kids, it was a disaster. They were raised by maids. Even the old grandmother, she was sweet, she paid for things, but mostly she loved her dolls and her stuffed animals more than she loved any actual people. And then, more and more, she seemed to be off in outer space.

"So we sat there and talked; and finally I said, look, Bobby, I have to get back to work. And he said, well, will you have dinner with me, and I thought, well, why not? And we went to this restaurant, in Palo Alto, very nice place, Spanish food basically, and it was quiet, we had a booth, and we talked and talked some more, and ... I heard everything, more details, his life, how he married this older woman, it was a terrible mistake, and it was disastrous, and he has a little boy, but she doesn't let him see the boy, and he cried and cried; but then we talked about other things, about food, about politics, all sorts of things, about religion; I never cared for religion, especially because my mother was some kind of fanatic, but Bobby said, he didn't like churches, but he had this spiritual side; and I said, I can see that. And then it was getting late, and I said, Bobby, this is great, but I have to get up early, maybe I should go home, and he said, I'll take you. I said, no, I've got a car, and then he said, I can't go yet, I can't leave you now, can I come to your place, and of course I hesitated, but when I said, no, no, he looked so sad, and honest to God, he started crying! He was embarrassed, and I was embarrassed, but somehow, he looked so pathetic, so ... you're going to think I'm crazy, but I said, OK, come to my place, we can talk some more.... And please don't cry. And that's what we did."

I knew what was coming.

"Frank, I'll be honest with you. I made him some coffee, and we sat and talked, and then it was getting later and later. And he spent the night. I don't have a spare room, but ... Frank, I don't have to draw you a picture. He's such an unusual person, but so warm, so much feeling. I just suddenly felt: this is the one. Finally. I told you, I'm starved for love. My mother, all that stupid guilt, as if she had some kind of scarlet letter ...

and my stepfather.... Well, you know the story. And then, when I moved out of the house, went off on my own, I mean, I've had male friends, and ... well, I don't have to tell you everything. Bobby is so different. I had the crazy feeling this is what I've been looking for, this is the one. Anyway, he spent the night. And in the morning, when I woke up, he was up already, and I got out of bed, and he was in the kitchen, in his underwear. He looked like a little boy, well, not really, but you know what I mean; and when he saw me, he said, Ashley, I'm so happy, I've never been so happy, and he burst out crying.... He's so emotional."

"Ashley," I said, "it's nice, but be careful."

"Oh, Frank, that's the trouble with me. I'm careful. Too careful. I don't want to be careful any more. I know this is different. This is for real. And Bobby thinks so too. He said to me, Ashley, this is like Romeo and Juliet, we're supposed to be enemies, you know, the Montagues and the Capulets, but this isn't like Shakespeare, this is real life. And I said, I hope so, they both ended up dead, Romeo and Juliet, and we're not going to do that. He said, no, no. Frank, it's really exciting, I mean, in love with a person you're supposed to hate. I just think it's so romantic, how Bobby fell in love with me, just seeing a picture of me on Facebook. People would think it's crazy, but I want crazy. I've never had crazy, and now I have it. And, Frank, he's not going to sue me; he's on my side. I mean, that's not really important. The important thing is we love each other. But this lawsuit, well, he couldn't care less."

"That's good news, Ashley. Still, he's only one of the grandchildren; the others are still part of the lawsuit, as far as I know."

"But Bobby's going to talk to them. He's going to try to get them all to drop the lawsuit. Though really, Frank, I honestly don't care. They can have the money. It doesn't mean anything to me. If they wanted me to do it, I'd give the money back. I really would. All I want is Bobby."

"Well, let's wait and see," I said. This was a new Ashley. She was like a little girl with a lollipop. Well, I was glad about the lollipop; but it wasn't *my* lollipop. I'm a lawyer, after all.

People pay me to be sensible, even when they're not. "Eight million dollars isn't peanuts, Ashley," I said. "My job is to protect your interests." But she wasn't listening; she was completely besotted. She kept saying it didn't matter, and Bobby doesn't care either, and so on.

"Ashley," I said, "I don't want to be a killjoy; but you know, it's been so recent. He just spent one night...."

"Oh, Frank, it's not one night. It's a lifetime; I just know it. I could hardly concentrate at work, I couldn't wait to see him again. I just want to be with him. I even switched my yoga class, so I could go with Bobby. Incidentally, at this class, there was this tall woman, very tall, woman with a hook nose, Zelda she calls herself, very friendly. She and Bobby are friends. I told her I was Ashley Savage. She asked me a lot of questions, about my father.... I mean, I liked her, but she seemed awfully nosy. Bobby, he's so naïve, he didn't see anything wrong, but I was wondering.... I do like her, but ... what's this all about, Frank? She sort of hinted she was working for you."

"Oh God. That's Zelda. No, she's not working for me, Ashley. I think she's OK, she's nice, she means well; but, well, just don't pay any attention."

I couldn't bring myself to tell her that Zelda fancied herself some sort of sleuth.

I was happy for Ashley, she seemed so delighted with her new romance, but I felt a certain amount of caution. This was all very sudden. Was Bobby really as child-like, as innocent as he seemed? Bobby Risley was emotional, unstable, impulsive. Those are traits that could be problems in a relationship. I wondered if Ashley knew what she was getting into.

And, after all, somebody murdered Langley Savage, in his hotel room. Who had a motive? The grandchildren felt he had robbed them of part of their inheritance. Was this enough of a reason to kill the man? The grandchildren: that included Bobby. Could he be a killer? It seemed unlikely. But who then? One of the others? Or was the motive something else entirely?

Was Ashley a suspect? Or her mother? Her mother must have hated Langley Savage. After all these years, he pops up. Do I dare ask Ashley whether her mother has an alibi?

Well, it was none of my business, I suppose. I couldn't really think of Ashley as a murderess. People don't kill their parents, unless they are seriously deranged; and she certainly wasn't that. They certainly don't kill a parent they had never met.

I told the story of Ashley and Bobby to Celia, after dinner. She was sitting in the living room, knitting. That was her new hobby: knitting. "It calms the nerves, Frank," she said. "I'm making a scarf for Adam Finkel." Adam was her project—the math teacher, painfully shy, the one with an awful skin condition. Celia would never give up her desire to save him from a life of loneliness. As the needles clicked, she listened to my story, about Ashley and Bobby. And, oh yes, about Zelda.

"Frank," she said, putting down the needles for a moment. "You're not getting involved, are you? You promised me."

"I'm not getting involved, dear. Really. I'm just representing my client, that's all."

"There's such a thing as a police force, Frank," she said. "Let them figure out who killed that doctor. It's absolutely none of your business."

"I know."

"Frank," she said, "tell me the truth. You're not trying to track somebody down. "

"No. I'm not. I don't even care," I said, which was a bit short of honest, "I'm not thinking about it at all. I don't intend to do anything."

And in fact, I had no suspect in mind. Not really.

But I was soon going to get one. From Zelda.

9

I had made a promise to Celia, and I did intend to keep it. No meddling with the murder investigation. But the legal side—that was another question. Ashley Savage was my client, but the Risley family kept intruding. First there was Bobby. Next came his half-brother Christopher, who showed up at my office and demanded to speak to me.

He seemed about as unlike Bobby as anyone could possibly be. He was tall, dressed in a conservative suit and tie, with a face that looked as if was chiseled out of granite, and dark hair with hints of gray. He was, I would guess, about 40 or 45.

He also looked anything but friendly.

He introduced himself as Christopher Risley, handed me a business card, which I hardly looked at, and sat down ceremoniously in my office. He stared at the office—the furniture, the layout—and I could almost feel his contempt. A solo practitioner, in a modest suburban office, no oriental rugs on the floor, no abstract paintings on the walls; in a building flanked by Chinese restaurants, coffee shops (three Starbucks' within half a mile) and offices of dentists. Christopher Risley, I imagined, was used to more elegant legal surroundings. But maybe it would be unfair to try to read the mind of Christopher Risley. Yes, my office did not resemble, say, Gideon Grambling's office in San Francisco; but neither was it like Sam Spade's office in The Maltese Falcon, on a grubby side-street, with neon signs flashing in the window. And I kept my desk reasonably neat.

"You're representing this woman, Ashley Savage," he said. "Am I right about that?"

"I am."

"My attorneys tried to contact her; but she refused to speak to them. Instead, she referred them to you. I instructed them to do so. But I said I would try to speak to you first."

"And why is that, Mr. Risley?"

"I'm a person who likes to be direct, candid, and get to the point. I would be most unhappy if this whole miserable affair became something that teams of lawyers were wrangling about. I tried to talk to Ms. Savage myself, after she rejected a conversation with my lawyers; but she refused to talk to me as well. That's why I came to you."

I nodded my head. I asked him what the purpose of this visit was.

"Her father, Langley Savage," he said, in a dry but chilling tone, "he stole millions of dollars from my grandmother, did you know that?"

"I know absolutely nothing about any such thing," I said. "I never met the man; my client is his daughter, and my job is to protect her interests."

"Suit yourself. He did in fact steal money. My family had been about to file suit against him. We want every penny back. Now he's dead. Are you handling the estate?"

"Not that I know of," I said.

"Well, who is?"

"I have no idea," I said. That was not exactly true. Gideon Grambling had handled the trust. Whether he would handle the estate was doubtful. He clearly wanted nothing to do with Langley Savage and his sordid affairs; at any rate, not any more.

"Did he have a will?"

"As I told you: I have no idea."

That didn't stop Christopher. "Will or no will, I have information that he transferred a substantial sum of money to his daughter, your client, Ashley Savage."

"I won't comment on that, Mr. Risley," I said. "Anything to do with my client's affairs, I have to keep confidential. But you know that."

He ignored this remark. "Of course, since the man is dead, and I must say, good riddance, we will now be suing his estate. And naturally, if he disposed of some of the assets to his daughter, we will pursue that avenue as well, and whoever is the trustee of this trust is going to have to answer to us. I want to make that very clear."

"Who is this 'we' you're talking about, Mr. Risley? You and who else?"

"I have two sisters, he said, "Juno and Cassandra; and a brother, Bobby. My late father had four children. We all, of course, have the same financial stake in this matter. We are, as far as we know, the sole heirs of our grandmother, Hortense Risley. The lawsuits are in the name of all four of us."

"Mr. Risley," I said, "in the first place, it's quite irregular, you coming here in the first place. I represent Ashley Savage, that's true. Whether her father has an estate at all, I have no idea. And he supposedly had a will, but I haven't seen it yet. I have no information about whether he left money to his daughter, who never actually met her father. As for the trust, its validity, the source of the money and all that, I have nothing to say at the present time. If there is an issue, I assume the courts will resolve it. And," I added, because the man irritated me, "I do have to correct one statement you made. I do not think all four of you are parties to any lawsuit against my client."

"What do you mean by that?" he said, clearly annoyed.

"Your brother Bobby is not suing anybody. We've been in contact with him."

"Contact? With Bobby?"

"Yes. My client has been assured by him that he has no intention of suing her under any circumstances."

He was clearly shocked and surprised. For a fleeting moment, the carefully controlled expression gave way to something else. Puzzlement. Annoyance? "Bobby and your client? He knows her?"

I was dying to say: yes, he knows her, and in the Biblical sense, too. But I resisted the temptation. "I'm not at liberty to discuss your brother's personal affairs, or my client's. He isn't suing. That much is clear."

He sat there silently for a minute, absorbing the turn of events. "I'll speak to him," he said finally. "But even if what you say is correct, it doesn't alter the main point. I might be the only sane one in the family; sometimes I think so. Meanwhile, as far as I know, my sisters will be with me. Juno and Cassandra."

As it turned out, he was wrong about that too.

At any rate, there was nothing more to say; and I made it clear that, as far as I was concerned, our meeting was over.

Christopher Risley got up and left. Plainly dissatisfied.

10

Ashley called me on the phone later that day. She said, "Frank, I'd like you to come to dinner at my place. Can you come Thursday night?"

"What's the occasion?"

"Business," she said. "I need to talk to you; and I really can't get away from the office, not these days anyway, it's crazy at work."

It was unclear whether Celia was invited; probably not. And she would certainly refuse to go. She never went if "business" was involved. On the other hand, Celia does not like it if I'm not home in the evening, leaving her to face two teenaged daughters without auxiliary troops. I was hesitant "Can't it wait? Really, Ashley, I hate to be away from my family."

"Just this once," she said. There was something she wasn't telling me, I was sure of that. I told her, no, I couldn't do it. "Are you busy that night?" she asked.

"Ashley," I said, "look: you're a valuable client. But you have something up your sleeve. We can talk business, it doesn't have to be over dinner."

She said: "OK, no dinner. But can you come for an hour, anytime, Thursday, eight o'clock say, or even later; or before dinner, say six o'clock. You choose."

"Can't you tell me why?"

She hesitated. "I want you to meet Bobby's sister. Cassandra. I want you to talk to her. Bobby is trying to get her to call off the lawsuit."

"That would be great. But, Ashley, there's still Christopher. Bobby's brother. Did I tell you he came to see me?" I hadn't. I filled her in on the visit, and I added, "Christopher is adamant. I feel he's going to sue, come hell or high water."

"Bobby knows that," she said. "But if we could get his sisters to agree not to sue, that might help. And Bobby thinks he can do that, he really can. At least he can persuade Cassandra. Can you come meet her? Say yes, Frank; it's important."

I was still hesitant. First of all, it was somewhat irregular. I'm rusty on lawyers' ethics, it's been years and years since I took a course on professional responsibility, and as I recall it was crushingly boring, but the idea seemed a little dubious to me—the idea of trying to peel off the plaintiffs in a lawsuit against my client. But in the end I agreed. I told Celia that I had to visit a client Thursday evening, after dinner, just an hour or two.

"What client? Why can't they talk to you during business hours, Frank? I just don't like it."

"It's Ashley Savage. And her boyfriend, Bobby."

"Isn't that the night we're supposed to talk to the high school counselors, about the kids? Tell Ashley you're busy."

But she was wrong about the date we had to meet the counselors, and after some grumbling she agreed to let me go.

Ashley lived in a condo, near California Avenue, in Palo Alto. It was a typical California place, fairly new, well-kept up, with a tiny fountain in a central courtyard, in which water dribbled aimlessly onto a group of ceramic frogs. There were plants all about the central courtyard, with spiky leaves. There was something vaguely forlorn about the place. Ashley's condo was on the second floor. I got there somewhat after eight, and she answered the door in an apron. She led me into a living room, where I saw Bobby, sitting on the sofa, and next to him a woman who I imagined must be Cassandra Risley.

She looked to be a bit older than Bobby; she was wearing a pink blouse, with maximum cleavage; I had the feeling she was not wearing a brassiere; well, more than a feeling, but let's not go into that. She had on a short skirt, more or less red and blue, in big splotchy colors. She was wearing sandals. Something also gave me the feeling she was not wearing underwear either, but I dismissed this thought.

Bobby said, "This is my sister, Cassandra."

I mumbled something like, pleased to meet you. She gave me a stony look. She had piercing gray eyes; her hair was worn in a bun, and she had long, complicated, extravagant earrings in her ears, and rings on almost every finger. There was something about her face I can't quite describe; it was somehow lopsided. She resembled Bobby—I could see that; but he was good-looking, in a babyish sort of way, and she was not. Like him, she had a round face, but more irregular.

She said to me: "What are you staring at?"

I was embarrassed. "I wasn't staring."

"You were staring at my breasts," she said. "What is it with men? They're obsessed with breasts. It's ridiculous. Suppose I stared at your penis?"

We were off to a bad start. I could have said, my penis is not on display; your breasts are. Anyway, I tried not to look at her breasts, but she kept wiggling, and they kept bouncing; it was hard to avoid them. I could see she would be difficult to deal with. I said, feebly, "I'm sorry if I offended you."

"You're not sorry," she said, "but we'll forget about it. Let's talk business. You're Ashley's lawyer, aren't you?"

"I am."

"And my lawyer, too," Bobby said. "That's why I wanted you to meet the family."

Cassandra grunted; and I said, "Bobby, I'm not sure this is going to work. I mean, you and Ashley, you're on opposite sides."

"Not anymore," he said. "We're on the same side. And so are you, Cassandra. That's what I'm asking you to do. The lawsuit, it's just Christopher. And maybe Juno. I was hoping she'd come here, and maybe she will later on; she said she was busy."

Cassandra snorted. "Busy. With what, sitting in her condo, doing Sudoku, I suppose."

Bobby seemed upset by this. "She's our sister, Cassie. We have to get along."

"Ridiculous," she said. "Do cats and dogs get along? Our dear father, rest in peace," she said, turning to me, with a voice dripping with sarcasm, "he was married five times, did you know that? Or was it six. I don't even know the names of all of the wives, they came and went. Bobby is my actual brother, poor fellow. Juno is my half-sister. Christopher is my half-brother. I could do without them, frankly. "

"I've met Christopher," I said.

"Did you now? He's a real creep."

I was hoping to talk to Cassandra privately. I had taken a dislike to her, I have to admit. But I did have a duty to my client, and prying her loose from the lawsuit was of some significance. "Can we talk?" I asked.

She said: "Why not? I have nothing against talking. Freedom of speech and all that." She gave some sort of signal, and Ashley and Bobby disappeared into another room. "OK," she said, "the lovebirds are in the kitchen or the bedroom or wherever they are. Maybe they can have intercourse; it's a great opportunity. Look: As of now, I feel, I don't want any part of this lawsuit. The two of them, Christopher and Juno, they can sue your brains out, if they feel like it. I don't care. Count me out, that's what I said to him, to Christopher. I'm doing this for Bobby. Do you have something for me to sign? I'll go with Bobby. Blood is thicker than water."

"There's nothing to sign," I said. "Just—well, just don't join their lawsuit."

"Don't get me wrong," she said. "It's not that I don't want the money. I want my share of my grandmother's money. If that money doesn't come my way, I might have to reconsider. Ashley's father stole some of our money. Grandma's money I mean. But you know, I don't care; she had plenty more of it. Christopher, he gets all hot and bothered, all moral and Goody Two Shoes. As if grandma *earned* the money. She never worked a day in her life. She inherited every penny of it, from her father, and he was a lying, cheating wheeler-dealer. Listen, *he* stole the money; is there such a thing as a millionaire who got his money honestly? Not one. So none of us deserves the money, it's dirty money. But I'll take it. There's plenty there for all of us, as far as I know. Unless.... But let's wait on that."

Of course, the estate of Hortense Risley was no concern of mine; my client was Ashley Savage, and as long as she was allowed to keep her interest in the trust fund her father had set up, the rest was irrelevant.

There was a bowl of fruit on the coffee table, and she reached out, took an apple and bit into it. "I'm being honest," she said, "I do want money. Or enough money anyway. For my career. That's the main thing."

"Oh, yes," I said. I wondered what kind of a career she had. I soon found out.

"I'm an artist," she said. "A performance artist. I want to this wretched art school, but I quit. I couldn't take it. It was a bunch of zombies teaching other zombies. I thought: why does art have to be so damn *conventional*, same old, same old stuff. Canvas. Or marble, stone, or any of that. Dead things. *Things*. Art has to be alive. It has to be people. I'm art. I personally. That's what I felt. It came over me, suddenly. I was in this class, trying to draw a vase of flowers, and I thought, screw the flowers. I should draw *me*, metaphorically speaking. I should turn my life into art. I think some people, if you explain it to them, and if they're not idiots, they understand it. I'm trying to get people to think outside the box."

I nodded my head. Actually, on the issue of art, I was probably more likely to be inside the box, as far as taste is concerned. Certainly I would be outside any box that included Cassandra Risley.

"I was a sensation," she said, "in the Wichita Art Museum. They had a show, avant garde art, they called it. Avant garde indeed. There was nothing avant garde about it, in my opinion. If I had my way, I would have gone through the whole gallery and sprayed paint on all that crap. People just trying to break into the market. Meaningless. Anyway, I brought in an old wicker rocking chair, it was missing some of the wicker: good, that's what I wanted. And I took off my clothes, and I sat on the chair, rocking back and forth, in one of the exhibition rooms, sucking on a lollipop. I started people talking. That's what I wanted to happen."

"I see that," I said.

"Some people got the point. I was written up in the newspaper. I got fan mail. Even there in Kansas, where most of the people are scarecrows, with corncobs for brains. But there's always a few who are different. This one woman, she brought me sandwiches. I sat and ate them, right there. People were staring all the time. Believe me, it's work, sitting on a chair, rocking, for hours on end. A piece of the wicker kept poking me in the butt. The museum closed at 5:00, so I could get dressed and go home. I wanted to sleep in the museum, but they said no. You should see the reviews. I kept all the clippings. One of the critics, he was from the University of Kansas, he was positively enthusiastic. He said I was testing the boundaries of art. Somebody from the newspaper though, a guy who called himself a critic, hated the stuff. Critic my ass. Anyway, he came to the museum and stared at my body, he said I ought to be ashamed of myself. I said, thank you. *You* ought to be ashamed, covering yourself up, and hiding the inner rot."

I nodded my head.

"In Trenton, New Jersey, I did a different sort of thing. In their museum. I brought in a chair again, ordinary wicker chair, and I sat on the chair. I was naked, but painted different colors, red, white, and blue; and I clipped my toenails, and did all sorts of things. And I walked around the room, humming, and sometimes singing American the Beautiful. Making fun of patriotism, that was the point. And sometimes, my boyfriend at the time, Chester, he would come and sit next to me. On the floor, and he was naked too. And people would stare at us, and we would stare back. I wanted to have sex with Chester, right there in the museum, at a particular time. My idea was, we would announce it, the way in the zoo they say, the lions will get fed at three o'clock. We'd say, sexual intercourse at 3:00, in Room 21, or whatever it was. But the museum director, he said absolutely not. He said something about children in the museum. I said, why do we assume this would be bad for children? Might be good for them. To tell the truth, my boyfriend wasn't thrilled with the idea. I guess he was worried, he was afraid he wouldn't be able to perform in front of all those people. He was a pretty narcissistic guy—thought he was God's gift to woman, great lover, and so on, like all the rest of them. After one week, he said, Cassandra, I'm not coming any more. We broke up then and there. Anyway, a lot of the customers in the museum, I call them customers, but they were pretty hostile. The director said, I'm getting bad publicity. I said there's no such thing as bad publicity. But some local nut, from some church, maybe a Baptist church—what's with Baptists, they always seem the worst ones—anyway, he threatened a lawsuit, and one day, they even had to call the police."

I nodded my head again.

"Why do people have this hangup about nudity, anyway? The kids nowadays, they don't care. They send naked pictures back and forth. And why not? The whole clothing business, it's ridiculous. Why should we always wear the stuff? OK, in winter, you can't run around naked, it's freezing outside, even in California. But in summer, why not? We have zillions of photographs of famous people, like President Kennedy, or Franklin D. Roosevelt, but not a single naked picture. Now does that make sense? What kind of penis did George Washington have? Did Jane Austen have big boobs or what?"

I had trouble wrapping my mind around George Washington's penis, or Jane Austen's breasts; but I suppose Cassandra wanted me to think outside the box.

Mentally, I crawled right back into the box. I had this terrible fear that she was going to illustrate her point by taking her clothes off. If not here, then maybe in my office. God forbid. Maybe I need a sign in my office: "Law Offices of Frank May. No Nudity Allowed." Not that a sign would dissuade Cassandra Risley. I could see that.

"I'm a very political person," she said. "I had this great idea for the San Francisco Zoo. I'd be in a cage, naked of course, nothing there in the cage but a bunch of straw, and I'd pace back and forth and make noises, so people could see, this is what it's like, life in a zoo. So maybe they'd ask themselves, what are we doing to these animals. Of course the zoo people, they absolutely hated the idea; and nothing came of it. But I've got something new going, something I'm going to do in an art museum in Fargo. People actually live in Fargo, believe it or not. You have to ask yourself, why. There's oil and gas in North Dakota, but is that any reason to live there? I'd rather be dead. Anyway, this museum, it's in some old house, hundred year old house, it's a miracle nobody tore it down, and it has a lot of local artists. Wretched stuff. If they had any talent, would they stay in Fargo, North Dakota? But the director, he likes my work. My idea was, I'd take this room, take everything out of it, so it'd be absolutely empty. And then when somebody would come in, you know, a visitor to the museum, they would hear a voice saying: 'You're worthless. You're a worm. No, you're lower than a worm. You're nothing but a pinprick in the galaxy. You're meaningless.' That would be my voice on a recording. And then I'd laugh hysterically."

"I see," I said. But I didn't really see. I had my doubts about whether this would go over well in Fargo, North Dakota. Or in New York City, for that matter.

My tone of voice must have given me away. She gave me a look of withering contempt. She probably dismissed me as a hopeless Philistine. Could she be right? I've been to the Museum of Modern Art in San Francisco a number of times. It's a beautiful building, designed by a prominent architect. They have a permanent collection, nothing as good as New York, but I suppose it's a lot better than Fargo, North Dakota. They also have shows, exhibits, usually of new artists, up and coming artists. I almost always hate these exhibits; I don't know why I even bother to look at them; a glutton for punishment, I guess. Isn't art supposed to be beautiful?

Even more than the paintings and sculptures, I hate the explanations they give, the statements next to the works themselves, conveying to the ignorant masses the deeper meaning of it all. These never make any sense to me. The work, let's say, consists of an empty canvas, except for a piece of string stapled to the canvas, and a small area smeared with dog turds (a recent masterpiece). And then you read: "In this startling oeuvre, the artist challenges us to re-examine our notions of space and time, the real and the unreal, the parameters of art and life, and the psychology of the everyday object, only at another level, that is subjectified and positioned in our field of vision." I'm actually quoting this from the last exhibit I saw.

Rembrandt, poor soul, never made this kind of brilliant explanation.

Cassandra was going on about plans she had to revivify the art scene in Fresno, or was it Fargo, where one of the "very prominent local business people, a man I met on my last trip, he's in cotton futures, and he's eager to support my work. He found it dazzling. Of course, he wants to fuck me, too." I interrupted her at this point, and brought her back to the subject. "Cassandra, can we talk about Ashley? First of all, how was dinner?"

"I don't care about food very much," she said. "It's fuel, nothing more."

"Well, was it decent fuel?"

"I'm vegan," she said. "I told Ashley that. I do eat oysters, though. They have no nervous system. An oyster can't feel pain."

I wanted to ask her about shrimp. Perhaps a shrimp has deep feelings. No, she said, when I posed the question, she doesn't eat shrimp. Was I supposed to feel guilty when I inflict pain on a shrimp? I changed the subject. "You said you would withdraw from the lawsuit, like Bobby. That's very good news."

She said: "I'm doing it for Bobby. He has this mad passion for your client. He could hardly sue her one minute, and have sex with her the next. I mean, maybe Bobby could; he's so flighty. I'm unconventional myself, and proud of it; in some ways he is and in some ways he isn't. Right now, he's so involved, he can't think straight. OK, it's his business. Whatever he wants."

"You won't change your mind, I hope."

"Look: I'm not a money-grubber, like Christopher. I *need* money, I'll admit it. But I'm not greedy. Christopher is just greedy. Bobby ... well, he doesn't really care. Listen: He'll have Ashley's money, I suppose. If she gets any."

"That's a question," I said.

"You know, Bobby's my full brother. The others are halfsies. I told you that. I have no feeling for them. With Bobby, it's different. I feel we're one flesh, if you know what I mean. He's an angel, he really is. Everybody calls him a puppy dog. He's terrifically shy, the opposite of me, I'm a reaction to him, I think, even though I'm older. He blushes all the time, that is, when he's not crying like a baby. I absolutely love him. I like to make him blush. He came to the museum, where I was sitting, you know, naked, and he blushed from ear to ear. Funny thing, he attracts women like honey attracts bees. Even though he's so painfully shy. It's a paradox. I told him once, Bobby, I love you. He said, I love you too Cassandra. I said, no, I don't mean that brother-sister shit, I mean I really love you. You saw me naked, but, you know, I never saw *you* naked. I'd love to see what your butt looks like. Let me come over next time you're going to take a shower. You're incredibly sexy. He was embarrassed, turned beet red, he blushes so easily. But then he said, of course you're joking. Actually, I wasn't. I told him so. I really wanted to have sex with him. I propositioned him. He said, Cassy, no! Really, stop it: that's incest. I said, so what, Cleopatra slept with her brother, all the Egyptian pharaohs did it with their sisters. He said, that was in the old days, and I'm not the pharaoh, please don't say such things. They say men are the aggressors, and some of them are, look at all the rapists, but I think a lot of men are pretty chicken, they're actually scared of sex; and maybe even the rapists, you know, they can't do it any other way, they're like eunuchs otherwise. Disgusting."

It was hard to keep her on track. I tried to get her back on the subject, I started talking about the estate, and about the lawsuits, the legal issues and so on. She obviously paid no attention.

"I wish you wouldn't talk like a lawyer," she said. "Try talking like a human being. I'm not interested in that legalistic crap. But yes, of course I'm with Bobby. If for no other reason than to spite Christopher. He's a total pain in the ass. I told him once, you know, I think you're an android, somebody who came from outer space. He's so uptight it's pathetic. Juno, there's another one. She'll go along with him, I suppose. She's also pathetic, so passive, you know what I mean? Well, I'm not sure about her. No idea what goes on in her frightened little mind. Anyway, why should I sue Ashley Savage? What do I have against her? Nothing. In fact, I like what she's doing for Bobby. Giving him a sex life, not that he's a virgin or anything like that, he's got a kid in fact, but the two of them, they're regular love-birds. I never saw him so happy."

Two down and two to go, I said to myself, although Christopher was going to be a tough nut to crack. And even Cassandra hedged a bit. She wasn't going to join the lawsuit, no, she was emphatic about that; but every few minutes she seemed to wobble. "Mind you," she said, "I could change my mind. If I don't get money from my grandmother's estate, well, you can't expect me to kiss those millions goodbye. My career takes money."

"I understand."

"Bobby keeps telling me how wonderful his Ashley is. Bobby is a baby, he really is. You should meet his former wife, Hildegarde. A real witch. She got her hooks into him, and now she's blackmailing him, in a way, about his little boy. Snot-nosed brat, but to Bobby he's the world's most marvelous infant. Now he goes on and on about Ashley, this is real love, blah blah; but of course *she* isn't the one we're suing, not really; her father, Langley, the quack doctor, he's the one. I know he's dead. Deserved it, too. Whoever killed him should get a medal. He would have taken every penny from my grandmother, if he could. As it is, he got mega-millions."

"Did you know Langley Savage? Did you meet him? Like, at the hospital?"

"I did see him at the hospital. I went to visit my grandmother. Frankly, I wanted money for my career. I hadn't gone for years; I was busy, trying to make a life, and to be honest, I just wasn't into old people, I didn't like them, always whining, and creeping along, blocking the sidewalk, I mean, you wonder why we keep them alive, I think I read somewhere, the Eskimos got rid of old people. Sent them onto the ice, like, good rid-dance, it's time to die. Anyway, I used to send her clippings, my grandmother, clippings about my shows. When she was younger, she seemed to have some sort of feeling, about the grandkids, including me, but then she sort of retreated into her shell. Christopher, of course, he tried to get through to her. Money, of course. That's what he wanted. She never said boo to him. Maybe she was already gaga. Anyway, I thought, I'd better go, no harm in trying. And of course he was there. The doctor. Langley Savage. Like some sort of bodyguard or I don't know what, monitoring everything that went on there."

"Did you speak to your grandmother? And when was this?"

"When? Who knows. I don't keep track. A while ago. Did I speak to her? Can you talk to a turnip? She was practically a vegetable. I mean, I don't think she had the slightest idea who I was. There she was, and this quack doctor, and the other guy, rubbing her feet, and she was going ooh and aah, maybe she was getting a sexual charge out of it, I mean, the foot rubbing, even though she was a million years old. And the room, it was disgusting, filled with stuffed animals and dolls, and positively stifling. I said to the doctor, can't you open a window? And he said, well, Mrs. Risley gets cold. Cold! She had like a dozen blankets on. I said, 'hi, grandma.' No response. And all the time, the creep, the foot doctor, he was rubbing her toes, as I said, sort of massaging then, and her ankles. It was nauseating. I didn't stay long. Those doctors, I think they were drugging her. Dr. Savage, he was an absolute criminal. Robbed her blind. And then she died. Well, it was time, she was so old, no use to anybody. I guess her money kept her alive: she could buy the whole hospital if she wanted. I guess *they* wanted her alive, those robbers, so they could milk her some more. There was no funeral, for some reason. I guess she was cremated. Who cares. We heard from some lawyer, about her estate. I couldn't follow a word of it, it might as well have been in Chinese. And then he showed up, the doctor, Dr. Savage, I mean, the colossal nerve of him. He starting making phone calls. Called all four of us. All the grandchildren."

"He called you too?"

"He called all of us. That's what I said. Told us he wanted to talk to us individually, and it was very very important, he said this in some sort of tone of voice, like it was life and death, and it had to do with our grandmother's estate, and that millions of dollars were at stake. I said, yeah, what about the estate, what business is it of yours? And he said, oh, it's my business all right. I said, OK, tell me, what's this all about. But he wouldn't say anything. He said, I'm staying in a hotel, in Palo Alto, you can come meet me there."

"And did you go?

"I said I didn't have time. I was all busy with my plans for doing a gig in Little Rock, Arkansas. An installation, I'll tell you about it some time. So, no, I didn't go. I would have, I guess. I told Bobby to go and let me know what this is all about. And here's a surprise: That bitch, Hildegarde, she had the gall to call me on the phone. I said, what do you want? She said *she* had a call from Dr. Savage. I said, you? Why on earth? Well, she said, maybe he didn't know we were divorced; he thought he was calling Bobby, something like that. And he wanted Bobby to go see him. I said, well, you're the last person on earth who could talk Bobby into something. She said, I know that, but you're close to your brother, you do it. But I didn't. I slammed the phone down. I wasn't going to talk to that bitch. The way she treated Bobby, poor guy. And you know what? I found out later, she ended up actually *sleeping* with Langley Savage. Bobby's ex-wife, can you beat that?"

"Did Bobby go? To see Dr. Savage?"

"He says he didn't and maybe he was telling the truth, maybe he wasn't; anyway, that's Bobby's business, and I wasn't about to suck up to Christopher or Juno, so I never found out what Dr. Savage was up to. It was *something*, I'm sure. The man was as crooked as a three dollar bill. Maybe he was going to shake us down for more money. For medical services or whatever. I wouldn't give him a nickel."

At that point Ashley and Bobby came back into the room. We talked for a bit, small talk, while Bobby kept nuzzling Ashley, twisting his fingers around her hand and acting like a lovesick adolescent. Cassandra left a few minutes later and I thought it was time for me to go. I asked Bobby about the call from Dr. Savage, did he know what Dr. Savage had in mind; he said no. I asked him if he had gone to see Dr. Savage.

He said no, he hadn't. But he turned beet red. Of course he was lying. With Bobby you didn't need a polygraph.

So he did go. But why keep it a secret? I wanted to ask him that; but I didn't dare. I said goodbye and left. I could hear, inside my head, Celia's voice, which was in a way implanted there; she was telling me to stop probing. It was as if she had some kind of space-age machine, sending messages through the ether, right into my brain. I drove home in a sour mood. Somewhere in the wilds of suburbia, I took a wrong turn, went too far, made a U-turn, which was apparently illegal, and was stopped by a policeman, who gave me a ticket.

It wasn't my day.

11

The next morning was extremely busy, and full of client-based irritations. I decided to treat myself to a good lunch, and I headed out the door intent on gobbling down some sushi at an excellent Japanese restaurant, Bengoshi, which was only a block away. It was a brilliant sunlit day; and the air was clean and clear. According to the calendar, we were in the very middle of the rainy season, but California was suffering a horrendous drought, and we're not getting the rain we need. All winter, almost no rain, every day bright and sunny. If you must have a weather calamity, I suppose, this is the kind I would choose.

Hardly had I gone out the door, when I saw Zelda, crossing the street in my direction. She was in a huge hurry and almost out of breath. "Frank," she said, "I was hoping to find you in."

"Hi Zelda, well, as you see, I'm not in. I'm on my way to lunch."

"Can I join you? Is this a business lunch?"

I could have lied; but I didn't. "No ... just me."

She said: "I have a lot to report."

We settled into a booth in the restaurant and placed our orders. "I love sushi," Zelda said, "it's so spiritual, in a way. It reminds me of the sea, all that seaweed. It's good for the brain, I really think so, Frank. Good for my brain, anyway."

"It doesn't do anything for *my* brain," I said. "At least nothing I've noticed. Maybe it's different for different people. I do like it though. Except for sea urchin. I don't like sea urchin."

"Frank," she said, "I've been making progress on your case."

"Zelda, dear Zelda, really, it's not my case. I don't have a case. I mean, my case is Ashley Savage and her legal affairs. Not who killed her father."

She brushed this aside, "Yes, yes. OK, Frank, let's pretend you're not working on the case. Which I don't believe. Ashley surely would want a person with your talents...."

"Oh God."

"I won't pursue this," she said. "So let's just say, I'm doing it on my own, but I like to tell you how it's going."

"Fine with me," I said, fumbling with my chopsticks.

"I've been talking to Hildegarde," she said. "Hildegarde Risley. Bobby's ex-wife. Did you know that Dr. Savage called her? Or called a number, trying to get Bobby, and she answered. Whatever. Did you know about that?"

"As a matter of fact I did," I said. The minute I said this, I was sorry. There was a look of triumph on Zelda's face. I know what she was thinking: he *is* working on the case. "But so what? She has nothing to do with this."

"Oh, but she does. That phone call, it was fateful. It started something. Sometimes, life, it's like a movie, or one of my romance novels. Well, not quite. I think they met somewhere, maybe at the hospital, but still, the phone call, it made a difference. I didn't realize it at the time, but she and he, well, soon they had a love affair going. So she knows a lot of things. Now I didn't get details, mind you. She didn't want to talk to me. She's not an easy person. I hope she'll talk to you, Frank."

"To me? Why on earth would she?"

"Well, I told her, I was working as an investigator, private investigator, looking into the death of Langley Savage, of course she didn't believe me, she asked me for identification, my license, and of course I don't have a license, I didn't even know they needed a license, but anyway, that was terribly embarrassing. So I said, well, I don't have a license, but I'm working for an attorney, Frank May, and he's representing Ashley Savage; and also, he is involved—that's what I said, 'involved'—in the investigation of Dr. Savage's death.... I love that word, 'involved,' it doesn't mean anything, it can be anything, if you say you're involved, that could mean so many things. Anyway, I told her, well, if you won't talk to me, why don't you talk to Mr. May...."

"Zelda, you didn't!"

"I did. What's the harm? Don't you want to talk to her? She's a suspect, isn't she?"

"For one thing, Zelda, I know you don't believe me, but honestly, I'd rather not get too entangled in this affair. For another thing, why is she a suspect, Zelda? Why would she want to kill Dr. Savage?"

"I know, Frank. Motive, motive, motive. It's so important. But maybe a lover's quarrel? I'm trying to figure all this out, why somebody wanted to kill him. This Hildegarde, she's tough, she's just the kind who might kill somebody. I had a woman just like her in one of my romance novels. The one about the pirate who fell in love with a nun, in the Caribbean. I told you about it—one of my most successful books. For a while, it just leaped off the shelves. It had a wonderful picture on the cover. There was Sister Santa Cruz, in her habit, and the pirate, all bare-chested. Anyway, Hildegarde, she didn't look at all like the way I pictured Sister Santa Cruz; but she was the way I pictured the Mother Superior. Cold, hard, mean. She's the villainess in the book, along with a British admiral, Lord Fingerdrum, who was hell-bent on catching the pirate, Rodrigo, and hanging him from the tallest mast. Anyway, the book made money for a change."

"Zelda," I said, "I really don't want to see her. I ... I promised my wife I'd stay out of this affair, and there's no reason for me to talk to this woman, I mean, no reason connected with my actual role, which is as Ashley's lawyer."

But Zelda was not the kind of person you could easily talk out of things. Was I finally getting through to her? Maybe. She said: "Aren't you also the lawyer for her father, I mean, for his estate?"

"No, Zelda, I'm not; and why would that make a difference?"

Zelda brushed that fact off, as if it was some minor technicality. I felt, in a way, helpless. Zelda was a force of nature. In the end I promised her weakly that I would see Hildegarde Risley in my office. After leaving the sushi bar, I consoled myself further with a hot fudge sundae at an ice cream parlor down the street; in a minor concession, I left off the whipped cream. I walked back to my office and consoled myself further with the thought that *maybe* there was a valid reason to talk to the woman. I'm Ashley's lawyer, and Ashley is now connected to Bobby in a way, and she's Bobby's ex-wife, so that gives meeting her some sort of relevance. This was thin soup, I know, and I cannot honestly say I was able to convince myself entirely. Nor would anybody else probably buy it.

Anyway, some four days later, in mid-afternoon in my office, there was Hildegarde Risley sitting across from me. She was a woman in her early forties, I would say, which surprised me, since Bobby was not even thirty. She was thin and bony, with a longish nose, dark eyes and graying hair; she was dressed in navy blue—a skirt and a matching blouse. She had a kind of severe look to her, or was I simply prejudiced by thinking of the evil Mother Superior in Zelda's novel? She had a deepish voice, and a distinctly unfriendly air to her.

She said: "This woman, Zelda Valdez, she said she was working for you and that you were investigating the death of Langley Savage."

"I think she's exaggerating a bit," I said. "But I do represent Ashley Savage, his daughter."

"Why is it any of her business, this Ashley person, whether I saw her father, or knew her father, or whatever?"

I mumbled something about the estate; what came out was, frankly, word salad: "It's, uh, complex, you know, there's lawsuits.... And this, uh, affects his daughter's inheritance, I mean, if she has one.... Anyway, I need to know as much as I can about Dr. Savage.... Ashley ... an only child after all.... And we don't know if he left a will, and the, uh, size of his estate...."

"His estate? Everything he had, he stole from the old lady. And the family is suing him; I'm sure you know that; they're trying to get it all back."

"I don't know anything about those lawsuits," I said, a bit

disingenuously. "And I'm not handling his estate, so I have no idea about ... well, what's in it. For all I know, he had plenty of money of his own; he was a doctor, after all. Doctors make money, don't they?" I wondered if she knew about Ashley's trust fund. Did that kind of money come from the normal practice of medicine? Did he operate on a lot of people's brains, or give MRIs and CAT scans to anybody who walked in the door? Or did he invest some of his earnings in real estate, or in Google stock when it was pennies? There are so many ways to make money. Not that I've done any of them.

I had to wonder about Hildegarde. She had been having an affair with Dr. Savage. So they told me. Lovers. But she hardly spoke of him with affection—that was a striking fact. For instance she said he "stole from the old lady," which is hardly a loving kind of phrase.

"Everybody's suing him. He was in trouble," she said. "The medical board or whatever that is. Tax people. The Risley family. Everybody. And he gambled. Drank. Spent money recklessly. I don't think he had anything much besides the Risley assets."

I couldn't help asking, "You were, uh, friendly with Dr. Savage?" Of course I knew the answer already.

She gave me a look of total contempt. She realized, of course, what I meant by "friendly," and how dumb a label it was for her relationship. "Yes," she said, "we were friendly, if that's the way you want to put it. But he never talked business with me. I asked him questions about money, yes, but he said I'll talk to your ex-husband, not to you. I said to him, well, we're divorced, but I have a claim on his money, don't I? At least some of it. So fill me in. But he wouldn't do it."

I decided that she was probably lying, like everybody else. Surely she knew more about Langley Savage's affairs than she let on.

But I didn't need her as a source for *some* kinds of information. I made a mental note to ask Gideon who was handling the old lady's estate and whether he was handling Langley's.

I was happy when Hildegarde left; I could not imagine for the life of me how she had ever appealed to Bobby Risley, but then love is blind. And how had she managed to appeal to Langley Savage too? I was disappointed that Hildegarde had given out so little information. I was dying to know what Langley Savage wanted to say to the four grandchildren. Bobby and Cassandra claimed they never found out. Christopher probably did know; but he would certainly refuse to tell me what this was all about. He was, after all, The Enemy. That left Juno Risley.

I called Gideon later that day. Gideon was, as usual, reluctant to say anything much to me. Getting information out of him was like pulling teeth. Big teeth. Molars. But at least he was willing to tell me who was handling the estate of Hortense Risley. The family had retained Foster, Worcester and Fain, a boutique firm specializing in estate work, but with a very upscale group of clients. There are rich people, and there are super-rich people. The rich people fly first class. The super-rich own an airplane. Foster, Worcester and Fain was the go-to firm for families of dead people who had a jet airplane as one of their expensive toys. "And which partner?" I asked.

"I believe it's Wentworth Fain." Fain was the senior partner. Foster and Worcester were dead. Having left behind, I'm sure, very substantial estates of their own.

* * *

I went over the events of the day with Celia that evening, after assuring her that dinner had been absolutely delicious. It wasn't every night that Celia made dinner. She was, after all, a working wife, and I was perfectly satisfied with leftovers, take-in Chinese meals, pizza, and sandwiches. I could hardly expect her to come home from an exasperating day at her high school and prepare a dish from one of Julia Child's recipes, with twenty ingredients and seventeen steps in the process, including something left in a marinade for 48 hours. The girls perpetually grumbled about the quality of our dinners, and held up as a model some mythical mother of a friend, who made hot, cooked meals every evening. I doubted whether this paragon really existed.

But all this did make Celia feel guilty enough to do something dramatic on occasion. This night she concocted an elegant pasta, with mushrooms and a terrific sauce. She bought a fruit pie for dessert. The girls of course expressed no opinion, rejected the pasta with a loud "yuck," and fled as soon as they had gobbled down the pie, to spend the evening giggling in their rooms and texting their friends.

Celia was annoyed, of course. I had to bear the brunt of her displeasure. Not about our children, but about my connection with the late Dr. Savage. "Frank," she said, "you're completely incorrigible. I told you not to meddle, and here you are doing it. Why?"

I'm sure my explanation sounded weak. In fact, though, I was on slightly stronger ground than usual. Ashley was my client; and the trust fund was her biggest asset. She might conceivably also get something more from her father. Undoubtedly, Dr. Savage had wanted to talk to the Risleys about money—his money, or Hortense's money, or some combination. And that could very well be relevant to my client. At least that was something I had talked myself into.

I called Ashley the next morning, and told her I wanted to get in touch with Juno Risley, and could she ask Bobby about this? Were they on decent terms, Bobby and Juno? She called me back later: "He doesn't know her all that well, really, even though she's his half-sister. But he likes her, she likes him, and she's a lot easier to deal with than Christopher. I told him what you wanted, and he said he'd see if he could arrange it."

And he did. A few days later, Juno Risley, in person, was sitting in my office.

12

I have to be honest: Juno Risley was a most unattractive woman. She was, I would guess, in her late 30's. She was short like Bobby, but dumpy; her breasts were too big, so that she looked top-heavy, and she had a kind of unattractive paunch. She wore thick glasses and squinted from time to time. Her hair was dark, tinged with a bit of gray, and extremely messy; it seemed unruly, gathered in clumps. She wore it in a bun, but locks of hair escaped captivity and fell over her forehead. I can't begin to describe what she was wearing. She was, I suppose, a wealthy woman. A woman as rich as Hortense Risley had no doubt set up some sort of trust fund for her grandchildren, maybe after her son died, and before she retreated into the hospital. Surely Juno had had access to money in her life; but there was no sign of that in the way she was dressed. I am no judge of women's clothing, but Juno's long skirt, reaching to her ankles, struck me as more bag-lady than, say, Givenchy. Juno had thick lips and thick ankles, and a weak, receding chin. She had fat fingers, too. Not, on the whole, a woman of movie star quality. She had a sort of dim, faraway look. But not hostile or unfriendly.

"I'm glad you could come," I said. "I know that there are, uh, disagreements, in the family; and I appreciate that you're willing to talk to me."

Her voice was not unpleasant. I felt that, inside that unappealing body, there was a person who meant to be kind. Of the do-no-harm sort. "Family," she said. "We never really had a family, Mr. May. That's an important thing for you to remember. I know you mean well. Bobby spoke to me about you. Bobby said you want to help us."

"Whoa, Juno. I want to be honest with you. I'm a lawyer. Ashley Savage is my client. I want to help *her*. It's not that I don't want to help *you*; but that's not my job. And call me Frank, please."

"It's such a dirty business," she said. "Bobby and I, we were the only ones who cared at all for our poor grandmother. She was always somehow in a different world. Even before she went into that hospital. And she never had a happy life. I mean, people might think: all those millions, and a house here and a house there, and an apartment in New York, and an apartment in Paris. But she was a lonely woman. Her father was awful to her. He was a terrible man. All that money, but he was mean and vicious. And her marriage, a disaster. People took advantage of her. And her only child, *our* father, oh, he couldn't have been worse. I hate to say it, but it's true. No wonder we turned out the way we did."

"But your mother...."

"Who ever saw her? She was a society woman. Five marriages. Or six. Oh, I wanted so to have a real mother; but you don't get to pick your mother. She loved to spend money, but not on us. And she drank. I have these awful memories, mother drunk and sitting in a chair cursing and cursing. We were raised by nannies. I know, some people love their nannies, and some of them were nice, but then there were some that actually hated us. There was never any love in our lives. Never. That's why I think Christopher, my brother, is so hard, so tough. He had to be, to survive. Me, I was the ugly duckling, but I never turned into a swan."

I found this confessional embarrassing. I muttered something vaguely empathic.

"When my father married again, and had two more kids, Bobby and Cassandra, I hoped I could get close to them. Somehow it didn't happen I always liked Bobby. Cassandra hated me. I don't know why. I always liked school. I was good in school. I went to the University of California, after high school, Riverside. I majored in math. But the guys, the math guys, they were mean to me. They thought, a girl, she can't do math. Maybe I couldn't. I gave it up. The most I do is Sudoku. I love Sudoku. I do the puzzles every day. But I'm boring you: all of us talk too much."

I asked her how well she knew her grandmother. "Not well," she said. "I did try to visit her. Bobby did, too, once in a while. The others, I don't know. Grandma, she was sweet, in a distant sort of way. She didn't know how to relate to people, only to stuffed animals and dolls. And then, as you know, she went to this hospital, and she stayed there. I once said, grandma, don't you want to go home? She said 'this is my home.'"

"Did you know Dr. Savage?"

"Oh yes. And Dr. Christoff."

"You know, they're accused of doing, uh, bad things, stealing money from your grandmother."

"Oh, not Dr. Christoff. He was such a kind man. Grandma loved him. He massaged her feet, and he was nice to her. I think she had trouble with her feet, feet can be so painful, I mean, like if your shoes don't fit. I told him all about my feet. I have bunions. Dr. Savage ... he stayed in the background when I was there. I never had a clear picture. And of course, I know nothing about all this money business, the estate, taxes, all of that. I just don't want to be involved in that sort of thing, I never have been. I have a financial adviser, a man from Fidelity Investments, and he takes care of everything."

"Can ... I ask you.... Your brother Christopher is suing the estate, I mean, Dr. Savage's estate.... Are you part of this lawsuit?"

I was skating on thin ice, ethically speaking. At least I think so. Presumably the Risley family had lawyers—but here I was, talking directly to one of the Risleys, about a matter that concerned my own client, but was certainly not in Juno Risley's interest. But she squinted behind her thick glasses, took off those glasses, squinted again, wiped the glasses with a cloth, and said: "Oh, I don't know. Christopher can be so insistent. He says it's our money, and people stole it. Did you know that grandma set up trusts for us? Some bank manages the money, I get a check every few months, and I don't need more money, I really don't. They say grandma was very, very rich, and I suppose she was. She owned a lot of property. If I inherit some money, I want to set up a foundation. Do you know how to do that?"

The thought of Juno Risley as a client—and a rich one—was extremely tempting. I said, yes, I did know how to set up a foundation. "Oh, that's so nice," she said. "I don't like the lawyers we have. They seem so formal. Bobby said you were a nice man. An education foundation, that's what I was thinking of. I went on a trip to Africa once, I was in South Africa, and saw all the animals, but oh! The people in the villages, they were so poor, and I felt so sorry for them. I want to help people out, with my money. I loved math in school, I told you I was a math major, but I never did anything with it. I don't have a job. I do volunteer work, in a soup kitchen. My foundation, we'll get young people, math people, and they'll go to Africa, and work with little kids. Do you like math, Frank?"

Actually, I don't. I never took to it in school. Now, decades later, I put the blame squarely on Mr. Mitnick, my high school math teacher, a short, overweight man with a handlebar moustache, who wore tweed jackets and a blue necktie every day, and who worked very hard to make algebra boring and pointless, and succeeded beyond his wildest dreams.

The only worse teacher I had was Miss Buffins, who taught French. She was what we called an old maid, which in those days actually meant no sex; at least that's what we kids thought. Sex with Miss Buffins was simply inconceivable. She was prudish, as well as incompetent. I really don't think she knew much French, either, even though she taught it. Short of concentration camp guards, high school students as a group are among the world's cruelest people. And Miss Buffins was a born victim. We loved asking her embarrassing questions, like, "Miss Buffins, I was wondering, how do you say 'seal' in French, you know, the animal, the one that goes honk honk and balances balls on its nose?" And she would turn bright red, because the word in French is "le phoque," as of course we already knew.

Why was I thinking suddenly of Margaret Buffins, the high school French teacher? Because in some ways Juno reminded me of her. Physically at least. Miss Buffins was dowdy and several sizes too large. And short. Unmarried. To us, she looked like a total loser. And she wore thick glasses too. Still, after all, Juno was the granddaughter of a woman worth hundreds of millions of dollars. Poor Miss Buffins surely had no such luck, and her life was no doubt cramped and dreary.

Or maybe not. What did I know? Maybe Miss Buffins was a secret swinger.

I told Juno I would be more than happy to help set up the foundation. "Of course," she said, "I don't have the money yet. But if I get it ... and I'll name it after my grandmother, I'll call it the Hortense Risley Math Fund."

"Sounds great," I said. I told her a few things about foundations, their tax status, and the like. She listened carefully. Then I slowly steered the ship of our conversation into port. I asked her whether she had gone to see Langley Savage, shortly before he died, that is.

"Oh, I didn't want to. And Christopher, he can be very autocratic, he said, don't go; and then he changed his mind, and he said, yes, go; and then he changed his mind again; and I was really upset about the whole thing—but in the end I did go. I met him at the dining room, in that hotel, the one in Palo Alto, but he didn't want to talk there, he said he had confidential things to say, could we come to his room, and I felt so awkward but I went with him."

"And?"

"I don't think he wanted to tell me the whole story. I felt he was looking down on me; he thought Christopher was some sort of leader, and that I would just follow whatever Christopher said. Dr. Savage, he did say he had information, some sort of document, and that it had to do with grandma's money. And I said, well, I really don't care about the money, but of course he didn't believe me, and it's actually not entirely true, because I was thinking about the foundation. He said something about how this document might make a difference, and I said, what kind of difference, and he said, a difference between you getting nothing at all, and getting millions and millions of dollars. I said I don't understand, what're you talking about? And then he said, well, I'll explain it to you. I'm sure he explained it to Christopher, by the way. Anyway, I said, all right, but then the phone rang, and he picked it up, and I have no idea who it was, but he listened, and he seemed extremely upset. He put down the phone and said I can't talk to you, I'm sorry. I said, maybe some other time, and he said yes, yes and he practically pushed me out the door. So I never did find out."

When she left, I sat for a while in my office, thinking. What did Langley Savage have up his sleeve? Juno said he mentioned "some sort of document." What could that be? I had a general idea—after all, I deal with "documents" every day, it's my bread and butter. I couldn't be sure, but I thought, could he be referring to a will, or a trust perhaps, something that Hortense Risley had executed—but if so, where was it and what was it? No use asking Ashley, who knew less about her father than anybody.

How could I find out? The only person likely to know, I supposed, was Gideon Grambling. I had other questions to ask him, too.

So I found myself, a few days later, sitting in his elegant conference room, with the wrap-around view of San Francisco, the Golden Gate Bridge, and the Marin highlands in the distance. I hated visiting him. Gideon made me wait, as usual, after his receptionist, in an exceedingly frosty manner, showed me into the conference room. This receptionist was new. At the time that Gideon and I first had dealings—that was in connection with a different case—he was in the midst of a secret affair with his young receptionist, Miss Guthrie; the affair broke up his marriage eventually. But that was water under the bridge. His present receptionist, Miss Murgatroyd, had very little in common with Miss Guthrie, except for insufferable snobbery. She was a woman in her 60's, I would say, with a pencil thin body, dyed hair, flaming red nail polish, and an elegant blue outfit. Gideon must have told her I was an insignificant suburban lawyer, because she treated me more or less the way she would have treated a homeless bum who came looking for the key to the men's room. But in my business, you learn to swallow a lot of guff.

I cooled my heels in the conference room for a good twenty minutes, and then Gideon came in, with a brusque and unconvincing apology. "How are you, Frank?"

"Surviving," I said. "Each day is a triumph."

He gave me a look, as if to say, what on earth does that mean? I said, "I need to know some things, Gideon, about the estate of Langley Savage."

"Oh? Like what, for instance?"

"Like: what is the status of the estate? How much money is there? What's going on? Don't forget, I'm representing his daughter."

"Frank," he said. "So many questions. No easy answers. Is there much of an estate? That is exceedingly difficult to say. We're at a very preliminary stage, of course, and I can't comment on any actual or potential assets or, for that matter, liabilities...."

"Gideon," I said, "please don't give me the runaround. Is there money here?"

"If by 'here' you mean the United States, I really don't know. If you're referring to the Cayman Islands or God-knows-where...." But then he broke off, and said. "I'll be honest with you, Frank. I'm getting out."

"Getting out?"

"I don't want to handle this estate. This estate is nothing but trouble. Lawsuits. Offshore accounts. The late Dr. Savage was as slippery as an eel. I am so sorry I ever got involved. It was the mistake of a lifetime, believe me. I went to Ivy League schools, Columbia Law School, order of the coif, I clerked for a federal judge, and here, in San Francisco, I've built up a practice, everything done in accordance with the highest professional standards. My list of clients, well, it's confidential, but it's the leading families of San Francisco. Old money. People on the board of the San Francisco symphony. I get invited to the most exclusive parties, fundraisers, benefits, for the De Young Museum, the Asian Art Museum. Just last evening, I was at the Palace of the Legion of Honor, they were having a private affair, very exclusive. I have a reputation; it's my most precious asset. This man ... he pulled the wool over my eyes, I thought he was legitimate, a leading member of the medical profession, a man with money, and I was foolish enough to believe everything he told me. He told me money was no object. I should have investigated, but I didn't. Big mistake. The man was a charlatan, plain and simple. Now the FBI is involved, and the Medical Board, and who knows who else. If he were alive, I would simply drop him as a client, I could have done that, you know; and I was in process of doing that. Now, I don't know. I asked a specialist in legal ethics, can I simply walk away from this? This man was my client, and there are lawsuits pending. This expert, Rhoda DeBree—she teaches at Boalt Hall—she said, well, it wasn't so clear. I thought, am I trapped? But nobody can force me to represent this creature, or his estate."

"And the will? You said he had a will."

"Yes, he had a will. I told you that. Not an elaborate will. You know about the trust for his daughter. And he did fund it, that much I know. Heaven only knows where the money came from. At any rate: the will was a simple affair. He named me executor. He left half of his estate to the trust for his daughter, Ashley. Didn't I explain that to you?"

"You did. And you said, the other half is also in trust for his daughter but reserving the right to make changes."

"Yes. And, by the way, he did make a change. In a codicil. I just found that out, this codicil, it just turned up. They found it with his papers. Anyway, he named a beneficiary, for this second trust. Bobby Risley."

"Bobby Risley? Are you sure?"

"Of course I'm sure."

"But Gideon, I don't understand. Bobby Risley was nothing to him. Bobby is Hortense Risley's grandson. I don't believe they even knew each other. Well, I suppose they had met, at the hospital, but surely that doesn't amount to much. Half the estate? I can't believe it."

"Be that as it may, that's what the man wanted."

My mind was racing wildly about. What on earth could

this mean? Bobby and Ashley were now an item, but Langley Savage couldn't have known that; he was safely dead. Did Bobby know about this will? Suddenly, I started to wonder about Bobby: this sudden passion for Ashley—was that sincere? Or did it have something to do with the money in Langley Savage's estate? But how could he have known about that?

"But I should add," Gideon said, "that the will may be irrelevant. As a matter of fact, we can't find it."

"You don't have it?"

"No, he insisted he wanted to keep the original. I have a copy, of course; but as you know, only the original counts. He said he had a safe in his house. He told me he lived in Pacific Heights, in an old Victorian mansion. That was, it turns out, a complete fabrication. He rented a room somewhere, in the Mission District, and a few days before he died, he checked into a hotel in Palo Alto. At any rate, there's no trace of the will."

"He destroyed it?"

"I suppose that's possible. More likely, somebody took it. The hotel room was a pigsty, but there were, shall we say, indications that someone had been there, rifling through the drawers. At any rate, at the present time, there is no will."

"Which means?"

"Intestacy, I suppose. As far as I know, the only relative is his daughter Ashley. I said, as far as I know. A man like that, he might have wives and children scattered all over the globe. Nothing about Dr. Savage would surprise me. I have to say in my defense, that he was a very smooth, very slick operator. He had me completely fooled. And the assets for the trust, they were certainly genuine enough. Gilt-edged securities; stocks and bonds, mutual funds. Oh, he had money. But where it came from, the Lord only knows."

I almost felt a smidgen of sympathy for Gideon Grambling. Clearly, the less one had to do with Langley Savage, the estate of Langley Savage, the death of Langley Savage, the better off one would be. Was I better off, as attorney for Ashley Savage? I could see the eight million dollar trust, and whatever else Langley Savage left behind, as it disappeared into a giant sinkhole of litigation. Fees for lawyers—not my fees of course—and, for the rest, the hungry maws of the Risleys.

Yet there was more here than met the eye. What happened to Langley Savage's will? Did somebody destroy it? If so, why?

What I didn't yet know, but soon found out, was that there was another missing will. A will made out by the late Hortense Risley. Missing. Or perhaps it never existed at all.

13

I had an appointment to see Ashley; and when she showed up, she had Bobby in tow. "You can say anything you want in front of Bobby," she said. They were squeezing each other's hands and looking into each other's eyes. I suppose it was heartwarming. I found it vaguely uncomfortable. It's wonderful to see people who love each other, but do we want to see proof of their love in public?

Most of what I had to say to Ashley was not particularly sensitive. I had to tell her that I knew very little about her father's estate. Gideon had been in touch with her, but he too had very little to tell.

She had taken a dislike to Gideon, which didn't surprise me. "He was so obnoxious, Frank," she said. "So cold and impersonal."

"Ashley," I said, "I have no great liking for the man, believe me. Your father, though…. How should I put it? He left a mess behind, and Gideon is more or less stuck with it. He's trying to get rid of it, fob it off on somebody else."

"He could at least be polite," she said.

"He's polite, but only if you're a rich client, or old money, or on the board of the symphony," I said. "Anyway, I'll try to find out more. Your father's affairs were complicated. Nobody knows if he was rich, poor, or what. If your father had money, and we aren't sure about this, you might stand to inherit a considerable fortune. But there are going to be lawsuits, that's for sure. And, as you know, there's litigation brewing about your trust."

"I don't care. I don't want my father's money," she said. More hand-squeezing. "Frank. Bobby has things he needs to say to you."

"Fire away."

Bobby explained that he had gone to see his brother Christopher. "I told him I wasn't going to go along with him. Well, he knew that, as far as Ashley is concerned, and her trust funds. He said, what about her father? What about the money he took? And I said I don't want anything to do with that either. That's going to be Ashley's money, isn't it? She's his daughter."

"What did he say?"

"Well, he was very very angry. He said things to me, awful things, I won't repeat them," Bobby said, and a big fat tear rolled down his cheek. "Not very brotherly. I said Christopher, you're flesh and blood, and I want to love you, but you make it hard for me; and he said, screw you, Bobby, I don't want your love. I started to go, and he said, all right, wait a minute. He seemed to calm down. He said, maybe we can work out some sort of compromise. Suppose I dropped the lawsuit against Ashley, meaning against her trust, what then? And I said, what do you mean, what then? He said I still want to get the rest of the money back, the money that doctor stole from our grandmother, all those assets, millions and millions."

"And what did you say, Bobby?"

"I said, well, but won't that money belong to Ashley, now that her father's dead? And he said: but your Ashley, she's an honest woman, isn't she? Did she know where that money came from? Did she know that Savage was systematically looting our grandmother's estate? He got our grandmother to give him power of attorney, he cashed her dividend checks, he transferred property to himself, he gave himself an apartment in Paris, a condo in New York, and God knows what else, plus accounts in the Cayman Islands and other places, we can't even trace them all; the man was a fantastic crook."

"If that's true," Ashley said, "I don't want that money. It doesn't belong to me."

I asked whether Christopher said anything about his grandmother's estate, how much was left, what was the size of it.

Bobby said: "What Christopher told me was they were robbing her blind. But I guess she died before they could steal everything, and she was awfully rich. I don't understand people. Here was this poor old lady.... And they were taking her money. Maybe half of it, I don't know how much. I don't want to know. But anyway, I said, Christopher, didn't you know this was going on? And he said, he suspected but he never did anything about it, he had his own troubles, he had been all tangled up, his second wife was suing him for divorce, and he had a business, but it was going bankrupt. Wow. We're a pretty worthless bunch, Frank, aren't we? Anyway, Langley Savage quit the hospital the minute grandma died. Of course, the hospital is suing him, and Christopher is suing the hospital, and everybody seems to be suing everybody. Not me, I want to love everybody. I went to my psychic again, Madame Zarathustra, and she told me my future was full of love, and that I needed the love, and not to hate anybody. And that's what I'm going to do. I'm going to devote my life to love. Ashley and my little boy."

"That's a good attitude," I said.

I guess I didn't sound particularly sincere. "You don't really mean that, Frank," he said. "But I do want to love people. I want to love *you*, Frank. Madame Zarathustra said, people will take advantage of me, so I have to be careful. Love them, she said, but be careful. I need somebody like Ashley. She'll protect me. I'm too emotional, it makes me vulnerable. My psychiatrist, Dr. Wong, Serena Wong, she told me I'm vulnerable because I'm starved for love. I'm like a person who hasn't eaten for days, you know, starving for food. Can't think about anything else. I'm starving for love. All my emotions are near the surface. But now I have Ashley."

She hugged him. "Oh, Bobby. Everything is going to be great from now on."

"I want that so much," he said. "I want a new life. I'm made so many mistakes. I mean, like Hildegarde. I'd like to love her, but I can't. She hurt me terribly."

"That's all over," Ashley said. "She can't hurt you anymore."

"Oh, but she can," he said. "She's got little Bobby. Do you know how I met her, Frank? It was in group therapy. She told such stories. Her husband beat her, she said. I felt so sorry for her. I went up to her afterwards, and I said, I feel your pain. She had a drinking problem, too. I ... went home with her. I'm so impulsive. I let my emotions get away with me. I had pity on her, and I wanted to share her misery, I wanted to make her feel better. I was just coming off a relationship, I was with this woman, a school teacher, we were together for three years, and then she left me. I was heartbroken. It was like a big vacuum in my life. Hildegarde, maybe she saw that. Then she got pregnant. She said, what'll I do, and I said, it's my baby, I'll marry you. We got in a car and drove to Las Vegas. I knew right away that it was a terrible mistake. She hated me from the start. She absolutely hated me, why, I don't know. She told me flat out she hated me. She had the baby, and then she told me she hated me. She got a divorce. I think she's unstable. I need your help, Frank. Can you help me?"

"Help you?"

"Little Bobby: the minute he was born, I was in love with him. I looked at this baby, and I thought, this is mine. This is me. I could see it. I told Madame Zarathustra about the baby, she said, you see, you have a capacity for love, you will love it forever. But Hildegarde, she's fighting me. I have a lawyer, a family law person, somebody recommended her, she's trying to help me on the custody thing, but Hildegarde tells all these lies. My lawyer isn't tough enough I think. I'm not tough enough either. Hildegarde told the judge I abused the child. He's two years old now. She said I abused her too. I did slap her once, I lost my temper, I was so desperate. She hit me back, she's stronger than I am I think. And once she said, I cut her with a knife, but I never did any such thing. Can you help me, Frank? I need help so badly."

"It's not really my field," I said. "If you're not satisfied with your lawyer, Bobby, you should definitely make a change. I can give you some names...."

I don't think he heard me. He went on and on. "I couldn't

stand it, the way Hildegarde hated me. I'm a very emotional person.... She says I need anger management. I do get angry, but I don't hurt people, I turn things in on myself. Dr. Wong told me that. I think I have road rage. I'm trying yoga now, I think it helps a lot. And I go to Dr. Wong twice a week. She helps me. I sit there and cry like a baby. I love little Bobby, he was my whole life, except now there's Ashley. Imagine, Hildegarde said I abused the child, and it's such a lie, I love that child madly. I can't stop kissing him, I love him so much. She's a maniac, Hildegarde. I only married her because she was pregnant, oh, I told you that; I'm repeating myself. I must have been crazy, ever to get mixed up with her. On top of it, she told me little Bobby wasn't really mine. She keeps going on about DNA, I said to her, screw the DNA. I think it's all a lie, what she says, she says she was sleeping with some guy named Andy, and it's his baby; but you know what? I don't care. I love that baby. So what if it was somebody else's sperm. I'm the real father. Who cares about Andy? Sometimes she even forgets she said Andy and says it was a guy named Joshua. Who knows? We separated after the baby was born.... I told you, when I saw that baby, it was like wow, something inside of me, something happened, it was like an explosion, I thought, this is true love. This is my baby."

"Is it possible it's *not* your baby?" I asked, as gently as I could.

"It's my *emotional* baby. I bonded with that baby. I used to hold it and hold it, and I'd be crying all the time. That's the way I am. Cassandra laughs at me, but I can't help it. I'm the same way about Ashley, too. And I can't live without that baby. And that woman says I abused this child! I mean, she's a liar. I wish she was dead. I know that's wrong, she's a human being, but it's hard for me to forget the things she did. If she was dead, I'd take the baby, I'd be a house-daddy, I swear, I'd give up everything. I wish I could kill her, but I can't, I'm not a violent person, not at all, I'm the opposite, I never hurt anybody in my life. And if I did, they'd send me to jail, and then what would become of my little Bobby?"

All this time, Ashley was sitting there, and I wondered:

what does she make of all of this? But she was squeezing his hands, and staring into his eyes. I thought: they're both crazy. Crazy about each other, and maybe crazy, period. But probably it's a good crazy, not a bad crazy.

"I'll love that baby, too," Ashley said. "Because it's Bobby's. I want to help raise that little boy. And we'll have children, more children. I want to be a mother myself. That Hildegarde, she's an awful woman. I'm getting phone calls from her. Nasty phone calls. Did you know she was sleeping with my father? So she's somebody who was in both our lives, in a way, me and Bobby. She was part of our karma. I think that's terribly significant. It's like we were destined to be with each other, me and Bobby, don't you think? Anyway, I'm going to change my phone number, get unlisted, or get rid of my landline altogether, just to get that woman off my back. She's so terrible. My poor Bobby."

"Maybe you should try a restraining order," I said.

"It's so unfair," Ashley said. "Just when we have a chance at happiness. The two of us. Frank, you don't know how wonderful this is. I love Bobby. Before Bobby, I was feeling all depressed, and I found a little bird, I don't know what kind it was, tiny bird, and maybe it was a baby bird, you know, just born, wounded, I guess, fell out of the nest or something, and I picked it up. I stroked it and I tried to put it somewhere safe, in a bush, maybe it would get back its strength, and I hoped that bird was going to make it. I really did. You know, I think now, that was some sort of message. That bird, it was a sign. It was pointing toward Bobby. He's my wounded bird. I know you think this is crazy. But I really feel this way. Did you ever have that feeling, Frank? About getting a sign from who knows where, something that means something, but at the time you don't know it?"

"Oh yes," I said. But I was lying; I never had that kind of feeling at all. I know there are folks who believe in reincarnation, feng shui, omens, spectral visitations and God knows what, not to mention Eastern religions and the rest of that stuff. Signs and messages and whatever. To me, it's all rubbish.

And especially when it came to little wounded birds. We

had hummingbirds nesting outside the house, on a light fixture, just last summer. More than one nest. And there were bird droppings everywhere, and I suppose the little baby birds were cute and all that, but enough is enough; and Celia draws the line at bird droppings. We got rid of the nests and that was the end of it. I suppose the Audubon society would consider me a monster, but there you are.

I tried to steer the discussion away from life, love, wounded birds, and other irrelevancies. "We got off the subject," I said. "Did you tell me everything about your conversation with your brother?"

"Well, not exactly. There was something else," he said. "But I just didn't want to listen. I told him, I'm just not going to be part of this, it's crooked."

"Something crooked?"

"Really, I don't even like talking about it," he said. "After all, this was my darling Ashley's father. I know he wasn't much of a father. Mine wasn't either. But it's instinct, isn't it, to love your parents? My father was never around and he was drunk half the time. He told me flat out that he didn't love me, he called me a worm, a disgrace to the family, a namby-pamby. Then when I started crying, he would become totally enraged. But I still loved him. There was something *genetic* about it, I really believe that. When he died, I was heartbroken. I thought, I'll never have a chance to get him to love me. Never. He's dead. I kept thinking about that, with Christopher. It was his father too. I don't know, maybe he doesn't feel things the way I do. Anyway, I'm talking too much. Frank, the point is I just don't want to repeat what Christopher said about Dr. Savage; it's too ugly."

"Bobby, darling," she said. "I love you for feeling the way you do. But honestly, the man meant nothing to me. I never had those emotions you had. You can say whatever you want about him. I honestly don't care."

"It was a kind of blackmail," Bobby said.

"Blackmail?" I asked, "What do you mean."

"Well, according to Christopher, the man told him that he had some kind of document. I think it was a will. Grandmother's will, all handwritten, but legal. According to the doctor, anyway. And it left all the money to Dr. Savage, or most of it. But if Christopher would call off the lawsuits, and let him alone, he'd just tear it up, and nobody would ever know about it. Except of course now we do."

"And what did Christopher say?"

"He said no. He refused the offer. He said, the will or whatever it was wasn't worth the paper it was written on. A senile woman, nearly a hundred years old, leaving everything to her doctor; no court would uphold that. But Dr. Savage said, maybe you're right, maybe you're wrong, but do you want to go to court? It'll cost you money, a fortune. And, oh yes, it could drag on for years. You might as well come to terms with me. And by the way, if we do go to court, a lot of dirty linen will get washed in public. What do you mean, Christopher asked, what kind of dirty linen. Well, the guy said, stuff about your sister Juno."

"Juno?" I asked. It was a huge surprise. I asked Bobby if he knew what this "stuff" consisted of; but he shrugged his shoulders. "I have no idea," he said.

Still, I had learned something very important. Langley Savage claimed he had, in his own hands, a will, Hortense Risley's will. That was big news. I lost no time the next day trying to get in touch with Gideon. As always, when I called, I had to maneuver past his receptionist, who guarded him from the Unworthy like a savage police dog. Maybe I should have pretended I was an old-money client. At any rate, I finally did reach him. He was as usual impatient, but I ignored that. "Gideon," I said, "your client, Dr. Savage, we talked about his will. Did he have, uh, somebody else's will in his possession?"

"Somebody else's will? What on earth are you talking about, Frank? Why would he have somebody else's will?"

I didn't feel like telling Gideon the whole story. I said: "I heard a rumor that he had Hortense Risley's will; a holograph; that he was holding on to it."

"Why in heaven's name would he do that?" Gideon said, in a very annoyed tone of voice.

"I don't know," I said. "I just heard a rumor."

Gideon said, "I don't know what kind of a game you're playing, Frank. I don't have time for this. I'm due at a client's home in half an hour. In Pacific Heights. It's a very big deal, Frank, and very complex; so please, don't waste my time. I'd like to forget all about that wretched, cheating, fraudulent doctor. In any event, I had people go over every inch of Langley Savage's miserable apartment, and the room in the hotel where he was staying, and there was no will there at all. Not his will. Not anybody's will. Nothing."

So the holograph, if there was one, was missing. That might make *two* missing wills. Did Langley Savage destroy the Hortense will, as he promised he would—but only after he made a deal with Christopher Risley? Or did whoever killed him snatch the will and get rid of it, tear it into little bits and maybe flush those bits down the toilet? Or did it even exist? At least now I had a possible motive. Of course, if there was a will, and if it was valid (a big if), destroying it would be a crime. If the will simply vanished, any older will that Hortense had executed (and surely she had such a will) would be the last and presumably valid will. I would love to know if such a will existed. And what it said. I was willing to bet it left money to the family. The four grandchildren.

One of them could have taken the new will, destroyed it, and killed Langley Savage. Millions of dollars were at stake. Is there any motive more powerful than money?

Or suppose there was no older will. Then Hortense's money would go to her nearest relatives. The four grandchildren again.

But I was having trouble thinking of any of them as killers. Christopher was cold and calculating, but murder? It didn't seem in character. Juno: unthinkable, although what was her dirty secret? Cassandra? Maybe murder as a kind of performance art, but no, she simply wasn't the type. And Bobby? The least likely at all.

No, none of them seemed the fit the description of a killer.

Not to me, at any rate. And yet, thanks to Zelda, suspicion was about to fall on one of them.

14

I had always tried to ignore Zelda and her involvement; I had other things to do. It was Ashley who next brought her up. We were having a conversation, a business conversation, over coffee. Partly about her trust, but also about Bobby, and his financial affairs. It was mid-afternoon. We were having coffee. Coffee and (I admit) pastries, in the shop down the street from my office. I knew most of the workers there, especially Marigold, a woman of a certain age with a huge pile of hair-sprayed hair, and a nose for gossip.

"Have you seen Zelda?" Ashley asked.

"Zelda? No, not recently. Why?"

"I don't know. I guess she quit the yoga class, I haven't seen her around. I wondered what was up; I had her cell phone number, and I called her, I was trying to be friendly; she had been so nice to me and Bobby. But she acted really funny, like she didn't want to talk to me; and I wondered, what was going on? Is it something she's doing for you, Frank?"

"For me? Oh, no. Really, I have no idea."

"I was just wondering."

I put it out of my mind. I had other things to think abou, besides Zelda. Zelda could manage on her own. I have to admit, I was intrigued with the strange death of Dr. Savage. Who killed him, and why? There was also a whole host of subsidiary questions. The two wills, for example. What had become of them? I was also intrigued by the idea that Langley Savage had some sort of "dirt" on Juno. What on earth could that mean? Celia was also intrigued with Juno, but from a quite different angle. I had described her to Celia—I told her Juno was an un-attractive woman, with a penchant for mathematics, unmar-ried, overweight; and, of course, either rich now or potentially rich.

"Goodness, Frank," Celia said, "do you think she might possibly like Adam, if we introduced them to each other?" This of course was Adam Finkel, the math teacher with the terrible complexion, the one that the students called Frankenstein, a shy and lonely man. One of Celia's great projects in life was to find a woman for Adam. "Or a man," she said, "I don't think he's gay, but I don't care. Either way. The poor soul must be so terribly lonely. Lives with his mother, a truly dreadful woman. Can we have this Juno over for dinner?"

"Celia dearest," I said, "the answer is no. What excuse would I give? And she's more or less the enemy; I mean not literally, but the Risley family is hostile to my client, you know, to Ashley or at least her brother Christopher is, he's the ring-leader, they're suing my client, and it just wouldn't be right to have her over. It wouldn't be ethical."

Celia was silent for a while. All I heard was the clicking of her knitting needles. I know she thought I was just making excuses. "It's not ethical to introduce two lonely people to each other? What if we had her over with Bobby and Ashley? Wouldn't that work? And I'll ask Adam along." But I resisted. I had no faith in this plan. The poor man had all these bumps and boils on his face. Apparently nothing could be done about his condition. Even ugly women prefer handsome men. And ugly men prefer beautiful women. I suppose ugly people have to settle for less than their ideal. Juno, whatever her problems, was a *rich* ugly woman; I suppose they have more options. But I thought Celia's plan was a total non-starter.

"What do you think?" Celia asked.

"No, no, no. Absolutely not," I said.

But in the end I gave in.

15

I had mixed feelings about this dinner party, but I had lost the battle, and I knew better than to continue a hopeless struggle. I called Ashley and said, we'd like to have you and Bobby over; we can talk business, I said, but really, it's just a social event. She seemed dubious. I suppose, to her, the idea of socializing with her lawyer was a little like the idea of socializing with your dentist. It's not usually done in her circles. Or any circles, for that matter. She hesitated, and I tried a charm approach. I'm sure she was groping for an excuse; but I heard Bobby in the background, apparently in favor of the idea, so she did agree. Since I hadn't mentioned any specific date, it was hard for her to say no, we're busy.

Then I said we'd like to have Juno over too.

"Juno? What on earth for?"

What indeed. I said that we wanted to be friendly with her: "It's to detach her from Christopher, you know, get her on our side."

Fortunately, Ashley was not in the habit of consorting with lawyers. Had she been familiar with professional etiquette, she would have realized that this sort of thing was simply not done. It was bad manners, and probably not even ethical. At least the Juno part. She turned to Bobby and said something; and then she told me Bobby would contact Juno. I said, "We're thinking of this coming Sunday night," I said. "Around 7 o'clock."

They probably felt trapped, but they agreed to come. Bobby called me back later. "Juno's coming," he said. "And Cassandra, too." I felt like saying, "we didn't invite her," but I didn't dare. "That's great," I said. "And, oh, Bobby, my wife Celia has invited one of her colleagues, she's a school teacher, I mean, Celia is, and she has this colleague, math teacher, and we're having him over too."

If Bobby wondered why we were playing host to a man whose job was trying to cram algebra down the throats of adolescents, he kept it to himself. Celia, as soon as I had nailed the Risleys and Ashley down, called Adam Finkel and invited him. She also talked him out of bringing his mother along, which was his original idea.

I had a feeling that this dinner might be a disaster. I'm not sure why. Celia announced that she was going to try a new recipe. "I got it from Sunset Magazine," she said. "It sounded healthy and delicious."

"Healthy and delicious?" I said. "How can that be?"

"Easy," she said. "Adam is a vegetarian," she added. "It's a kind of pasta, with kale. We need olive oil, too; we're almost out of it. Pick up some olive oil on your way home. And, Frank, plcase don't get the wrong kind, the way you usually do. Just plain olive oil. Not with garlic. And get a good brand, don't just buy the cheapest one."

Bobby, Ashley, Juno, and Cassandra appeared promptly at seven. Cassandra had on, as usual, a very revealing blouse, and a skirt that was a bit on the short side; she was wearing sandals. Juno was wearing a lumpish gray dress. She seemed ill at ease. I introduced them to Celia, who then disappeared into the kitchen.

"Hey, Frank, I hear you're playing detective," Cassandra said.

"Not a word of truth in it," I said.

"Really?" she said. "I heard otherwise."

"Oh, from who?" I asked. But she gave me an inscrutable smile. I was really sorry they had brought her. She dominated the conversation; she went on and on about politics, about the sad state of the art world, and about life in general. Neither Bobby nor Juno got a word in edgewise. She had a thing about clothing, too, or rather non-clothing, that is, nudity. "Why do we hate our bodies?" she said. According to her there was no reason to hide our bodies. "Bodies are beautiful," she said.

"Cassie, they're not," Bobby said. "I mean, some are, some aren't."

"Yours is sensational, I'm sure, brother dear," she said. "Not that you let me see it." He turned bright red. I think Cassandra rather enjoyed embarrassing her brother. And it was, of course, extremely easy to accomplish this goal.

"I was living with this guy, couple of years ago," she said. "He was a nudist, at least he said so. Went to some camp or something every summer. I said to him, what's the point, a few fanatics, they live in this place, it's fenced all around, and they play volley ball or whatever they do all day long, and make grinning faces for the camera, and pretend they're just ordinary people, which they are, mentally speaking. People shouldn't have to go to these stupid camps, they should get nude in daily life, on the street, in their houses, get over these hang-ups. Some nudist he was. I wanted to take pictures of him, he wouldn't let me. He was afraid I'd put them on Facebook, and show the whole world his private parts."

"Cassie, please," Bobby said.

There was no stopping her, I'm afraid. "You know who had a beautiful body? Grandma, when she was young. I saw pictures of her, with clothes on, of course. In the end, even in bed, even a million years old, there was something beautiful about her. Maybe she liked beautiful people, too. Like Peter Christoff, the foot guy. He rubbed her feet every day. Don't tell me that isn't sexual. He was a handsome devil. With and without his clothes on."

What happened next was startling. Juno, who had been sitting quietly in the corner, got up from her chair, she was trembling, whether with fear, rage, or embarrassment, was hard to tell. "What do you mean, Cassie?"

"Just what I said, Juno. Plain English."

"But you didn't! You don't mean.... What do you mean? You and Peter ... I mean Dr. Christoff...."

"He had a beautiful butt, that's what I mean," she said. "And the rest of him too. A real Adonis. Do I have to draw you a picture?"

"Oh, Cassie, you're a monster, I swear you are," Juno said. "I don't believe you mean a word of what you say."

Just then the doorbell rang; and Celia said, "I'll get it." It was Adam Finkel. Celia opened the door, and he was there, with a bunch of flowers held awkwardly in his hand. But he had hardly moved into the living room when Juno got up, and said, "I have to go," and ran to the door, bumping into Adam on her way out. He stood there, with the bouquet in his hand, looking utterly miserable. Celia took him by the hand and led him into the kitchen. She told me later that he had been terribly upset; he was convinced he was the reason Juno left in such a hurry. "She took a look at me," he said, "my face ... I'm sure that's what did it." He was utterly devastated. Celia tried as best she could to convince him that, no, it was something else, she didn't know what, but it had nothing to do with him, and, "Really, Adam," she said, "I know you have a problem, skin problem; but honestly, it's not so bad, really, you're actually quite handsome."

The dinner was ready to be served. The evening was already bordering on catastrophe, and it got even worse. Adam said hardly a word. He sat next to Cassandra, who at one point asked him, "What on earth is the matter with your skin? Have you gone to a dermatologist?" and he mumbled some sort of answer. He ate virtually nothing. Bobby and Ashley whispered to each other and nuzzled each other the whole evening. Celia tried to make conversation in between running in and out of the dining room with dishes. And at that point—it was about 8:30—the doorbell rang again.

"Maybe it's Juno, coming back," Bobby said.

But it wasn't. It was in fact Zelda. I answered the door, and there she was. "Frank," she said, "are you busy? I need to talk to you."

"I've got people over," I said. "It's not a good time."

"People? Which people? I love people," she said.

At that point she saw Bobby, who had come out of the dining room, hoping to find Juno. "Oh God," Zelda said. "Not him."

"You see I'm busy, Zelda," I said.

"Frank," she said, "I really do have to talk. Can we go somewhere—a bedroom, the kitchen, any place, so long as we can talk privately, can we do that?"

"That would be rude, wouldn't it, Zelda? Anyway, I don't think people are going to stay very long. It hasn't been a great evening, frankly. We've finished dinner, well, almost, except for the dessert and coffee; really, Zelda, this isn't the right time."

"Frank," she said, "this is important. And what's the dessert?"

"It's a fruit tart, if you must know."

"My favorite," she said. "I'll stay, if you don't mind. We can talk when the other people go."

Celia, of course, was terrifically unhappy, and Zelda was no help. Nothing had worked out the way Celia wanted. Adam had left rather early, clearly miserable; Juno had bolted out of the house, as I mentioned. Cassandra had uttered one outrageous thing after another. Celia had gone to a lot of trouble preparing the meal; I had done the shopping (and got the olive oil right this time), set the table, and tried to be helpful. All in vain. I brought Zelda into the living room, where Bobby, Ashley, and Cassandra were sitting at a coffee table, having dessert.

"Who's this?" Cassandra asked, in a loud voice.

"This is an old friend," I said, "Zelda Valdez."

"Nobody is named Zelda anymore," Cassandra said. "You should change your name."

"I like my name," Zelda said. "It's brought me good luck."

"Really?" Cassandra said. "How's that?" But she didn't wait for Zelda to answer; she went right on talking. "Names are important," she said. "Your whole life might be changed if you stopped being a Zelda. I changed my name to Cassandra. I was Sandra when I was born, but as soon as I was old enough to know better, I realized, Sandra simply wouldn't do. It had no spark. A Sandra is a dull, suburban woman, without any charm. Cassandra: that has a ring to it, and there's the ancient Greek business, which makes it exotic, even dangerous. I tell you, it makes a difference. My brother here, Bobby, is a born Bobby: he's sweet and innocent. I don't think he'd be so sweet and innocent if they called him something else, say, Luke, or Rex, something strong, with one syllable. My other brother, his name is Christopher. I don't like him. It's an awful name, anyway—it's a name for people who like nothing but money."

"I love being Zelda," Zelda said. "My second husband, Milo, married me because my name started with a Z. We're divorced, but it's because he went back to his first wife; her name was Zoe."

"I think Z is a dreadful letter," Cassandra said. "Everything with a Z is ugly. X is much better. What do you do for a living, Zelda?"

"I'm a novelist," she said. "I write books."

"I'm not into books anymore," Cassandra said. "I'm into images. I create images. I'm a performance artist. I perform in museums, which is a bit hypocritical."

"Hypocritical? Why is that?"

"I'm really against museums," Cassandra said. "Look: if I'm performing in a museum, sure, you should come and see me do my thing. But otherwise, forget it. People should train their eyes to look at *things*, not splotches of paint on canvas. Take a look at trees, people, toilet bowls, refrigerators, anything; try to understand what they mean. 'Art,' with a capital A, it's mostly bullshit. Anyway: I was in this museum, in Chicago, and this famous artist, he gets millions for his stuff, and believe me, it's total crap. Anyway, they were putting on a show of his work. He had this sculpture, it was nothing at all, a couple of pieces of twisted metal, one on top of the other; and he called it 'untitled.' That did the trick. I knew already it was garbage, everything he does is garbage, but when he called his monstrosity 'untitled,' I was sure it was bullshit. If you don't have a title, you're nothing. Labels are what make something important. Everything I do has a label. It's not easy to put a label on performance art, but I insist on it."

Celia was smiling grimly; I knew that she was smoldering inside. Cassandra and Zelda: she had invited neither of them, and they were dominating the conversation. Cassandra took two huge pieces of fruit tart, and gobbled them down. In between bites, she talked incessantly, going on and on, mostly criticizing other artists, people who for the most part the rest of us had never even heard of, but then she started in on Picasso, how he was a charlatan, and a sexist beast, and so on.

Finally, Bobby said, "I'm really tired, Mrs. May. The food was delicious. Thank you for having us, but we have to go."

He and Ashley left immediately, and Cassandra left shortly afterwards. Adam had long since gone. Zelda stayed behind. I helped clear the dishes.

The fruit tart, by the way, was absolutely delicious.

16

So I was left alone with Zelda. It had been a long day, and I was tired. There were heaps of dishes to put in the dishwasher, and pots and pans to scrub. Celia had simply gone to bed. I know she was utterly disgusted with the way things turned out. "It's late, Zelda," I said. "Maybe we can talk some other time."

"Frank, this is important," she said. "I have to tell you about all the progress I've made."

"Progress in what? I don't care about progress," I said.

She ignored this remark. "Frank, I always thought of myself as a terrific judge of character, you know? I'm a writer, and people like me have insights. It's our stock in trade. But even a writer can be terribly wrong."

"I'm sure that's true," I said. "Zelda dear, I really need to finish up in the kitchen, I've got to take care of the dishes, and as I said, it's getting late."

She had followed me into the kitchen, stooping a little. Zelda was a very tall woman. "I misjudged somebody totally. Totally. I'm referring to Bobby."

"What about him?" I said, grabbing a pot and some steel wool and starting to scrub.

"I'm in between books at the moment, and I have lots of time to devote to this business. I thought, I should go to the scene of the crime, the hotel. You know, the Intercontinental. I went right up to the receptionist and said I was a private investigator, and I showed him a business card. OK, I bought it on line, it's a fake, but he didn't know that. I said I was working for a prominent local attorney...."

97

"Zelda, you didn't mention my name. Please say you didn't mention my name."

"I think I didn't. Doesn't matter. He wouldn't remember. I said we would be willing to pay for information."

I stood there, holding a dirty pot in my hand, and I said: "Zelda, how could you?"

"Oh, Frank, it's not against the law or anything like that. I'm having fun, what's a little money? I made so much money on that book of mine, the one about the pirate and the nun, it flew off the shelves. Of course, when I actually look at it, these days, I'm almost embarrassed by it; but it went into eight printings. They wanted to make a movie out of it, but in the end they didn't. Some studio bosses were against it. I think they thought Catholics would object to the story, you know, nuns having sex. I mean, I was very respectful of the nuns. The only one who had sex was Sister Santa Cruz, and only with the pirate, Horatio."

Believe it or not, I had actually tried to read Zelda's pirate book. I read ten pages in a drug store. There was a whole shelf of romance novels, all of them with lurid covers. I must admit, Zelda's book had a certain breathless and ingratiating quality. I never got to the juicy parts, like the one where the pirate takes the nun's virginity. I was turning the pages, but then I saw a woman from our neighborhood, someone I know vaguely. She was staring at me, and I was too embarrassed to go on. I never found out whether the book had a happy ending. I suppose it did. Don't all of these romance novels have happy endings? The hero and the heroine get married or something like that.

"This receptionist," she said, "at the hotel, he was a young man—quite good-looking, average height, brownish hair, he looked intelligent. His name was Johnny. I bonded with him immediately, and I think he liked me. Well, it turns out he was actually on duty the day Langley Savage was murdered. I said, would you talk to me? I offered him $50, but he wouldn't take it. He said it was against the rules. Anyway, I came back later, when he was through with work, and I asked him if he wanted to have coffee, and he said yes. He told me the police had been all over the place, and they asked a bunch of questions, but he had gone off duty, and he wasn't there when the police came that first day, you know, the day Langley Savage was killed. They did talk to him later. I said, well, can you tell me who was there that day, I mean, who could have been there, and gone up to the room. And he said, well, you know, a person could go right to the elevator and go up to the room, that is, if Dr. Savage invited them. They don't need to ask me or the concierge. But I said, well, *did* somebody come to the desk and ask. And he said, well, I don't remember in detail, but yes, there was at least one guy, he asked for the room number, for S. Langley, and I told him."

"Did this guy Johnny know who the man was?" I asked.

"Of course not. But I said if I show you some pictures, could you identify him? He didn't think so, actually; but I had a photograph, I clipped it out of *People*, they had a story about Hortense Risley and her family and the doctors and everything, and he looked at a photograph of the grandchildren, and he said, well, it could be this guy. Bobby."

"He could identify him from a picture in a magazine? A guy he saw for twenty seconds one day? Somehow I doubt it."

"You're right, Frank. He wasn't sure of anything. He said, well, maybe it was this one. But he did want to talk to me. I think he liked me. Maybe he's somebody who likes tall women. I very much liked *him*. And I kept on investigating. You know, Frank, I really enjoy this. Writing is such a lonely thing. I get up in the morning, and it's just me in the house, now that Milo and I are split. I read the paper, I make my coffee, and then I sit down and I try to write a thousand words. That's my quota. But I can't keep at it all day. So I'm thrilled to have this other thing to do. Anyway, I found out some stuff, never mind how, maybe I'll tell you later. But Bobby was actually there that day. The receptionist said, I remember another thing, because somebody complained, there was this weird guy, he was crying, this was on Dr. Savage's floor, or one floor below, I can't remember; the guy came out of the staircase, and he was sobbing. One of the staff people went up to him, and she said, are you sick? He said, no, no, but then he sort of broke down. They thought maybe he was a mental case, that's why they complained. But by then he was gone. And naturally, they had no idea who he was, what his name was, or anything, but they said he was young, blonde hair, short, kind of stocky. It has to be Bobby."

I couldn't help thinking of Gideon's story, about this person he found sobbing in the stairwell. That was certainly Bobby. The description fit him like a glove, including the sobbing part. But what on earth was he doing there in the stairwell? I asked Zelda if she knew.

"I have no proof of anything, Frank. But I think Bobby killed the guy, Dr. Savage. Maybe it was an accident, maybe he just went there, and somebody had a gun, and they struggled or something. I had a scene like that in one of my novels, 'Slaves on the Plantation of Love.' It's set in the Caribbean, eighteenth century, just like my pirate book. I think those islands are so romantic—palm trees and so on. Anyway, my hero, Rodrigo, is madly in love with this woman, Esmeralda, but she's the daughter of the governor of Barbados, Lord Brimstone, and Lord Brimstone wants her to marry a wealthy planter, never mind the details, and Rodrigo has it out with Lord Brimstone, who pulls a gun, and the gun goes off, and Lord Brimstone dies, and Rodrigo has to flee for his life; and the question is, what about his Esmeralda, the love of his life, now she has a terrible dilemma."

I ignored Rodrigo and Lord Brimstone. "You think Bobby actually killed Langley Savage? I can't believe it, Zelda."

"Well, what was he doing there, in the hotel? Isn't that suspicious?"

"I guess it is," I said. "But really, Zelda, Bobby's just not the type, violent. I suppose it could be some kind of accident. But still, there'd have to be a fight. I don't see Bobby fighting. He's too much of a softie. I mean, crying his eyes out: that's not what murderers do."

"Frank," she said, "how do we know what murderers do? How many murderers do you know? Maybe you know a few, from your experience; but still, it's not like you took a survey. Anyway, I think Bobby's unstable. We know he's emotional. Let's say he did it, but a minute later, he was just plain horrified: that's why he went to pieces, crying, having a kind of breakdown."

I assume that Rodrigo, hero of "Slaves on the Plantation of Love," was made of stronger stuff, and failed to go to pieces after dispatching Lord Brimstone. It was definitely true that Bobby, if he really did kill Langley Savage, would absolutely go to pieces. That would be totally in character. But of course I still thought the idea was ridiculous. Bobby was not the type to kill. Or even fight.

Still, what was he doing, crying his eyes out in the stairwell?

"The question is," Zelda said, "when should I go to the police? This is important information."

"Zelda," I said. "Maybe the police know all about this. Don't assume they're just sitting on their duff doing nothing."

"Oh, Frank, I wish. Actually, I'm sure they don't know anything about this case, but don't ask me why I think so. If they had a real lead, we'd hear about it. They'd arrest somebody, I suppose. But I won't say anything yet. I have another lead I have to follow up on. A mysterious woman, who was seen at the hotel. I don't know anything about her yet."

"A mysterious woman? What do you mean?"

"OK: Bobby was in the hotel and he was crying and all that. One of the maids told the receptionist that there was this man crying in the stairwell, and then Bobby appeared, he came off the elevator, and the receptionist saw him, and he took out a handkerchief. He wiped his eyes and sat down in a chair, and he seemed to be sobbing; and then he looked up and he saw this woman, and when he saw her, he got up and ran out the door, as if his life depended on it."

"Saw this woman? Where?"

"I don't know. In the lobby. Somewhere near where Bobby was sitting."

"Maybe it has nothing to do with anything. But listen, Zelda: don't you think your Johnny told this whole story to the police? After all, that afternoon, after the body was found, the whole place was a crime scene, and the place was probably swarming with police; I mean, it's got to be that they asked the hotel people if they knew anything. So they know all about Bobby, for sure. And probably about this woman, too."

"Maybe. I'm going to check on it. I've got some more information, too."

"Information? What about?"

"I've been hanging around the hospital.... I think that's important, too."

"The hospital? Why on earth, Zelda?"

"Well, two reasons. One of them has to do with my work. I'm thinking of writing about hospitals. I'll come back to that later, Frank. The other reason is, I wanted to see the scene of the crime."

"The scene of the crime?"

"Langley Savage and his crew, they stole money from the old lady, didn't they? Well, that's a crime. Look: for all I know, they actually killed her."

"Zelda, she was a million years old. And she was demented. She died of old age."

"OK, she was a million years old, but maybe she was healthy, and they got tired of waiting, you know what I mean?"

"It's quite the opposite, Zelda, isn't it? When she died, that was the end of the gravy train. As long as she was alive, they could take her money; but once she was dead, they couldn't."

She paused, and thought about this. In the end, she had to agree. "But maybe they were drugging her," she said. "Maybe she didn't have Alzheimer's. I have an aunt, she's 102 years old, and she's as sharp as a tack. Anyway, it doesn't matter. I found out some really important stuff. You think none of the grandchildren visited her much. Well, maybe at the end, you can't blame them if they didn't, she didn't know them from a vegetable. But actually, it turns out, three of them had been visitors, and that must mean they had at least some idea of what was going on. Maybe they were part of the whole scheme."

"Three of them? Which three?"

"Cassandra, Bobby, and Juno. I'm not sure why they came. Well, Juno. I know about her. She was there; but not to see her grandmother. Maybe at first. But then, she had a different reason."

"Oh? What was that?"

"She came to see Peter Christoff. They were having an affair. Honest to God."

"Zelda, he was young, and, from what I hear, good-looking. Juno—have you met her? To be brutally honest, she's fat and ugly."

"But she was a Risley. She was maybe rich. Besides, if he was robbing the old lady, he was potentially robbing Juno. So it was good to have her on his side. I tell you, he was doing it with her. And the nurse found out, what's her name, Nurse Barbash, and there was a huge rumpus. I have my spy network in the hospital. It's because I'm looking for a new subject. For a book. Hospitals might be something worth doing. I'm not doing romance any more. Or vampires. That's out. Zombies too. It's a crowded field, zombies. It's been done to death."

"Has it? The zombie thing passed me by, I guess."

"It's so yesterday," she said. "I'm thinking of a different kind of book, a thriller. I'll place it in a hospital. I have a title already: 'The Devil Wears Scrubs.' It'll be about what goes on in hospitals, doctors and nurses, the way they carry on; and the patients, too, if they're not too sick, or infectious, of course. Regular orgies. Of course, it doesn't really happen. Anyway, I met this nurse, Millie Boggs, she worked on the same floor that Hortense Risley was on. I thought she'd be an excellent source about Dr. Savage and the foot doctor and Nurse Barbash. This woman, Millie Boggs, she's a lovely person. She has six grandchildren. Five boys and a girl. Anyway, I told her I was writing this book, and Hollywood was interested in the script, and she could be a consultant, well, that was a little white lie, but she was terribly excited. She's filling me in on technical details. She's the one who told me about Juno Risley and Peter Christoff. Hortense, the old lady, she had this big room, actually a suite, with a little side-room, and that's where they went to do it. And Nurse Barbash, the evil nurse, she's going to be in my book; she got some of the money, you know; that's not the point, though. The point is, she apparently caught them in the act, Juno and the foot doctor, and she made an enormous fuss."

"Really!"

"Millie told me all about it. This Peter Christoff, the foot doctor, he was young and handsome. And he had a way with women. He knew what to do. The way to a woman's heart, I guess, is through their feet. That's how it all started with Juno. As I told you, this Millie was on the same floor of the hospital, so she knew whatever went on. Anyway, Christoff used to massage Hortense's feet. And here's Juno, and he offers to do it to her too, and that's how it all started. First he was rubbing her feet, and she's going ooh, ah, ooh, ah; then, he kind of moved his hands a bit further up. I've got to put that in my novel, it's too good to leave out. "

I said, "Maybe he killed Langley Savage. I mean, the foot doctor did. Is he a suspect?"

"Would have been. But no, he's not even in the country. When Hortense died, and the whole scheme sort of unraveled, he got out of the country as fast as his legs could carry him. He's in Brazil, or Paraguay or someplace like that. South America, anyway. Ran off with the nurse, you know, the wicked one, Nurse Barbash, she went with him. I guess she forgave him for Juno. I don't think Juno knows that he ran off with Nurse Barbash. She thinks Peter's in hiding, somewhere, and he'll come back to her. He never will."

"Wow, Zelda," I said. "You've been busy."

"Oh, but I love this, Frank, you know that. And it gives me so many ideas for new books. Like the hospital book. I was going to make the villain a podiatrist, you know, like Peter Christoff. He'll be in the book, but I don't think the villain can be a foot doctor. Too unromantic. So my real villain has to be a surgeon, I call him Vlad Romanescu, he's Romanian, you know, same first name as Dracula, and he was born in Transylvania, he tells people they need an operation, and he takes out their kidneys, and he sells the kidneys on the black market. And he's sleeping with this nurse, Olga, and she falls in love with a young resident, and that causes all sorts of complications."

"Sells the kidneys, Zelda? Plural? He doesn't take both kidneys, does he? You can't live without at least one."

"That's what so devilish," she said. "But I have to work out the details. These hospitals, if a patient dies, they have some sort of investigation, I'm not sure how I'm going to deal with that. Not that the readers would care. I mean, if it's not accurate. Nobody cares about accuracy. I'm putting in lots of sex. You know, like *Fifty Shades of Grey*, it's what women want to read. Vlad is very attractive to women, dark, sinister, you know. A bit rough in the sex department, but that's what sells."

Zelda was a woman with enormous energy and enthusiasm. For all I know, "The Devil Wears Scrubs" might make a million dollars. I doubt that I'll ever read it. I'm not immune to trash, but Zelda's book didn't appeal to me. Not the way she described it.

Zelda was eager to talk about plots, characters, twists, and this climactic scene in the operating room. But I steered the conversation back to non-literary subjects. "And Bobby used to come to the hospital, too? What for? Don't tell me he was sleeping with a nurse."

"Oh, no, not Bobby. Yes, he's my chief suspect, I mean, killing Langley Savage, but in the hospital, he behaved himself. As far as I know. I think he went there maybe because he honestly wanted to see his grandmother. Now Cassandra, she went for the money, plain and simple. I found that out. She wanted some of grandma's money; and when she saw what was going on, she wanted money from Langley Savage. After all, he controlled the money. Power of attorney and all that."

"Did he give it to her?"

"I don't know. I don't think so. But the whole situation, Frank.... Just imagine, the old lady, there she was, getting dimmer and dimmer, and surrounded by vultures. It's dramatic. I've got to put that in my book. It has to be a subplot, though. I haven't worked things through yet."

We talked on for a while. I have to admit, I was enjoying myself. Zelda was irrepressible and the subject was deliciously entertaining; we discussed every aspect of the case. And because I know Celia would disapprove, the conversation had a bit of the flavor of forbidden fruit. Mango or papaya, let us say—tropical fruit. Caribbean fruit; the kind that Rodrigo and Sister Santa Cruz and Horatio and Lord Brimstone and all of Zelda's characters might have eaten. Mainly, we talked about what we knew, and what we didn't know. And who the killer might be. Zelda argued for Bobby; I argued for Cassandra. We left each other on a note of giddy exuberance.

17

I should have known better than to voice my suspicions to Zelda. Cassandra appeared in my office, unannounced, and in a state of high dudgeon. High dudgeon in her case went along with big cleavage.

"Listen, Mr. Lawyer," she said, "I don't appreciate what you're doing. I deeply resent it."

"I'm not doing anything."

"Oh yes you are. You're using this Zelda creature to worm information out of people. I went to see my grandmother, is that a crime? Did I want money? Yes, I wanted money. She was as rich as Croesus, whoever that was. Of course, the doctor, the foot doctor, and some bitchy nurse were robbing her blind, I could see that. I should have reported them. But I don't believe in going to the police. The police, you think they're any better than Dr. Langley Savage? No way. Bunch of racist crooks. I made my complaint directly to Langley Savage, he was the ring-leader. I said, listen, this is my money you're stealing, I said that openly, to his face. It's grandma's of course, but a quarter of it belongs to me, really, once the old lady is dead. So you owe me money. You owe me big. I'm an artist, I said to him, but I need money; artists need money like everybody else. This is a capitalist society, I said. I told him he was robbing an old lady. He laughed and he said, so you want to be an accomplice? If I deal you in, he said, and if I'm violating some law, or stealing money, then you'll be part of the scheme, too. I told him I didn't give a rat's ass for that. I just wanted some money."

"And did you get the money?"

"I got promises. Not cash, but promises. He was as crooked as Lombard Street. Maybe he had a gambling habit, Las Vegas or something, who knows? They had a nice little racket going there, he and this foot doctor and that nurse. The young one, the foot doctor, he had a greasy smile, and I had the feeling he would screw any woman who walked through the door. It's a miracle he let the old lady alone, except that is for her feet. Of course he made a pass at me. I wasn't having any of it. I know his type. I told him my boyfriend would come and cut off his balls. Do you know who he was sleeping with? My sister Juno. Pathetic. And Langley, you know who *he* was sleeping with? My sister-in-law, for God's sake."

"Your sister-in-law?"

"I should say, my ex-sister-in law. Hildegarde Risley, Bobby's wife. I should have made that clear. Christopher is divorced too, twice in fact: both wives took him to the cleaners. I have no idea where they are at the moment. Living in style somewhere I suppose."

"How did she get into the picture, Cassandra? I mean, Hildegarde."

"No idea. Maybe she came with Bobby when they were still together. Or maybe she saw what the money situation was, and this was going to the source to get it. The old lady wasn't giving anything away, she was totally gaga. No, the money machine was Langley Savage."

"You wanted money, Cassandra? But weren't there trust funds? Didn't your grandmother set up trust funds for the four of you?"

"Maybe you don't understand the situation. I'm an artist but, to be honest, I'm not making much money from my art. I mean, performance art, in little museums, like appearances in Pumpkin Junction, Arkansas, places like that—I mean, there's no such place, but you get my point. And, OK: I had this really rich grandmother and I had a lot of privileges in life, she gave us all big gifts when we reached 21, but frankly, that money is gone. Some stingy bank manages the trust funds, and Christopher was co-trustee, and he either stole the money, I wouldn't put it past him, or talked the bank into putting it into risky things, and it's not what it used to be. I'm not exactly on welfare, but I thought, why don't I get some of the gravy? I mean, she was practically a vegetable, but she kept right on living, nowadays they can keep you alive for a zillion years; and these guys were robbing her blind. I wanted my cut. I want to be rich, then I can put pressure on the galleries, and maybe sell some of my work. I don't just do performance stuff: I'll be honest, I want the big money. The hot artists, they make a lot of money. You splash some junk on a canvas, and you talk it up, and you get some critic to say it's a masterpiece, and you sell it for millions of dollars. I have a head for business, did you know that?"

"I'm not surprised," I said.

"I do. I live in Silicon Valley, and everybody is talking about start-ups. You know, kids just out of high school, they can make a billion dollars with apps, whatever. This guy, Joshua, comes from Tennessee, he and I were together for a while, a real geek, I don't know what I saw in him sexually, although, for a guy who wore glasses and had pimples on his rear end, he had quite a repertoire of moves. But that's not the point. He's into computers, he's a real techie. But he doesn't know shit about business. He and I were going to be partners. I mean business partners, not the other thing. Actually, he decided he was gay, and he's with some guy now, an older guy, a chef at a Mexican restaurant in Mountain View, they're even talking about getting married, can you believe it? I said, Joshua, OK, you say you love the guy, but a wedding? Get serious. OK, I'm talking too much. We had this scheme; well, Joshua had this scheme. We were going to market condoms, they would be in different colors, and they'd have slogans on the wrapper, political slogans, like 'frigging, not fracking,' or 'screw Wall Street before they screw you,' or we could use them to advertise candidates—like 'spend your sperm for Hillary Clinton' or something along those lines. I think they'd sell like hotcakes, we'd advertise on the web and all that. But when we tried to get venture capital from those business types, the creeps on Sandhill Road in Palo Alto, they just showed us the door."

The Risleys, I could see, all loved to talk. I preferred Bobby's talk to Cassandra's; but they were both, in their own ways, narcissistic. I had my doubts about Cassandra's business model. I didn't think the condoms would sell, but what do I know? I'm not part of the target market. I love my wife, menopause and all, hot flashes and all. We're comfortable with each other. I don't think the people I know, the neighbors, the members of Celia's book club, I don't think purple condoms with slogans would fit in their world. Cassandra Risley and her set were like a foreign species to me. At any rate, I didn't want to talk about her plot to succeed in business. I tried to steer her back to the subject that really interested me. I was particularly intrigued by Hildegarde.

"What does she have to do with all of this? " I asked.

"She's a real bitch, I tell you. Bobby is like a baby, he never grew up, and people take advantage of him. I hope this Ashley doesn't screw him over, like the other women did. Anyway: Hildegarde, the bitch, she's trying to steal the baby from him, little Bobby junior. She's trying every trick. Says Bobby abused the kid, which is a damn lie, Bobby wouldn't hurt a fly; now she claims it's not Bobby's kid, the father is somebody else, maybe it's Peter Christoff, maybe Langley Savage, but who knows? She wants to test Bobby, get his DNA, and he won't cooperate. I don't blame him. What difference does it make? We had real fathers and real mothers, genetically speaking, and where did it get us? All four of us are emotional cripples, one way or another. Me, I'm an artist, that's what saved my ass."

Cassandra, by now, was in high gear. I saw I wasn't going to get a word in edgewise. "Naturally," she said, crossing and uncrossing her legs. Her breasts were bouncing under her thin blouse; I tried to avoid staring at them. "This Langley.... What a creep. He was dealing and finagling to the very end. He offered me a deal. He offered all four of us a deal. Only I guess not necessarily the same deal. He was a real con man. He said to me, a bird in the hand is worth two in the bush. Your grandmother gave me power of attorney years ago. I controlled her finances for her own good. I said oh, really: Tell me another story. The woman was gaga. He said, Cassandra, are you listening? I controlled her finances, and it was for her own good, it really was. I said, oh, yes, for *your* own good, you mean. You were robbing her and her family. He said, what family, you, the four of you? He says, give me a break, you all meant nothing to her, and she meant nothing to you. Did you ever go see her? Let's talk frankly here, he said. She was a woman who knew her own mind. Her money was going to go to her *real* family. I said, oh? And who was that. He said, myself and the hospital staff and her favorite charities. She owed you nothing. But I'm willing to be reasonable. How much do you want?"

"And what did you say?"

"I said, no deal; you're bluffing. He said, well, think it over. If you sue, it'll be years before you see a dime; and meanwhile, you'll have nothing. I said, go to hell. And I called Christopher. I can't stand him, to be perfectly honest, with his pin-striped suits, he's a complete phony, my dear brother. But I told him what happened. And he told me about *his* deal."

"Which was?" I asked, although I more or less knew the answer already.

"He didn't want to tell me, at first. That's Christopher. Always playing games. I insisted. He made me promise not to tell anybody, but I don't care. So I told a lie, so what. I don't have any scruples, you know that, don't you? Artists can't afford scruples."

"You haven't told me anything yet."

"It was about a will. A handwritten will, he said it's perfectly legal in California. Sounded ridiculous to me, but what do I know. Somebody scribbles something on a piece of paper, and that's a will?"

"It *is* legal in California. They call it a holograph. It has to be handwritten, well, the basic parts anyway. You just take a piece of paper, and write down your wishes. That's a holograph. They don't have it in some states."

"I didn't know that. Anyway, he says he has this will. The old lady made it out. And it disinherits us. That's what he told Christopher. It left all the money to Langley the bloodsucker and to that foot doctor and the hospital, and some half-ass foundation for the dolls, I didn't quite get the point of that. And he said to Christopher, he's got this document, and nobody knows about it, and he was proposing to tear it up, get rid of it; and then the money would go under some other will, some earlier will. So Christopher said, and what kind of will was that? And he said, oh, a regular will, with witnesses and all nice and proper; and Christopher said, well, what's in it for you? And he said, well that will leaves some money to me and to Peter Christoff and to the hospital, but a lot goes to the family, and she was filthy rich, so you'll all get a lot of money, and everybody can be happy, happy, happy. So that was the deal. Drop all the lawsuits, let things be, and he'll flush the old lady's will down the toilet, or whatever."

"And what did Christopher say?"

"He said, like I said, you're bluffing, I don't believe you, something along those lines. And I think Christopher is right this time, it was a bunch of bullshit. I've been talking to a lawyer, one of my boyfriends, Byron's his name, he's a student at Stanford Law School, third year student, he's really smart, he's going to go into venture capital, I know he's a lot younger than I am, but so what; that doesn't mean anything nowadays. One of my boyfriends, once, was 17; Chester, the guy I was going with last year, he was 40. Lied about his age though. Anyway, this Byron, he gave me some advice, how we should handle the situation, he told me what the law was. He's a fan of mine, I met him at one of my performances, and I could tell from the way he looked at me, that we could have some fun together. Never mind that part. Anyway, we started having sex on a pretty regular basis, he says it helps him with his exams, can you believe it? I said to him, what am I, a cram course? I told him I wanted him to be in my next performance, but he said, Cassie, I don't want to strut around naked in public: you can have access to my body parts, but I don't want to let the whole world in on my secrets. That's what he said. Secrets. I said to him, what's the big secret? What have you got that a zillion guys don't have? And he just laughed. He's smart, but I don't trust him. He wants an open relationship, which is fine with me, so long as we're honest with each other. Me, I think

I'm honest; but I don't think he is. And deep down, he's got a prudish streak. I mean, about nudity, for instance."

She could, I felt, go on and on about Byron and Chester and who knows who else. Not that it didn't have a certain fascination, but I needed to know more about her visit with Langley Savage. "So Savage never mentioned the will."

"Not to me he didn't. Christopher told me the will isn't worth the paper it's written on. She was a senile old lady, she didn't know whether it was Tuesday or December, and he controlled her like some sort of puppet, and the other quack rubbed her feet and gave her a charge, but she was barely conscious. Christopher said that any court would throw it out in a heartbeat. He told that to Langley, he said, and Langley said, oh don't be so sure, Mr. Risley. Courts do funny things, he said. Byron agreed with Christopher's opinion. I told him the whole story. He was taking some course called estate planning, and he said that sort of will was basically worthless. I called Langley on the phone, and gave him hell."

"What did you say?"

"Byron had prepped me. So I told Langley Savage I knew all about the will, the phony will, the handwritten one. I said, I know about what you said about an earlier will too, and you know as well as I do, my grandmother was bonkers for years, so that will is probably worthless, too, and if we throw out all the wills, well, then the next of kin get the money—and that's me and my brothers and sister. Not to mention putting you in prison, and getting back all of your ill-gotten gains, plus the money you gave to your daughter, and whatever you and that foot doctor and that nurse squirreled away God-knows-where. He got quite annoyed with me, and he said some nasty things, implications about my sex life, which of course is none of his business. He doesn't know the half of it anyway. And I gave him back as good as I got, I said, yeah, and what about *your* sex life, how would you like that to come out?"

"Langley's sex life? You mean Hildegarde Risley?"

"Well, he's not exactly a Trappist monk, you know what I mean? God knows how many women he's had, he was an oily creature; and he had a way of looking right through you. I can imagine some stupid women falling for him; he probably preferred rich ones, maybe he could get hold of their money, but who knows? He had my grandma eating out of his hand, she was his cash cow, maybe that meant he could go for something different. So why not go for Hildegarde Risley, not that I can see what the attraction was for either of them. She came nosing around the hospital, that's what I was told anyway. She's rotten to the core. She only married Bobby, the fool, because she thought there was money there, you know, Hortense Risley's grandson; and when it turned out there wasn't that much money there, not yet, and meanwhile it was all siphoning out into Langley Savage's pockets, suddenly the doctor's sex appeal went way, way up. Now the real question is what did he see in Hildegarde? But men are funny like that. You can never tell. Anyway, she was available."

I found this intriguing. I also liked the idea of Hildegarde as a suspect. I didn't want to think of Bobby as a killer. Dr. Savage was obviously a liar and a cheat: maybe he did something that got Hildegarde furious enough to put a bullet in his brain.

"You told me your deal and Christopher's; do you know what Savage offered your sister?"

"Juno? Well, maybe he told her about the will; I don't know. I suppose she wants money, like everybody else. She wanted the doll collection, I know that. She wants money for her favorite charities, and some nonsense about algebra in Africa, as if that's what they need, they're dying of hunger and diseases, and she's worried about whether they can do equations. That's Juno. She's a simple soul. More than money, she wanted Peter Christoff. Like I told you, we're all emotional cripples. Me least of all, thank you. I had therapy for years. It really worked. The therapist fucked me, but you know what? I think that's what made me sane."

She wiggled and bounced some more, and went right on talking: "Now, take Christopher: Don't let that three-piece exterior fool you, he's just as crippled as the rest of us. Emotionally, I mean. Anyway, Juno: she's hopeless, worse than Bobby, at least he's a man, and this is a man's world. She's frumpy, she's ugly, she's charmless. She looks like she's spastic and retarded, even though she isn't. Dresses like a bag lady; doesn't matter if she has money or not. So who would go for her? Well, somebody might. There was some guy in her AP math class, in her high school, a miserable young punk, a guy with thick glasses like Coke bottles, and a face full of pimples. He started in with Juno. I mean, who else could either of them get? Anyway, this punk, his name was Elmer, he got her pregnant. Elmer Schmidt. I think people come to look like their names, if you know what I mean. He looked like an Elmer Schmidt. I suppose she couldn't resist him, simply because he showed an interest in her. She had an abortion, of course. Her mother, my stepmother, a colossal bitch, she had a cow, insisted on getting rid of the baby, and she had to get rid of Elmer Schmidt, too, so she made Juno change schools. If you ask me, he was probably just as happy. Didn't have to pay a cent for the abortion, either; he got away with murder. I wonder what ever happened to the guy. Look, who knows. Maybe he invented something and made a fortune."

I was, of course, not the least bit interested in Elmer Schmidt. I wanted to know more about Juno. She was happy to oblige.

"Juno," she said, "the poor thing, she's starved for love. The reason I'm telling you this is because that miserable podiatrist, Peter Christoff, she fell madly in love with him, practically threw herself at him, and he didn't exactly say no. Must have been quite an orgy there, with Christoff and Juno in one corner, and Savage with Hildegarde in the other. Of course, I'm joking, they wouldn't do it at the same time, and I suppose they didn't do it in front of grandma, not that she would know what was happening if it went on right in front of her face, but the grunting and moaning might have scared her, I suppose. Anyway, that was Peter Christoff. Of course, he was married with three kids, but he never bothered telling Juno that. I did tell her though, I warned her, I said, Juno, don't trust the guy, he's married, and he's just using you but she said she didn't care, and besides, his wife didn't understand him, it was no real marriage, and all that sort of rubbish. Meanwhile, he's left the country. Who knows? Probably there's a warrant out for him. But you can forget about her, as far as the lawsuit is concerned, she wouldn't do anything that might hurt her precious Peter.

'"I tried to talk to her, told her over and over again, this foot doctor, he's rotten to the core, but you know, it's useless. Love is blind. She's totally gaga over that turd. He knew how to get to her. Maybe he rubbed her feet or whatever, and that's when she probably had her first orgasm in years; and from then on, she was like some sort of lovesick cow, it was downright disgusting. It makes me sick to my feminist stomach. Anyway, Langley Savage, he knew what to do, he said to her, Peter was a fugitive, but he, Langley, knew where he was, and he could more or less deliver him to Juno, or deliver Juno to him, whatever. Complete lie, and of course she wanted to believe every word of it; she promised not to sue, and I told her, Juno, the man is completely dishonest, he would blush if he actually slipped up some day and told the truth. Besides, he's a desperate man. They're closing in on him, and if we do sue him, he'll end up penniless; and in prison, too, where the big tough gangs can cut him to ribbons. But she doesn't listen."

"And where *is* this Peter Christoff? You said he was out of the country."

"I don't know and I don't care. Who knows? Like I said, Brazil, I think. Isn't that where people go, when they don't think they can come back? Something about extradition. Or maybe it was Paraguay. I assume he took a bundle of cash with him. And, oh yes, the nurse, whatever-her-name Nurse Barbash, she went too; he'd been balling her for years. Dumped his wife in the process. No chance at all he'll come back to Juno. Well, unless she ends up with money, which is possible I suppose; if she gets enough millions, that might tempt him. I can't imagine the nurse had much of her own. Juno, poor soul, I told her to forget him, but she won't. The only thing that would work with her would be if she could get somebody else. Maybe I'll put an ad out, on the web."

She switched at that point to another disquisition on performance art. I know nothing much about performance art, and Cassandra's notions made no sense to me. And whatever the artistic merits, I could see one huge difficulty, as far as she was concerned. How could you go about selling it? I mean, the hot painters and sculptors can get big money for their work, but what did Cassandra have to offer to some rich Russian oligarch or a Saudi prince? A week sitting in their living room naked, cutting her toenails?

After she left, I went for a walk, taking a break from my humdrum everyday work, and trying to clear my head. It was a cool, crispy, sunny day—California at its best. The murder of Langley Savage kept swirling about in my head. Was I making any progress? A little, I suppose. If Cassandra was right, I could eliminate Peter Christoff from my list of suspects. And Nurse Barbash. They could hardly manage a murder from Brazil. Assuming they were there.

I sat down on a bench to think things over. Inside my head, it was as if I could hear Celia's calm voice telling me, once again, that the case was none of my business, that I should forget it and concentrate on my regular practice. But still....

I was at least learning more about the cast of characters. I now knew the four grandchildren and something of their character and foibles. Then there was Hildegarde. I needed to know more about her. We had met, of course. Once. I felt we should meet again. But surely Bobby and Ashley would not want me to get cozy with that woman.

And I needed to know more about chronology: what happened at that hotel on that particular morning, the morning when Langley Savage died. Who was there. And when. And why.

As it turned out, I would soon get some of the information I needed, from Zelda.

18

After my little spell of rumination, I went back to work. I had no time that day, or the next, for the Langley Savage case, even assuming I had a plan of action, which in fact I didn't. But, as I soon found out, my friend Zelda was buzzing about in a flurry of activity. A day or two later she called me, said she had things to say, and arranged to meet me for coffee in the afternoon. We went to my usual place, at 3:30, and Marigold, the woman with the hairspray, waited on us.

"She likes to listen in," Zelda says. "Let's wait until the coffee comes."

I hated to disappoint Marigold, who was a sponge, soaking up gossip, and she looked on me as a valuable source ever since Maggie Swift, the dentist's receptionist, right across the street, was murdered in broad daylight and I was somehow in the thick of it. We got our coffee, sat in a nice quiet booth, and waited until Marigold was off dealing with other customers.

"Frank, here's what I think," Zelda said. "Somebody was there with Dr. Savage, overnight, at the hotel. And he had visitors in the morning."

"Well, Hildegarde Risley, I suppose, might have been there in the room," I said. "She was having a thing with Langley Savage."

"Maybe," she said. "You know, I'm friendly with some of the staff there. You know, at the hotel they think I'm a private investigator. They're oh so cooperative. Partly because of Johnny, the receptionist I got friendly with. Everybody likes Johnny: such a dear man. And Johnny introduced me to his boss, a Mr. Potts. They know a lot because of the police, and the questions, and the constant investigating; and it's supposed to be confidential, but your Zelda is terrific at getting cooperation."

"I know you are." Of course, I would prefer if she didn't claim to be a private investigator; or say she was working for me, but I knew there was no point trying to rein Zelda in.

"Anyway," she said, "Langley registered all by himself: he was the only one supposed to be in that room. But that doesn't mean anything. Those big hotels, they have no way of knowing who's in the room, if it's one person or six dozen. I thought, well maybe he ordered something from room service, enough for two people, you know what I'm saying? But I don't think he ordered anything at all...."

"Then why do you think there was somebody there overnight?"

"Well, he called downstairs, in the morning, front desk, talked to Johnny, and he said he didn't want to be disturbed, and Johnny remembers it distinctly, and he said, of course, Mr. Langley, that's what he called himself, he used an assumed name, anyway, Johnny said, that's no problem, just put the 'do not disturb' sign on your door. He said, well, I know that, but I don't want any phone calls, or messages, and I don't want the maid knocking on the door or anything. And in the middle of the phone call, he said, one second, and Johnny had the impression he was talking to somebody in the room, saying something, muttering something, and then he came back on, and repeated what he wanted. Frank, I think somebody was there. Was it Hildegarde? Who was with him?"

"How did your Johnny remember all this?"

"Well, first of all, it was pretty unusual, that kind of request; and then, after all, the man was murdered that very morning and the police were swarming all over the place asking questions; and when Johnny went back on duty, they grilled him. It had been just that morning, and somehow it stuck in his mind."

"This other person: did your guy know if it was a man or a woman?

"He had no idea. He couldn't be sure of anything. Just an impression, from the way Langley Savage handled the phone conversation, a feeling that he was talking to somebody, checking something out. Frank, it's clear, isn't it, what happened? Somebody was there, and there was an argument, and that person shot him."

I had to admit that made sense, although we had no clue who this person might be. Nor what the motive was. Of course, there was the missing holograph, the holographic will that Hortense supposedly made.

That holograph, after all, was a powerful motive. If it existed. I wondered, did the grandchildren have alibis? Where were they that morning? I had no way of knowing. "And what time was this," I asked, "this phone call to Johnny, the one where you think somebody else was in the room?"

"He doesn't remember. Eight o'clock in the morning maybe."

"Doesn't that leave Bobby out? He came by later on—around ten o'clock, I guess. And the guy was already dead. We think."

"Oh, Frank, that doesn't mean anything, Bobby coming by at ten. He could have gone and come back."

So the question was: Where were Bobby—and the others—at eight o'clock? If it was, in fact, eight o'clock when Langley Savage phoned the front desk—and presumably shortly afterwards was murdered. It was all so indefinite. I felt we were groping in the dark. I had no right to ask Zelda to do anything more; but she seemed eager to keep up her pose as an investigator. I asked her if she could find out about the Risleys, where were they that morning, at 8 or thereabouts. She said she'd try.

I was more or less breaking my promise to Celia. But I was helpless in the grip of curiosity.

* * *

One thing was clear: it was really important to figure out the chronology of that fateful morning. We know Bobby was at the hotel. We know that Hildegarde had been sharing the room with Langley Savage but presumably left at some point. Very likely the murder took place some time shortly after 8 o'clock in the morning.

We know that one other person had been at the hotel: Gideon Grambling. Exactly when he arrived was unclear. We know that he knocked on the door around 10 or so, and we know he saw Bobby sniveling in the stairwell. Unpleasant as it was, I felt another phone call to Gideon was in order. Of course, Miss Murgatroyd said he was in conference. Eventually, he called me back.

"What do you want, Frank?" he said. "I'm really busy these days."

"Gideon, it's about the late Langley Savage. You went to see him, at his hotel, the day he died...."

"Frank, what is this? I know his daughter is your client, and we've had a common issue, I'm referring to the trust. But you seem to be meddling in affairs that hardly seem appropriate for a lawyer...."

"I think I'm the best judge of what's appropriate, Gideon. Humor me. The whole affair is all screwed up, as you well know, and it certainly does concern my client."

"I really don't see how."

I ignored this comment. "The story you told me about the man in the stairwell, crying his eyes out. That had to be Bobby Risley."

"Yes? I suppose it was. So what?"

"I really don't think he killed Langley Savage. But something weird was going on there that morning and I was hoping you could help me."

"Really, Frank. I know nothing about this, and furthermore I don't want to know anything about it. If you must know, the day before he died, I called Savage. I told him I could no longer represent him. I said I was phasing out his affairs. I said to him, to be perfectly candid, you are not my type of client. I said, I do not wish to pass judgment on you, but for good and sufficient reasons I feel I must take certain steps to terminate our relationship."

"And what did he say?"

"He said he understood. Then I reminded him that, although I would not handle his affairs in the future, we had had dealings, and he owed me a considerable sum of money. After all, I drafted the trust for his daughter, I set it up, and took care of various other matters. I named a substantial fee. He said he would make sure I was reimbursed. Of course, now he's dead and I can make a claim against his estate. You want my honest opinion? He had no intention of paying me. Ever. The man was rotten through and through."

At least I think I now understood the mysterious phone call. It was Gideon. I wish I could have asked Gideon for the exact time of the call; but that would be pressing my luck. In my mind, I toyed with a delicious idea: suppose Gideon had lied to me. Suppose he actually kept his rendezvous with Langley Savage. He demanded his fee. Savage laughed at him. Then Gideon shot him to death. Of course, the timing was off. But he could have done what Zelda thought Bobby could have done: gone away, then come back, knocked on the door, knowing the man was dead, giving himself some kind of flimsy alibi. Which wouldn't work. I conjured up a picture of Gideon, no longer in a three piece suit, but rather in an orange prison uniform. And, oh yes: handcuffs.

All of that was absurd, of course, but thinking of it made my day.

19

The next day, when I arrived at the office, I found Bobby and Ashley waiting for me. They were holding hands. Bobby squeezed Ashley's hand from time to time.

"Did you have an appointment?" I asked. "Did it slip my mind?"

"No, we didn't, Frank," she said. "But we need to talk to you. Is this a good time?"

"As good as any, Ashley," I said. "Come in, and sit down. Can I offer you coffee or tea?"

They both said no. Bobby, I noticed, seemed upset, even more than usual. I could tell by the look on his face. I asked him what the trouble was. He said, "I'm afraid I'm going to be arrested. Frank, is there something you can do? I don't want to go to jail. I think I'd die in jail. I read something about the jails around here, how awful they are. Do they have rats and cockroaches? I had this terrible nightmare, I dreamt I was in jail, I was in a cell, I was screaming, and roaches were crawling all over me."

"I wouldn't worry about cockroaches, Bobby. This is California. We don't tolerate cockroaches, like they do in Florida. I've never seen one around here."

"I'm really scared," he said. "I read that young white guys all get raped in jail. They have all those gangs, tough guys, criminals, with tattoos, and they have knives and razors, and things like that. Frank, I wouldn't last a day, if they arrested me. You've got to help me."

He was on the verge of tears. I keep a box of tissues on my

desk, for people with colds and allergies, and, incidentally, for clients who begin to cry. I've had a lot of clients crying in my office. But until now, they were exclusively women. Bobby was a first. I handed him a tissue. "You didn't tell me why you were worried about being arrested. Has somebody said something?"

He shook his head, and Ashley squeezed his hand. "It's because ... I was in the hotel. That was the reason. They keep asking me questions."

I felt I had to ask. "Well, Bobby, what did you tell them? Did you explain, why you were there? I mean, in the hotel?"

In novels, people are always described as wringing their hands; I'm not sure what that means, but Bobby was fidgeting and squirming, and moving his hands—maybe he was wringing them; anyway, he was clearly in misery. He said, "Don't ask me that, please, I beg of you."

Ashley too looked quite miserable. She said: "Bobby, talk to him, tell him the truth, the truth can't hurt you, I know it can't."

"I was there to go to a meeting," he said. "They had a meeting there, at the hotel, an organization I belong to."

"What organization, Bobby?" The poor guy was such a bad liar. "Bobby, please tell us the truth. You weren't there for a meeting. You went there to see Langley Savage. Don't deny it. It would be too much of a coincidence."

Now he was actually blubbering, and he grabbed Ashley's hand and kissed it, and said, "Ashley, darling, please, I didn't kill your father. You know that. I hate violence. It wasn't me. You have to believe me."

She said, "Sweetheart, of course I believe you, I do; but you have to tell us what this is all about, why you were there, we can't help you if you don't tell us everything. And you can talk to Frank, lawyers keep secrets, they have to. You can't even put a lawyer on the witness stand—they take an oath to keep everything confidential, it's part of their training."

I don't think he liked the idea of the witness stand, or going on trial. But he calmed down a little, wiped his eyes, and began talking. And talking. He still dodged the question, at any rate at first. "Frank," he said, "you have to understand us. I mean, the family. There's four of us. You know that. We're all so different. Me and Cassandra, we're the youngest two. Christopher, he's the oldest. He was born old, you know what I mean? He and Juno, they were the kids of dad's wife number one. Or maybe number two, I think there was some earlier marriage, they got it annulled. She was some kind of society type, their mother, but she had no interest in kids, and she drank a lot I think. Anyway, then there was wife number three, she didn't last long either, she was a show-girl. All of these women thought they were marrying money, and I guess they were; anyway, this third wife, Alba, she didn't want kids. Then there was our mother, she was wife number four."

"Bobby, why are you telling me this?"

"It's important," he said. "You have to know about my life. I mean, Frank, you need to hear it. In case they come after me."

I started to say something, but thought better of it.

He said: "I don't know why they had kids, my father, my mother. They never wanted us. I mean, it was terrible in the house, they fought like cats and dogs. They were both drinking a lot. Drugs too I think. And we were just furniture, you know what I mean? We were fobbed off on babysitters, nannies, and some woman who called herself a governess. She was a real sadist. I was six years old, Cassie was eight. Cassie, she used to protect me. Our father, he had girlfriends. All the time. Different ones. He had lots of them. Used to bring them in the house, can you imagine. When he thought our mother was away, which she was, a lot. I would hear him and his girlfriends, grunting and panting in the next room. Kept me up at night. Mother, she used to go visit her own mother, my other grandma, in Seattle, and she just dumped us on whoever was supposed to be taking care of us, it wouldn't be dad, he wasn't into that, but the nanny or whoever. Mother couldn't stand having kids I guess. She used to say, they're a pain in the ass. She'd say, I'm going to Seattle, to see my mother, you take them, she'd say to him, not that he was going to spend any time with us. He would scream and holler. As soon as she left, he'd turn us over to the nanny. He never paid us any attention. When they got divorced, it was so sad, neither of them wanted us. We ended up with mother, but she was never there for us. I mean, how did we ever grow up? And all this time, we had Grandma Risley, and she was filthy rich. I guess that was our salvation: she paid for stuff, for the nannies, and she paid for college. I dropped out of college, though, I couldn't concentrate, and I was afraid of the other guys, in my dormitory, don't ask me about that. Anyway, when I dropped out, that must have disappointed her. She was sweet, and she did love us, I think. She'd say, 'give gramma a kiss.' Not that we saw her that much. But she paid the bills. Until she lost her mind, and was a hundred million years old, and living in a hospital. And those people were robbing her blind."

I asked him how often he visited his grandmother in the hospital.

"Not that often. I mean, it was once in a while. She was my grandma, she was weird, but she was nice. She was sort of always out of it, always, well, different, if you know what I mean. But I went to see her. When I was little she used to give me candy. I'm the youngest, and I hardly remember when she wasn't in that hospital. I didn't really like to go. I hate hospitals. And she smelled of some kind of disinfectant. And then, you know, the last few years, she didn't even recognize me. I came once, she said to the nurse, who is this person? She had Alzheimer's I guess. I stayed a while, she just stared into space. The only time she seemed to come to life, was when that foot person rubbed her feet. When he started in, she would sort of make little cooing noises, and she seemed almost happy."

"Did you know what was going on? I mean, with the money."

"I swear I didn't. I don't pay attention to these things. Oh, once she said to the doctor, this was before she was really demented, she said to him, this is my little boy, he's the youngest, he's my favorite, isn't he nice? Give him something. And he said, what? And she said, do we have any money here? Don't I have some diamonds somewhere, are they in a drawer? And he said, no, Hortense, don't you remember? She said, remember what? What we did with the diamonds; but she just shook her head. And he took out his wallet and handed me

$100, and he said, Hortense, I'm giving your grandson some money. And she said, oh, I'm so glad. I must have been a teenager then, but she still called me a little boy. Yeah, later, I heard all those rumors, but I had my own troubles, I never thought about those things, the money. I got some sort of allowance, anyway. And by then, she didn't know what was going on, and there was no point even going to see her."

"Bobby," I repeated, "why are you telling me all this stuff?"

He had a pleading look in his eye. "I just want you to understand who I am, how I got this way. Ashley understands me. She knows I could never do anything really bad. I mean, I had no reason to hate that man, Ashley's father. OK, they were taking the money. But I don't want the money. I mean, I'd take it, if somebody handed it to me, I could do stuff with it, you know, help people; but I never earned the money, and, you know, neither did gramma. She had a rich father, that's all. And he was probably a crook, you can't make all that money honestly. I really believe that."

I said, "Bobby, I do understand. At least I think I do. I know you're not after the money; if you end up getting money, from the estate, you can give it away, or some of it; whatever you want to do. That'll be up to you. Your grandmother's estate, I don't know that much about it, but it's a mess, I'm sure you realize that. What with all these lawsuits…. But she was very rich. Whether you're going to get a lot of money, or not so much, that depends. Like, how big is the estate. How much is left, after all the money she gave to those people. And whether they can get the money back from Langley Savage's estate. That's a ticklish thing—for you, Bobby, and you, Ashley. I mean, you're in love, I think that's wonderful. But you really are on opposite sides, whether you want to be or not."

Bobby said, "I hate all of this, it's so awful. I know what you're saying. But are we really on opposite sides, I mean, me and Ashley? Anything I get, it's going to be hers. I'll give her every penny, I don't want it."

"Don't be ridiculous, Bobby," Ashley said. "I want you to get what belongs to you. My father had no right to do what he did. At least I don't think so. We'll let the courts decide, and however it turns out is OK with me. Frank will look out for our interests."

"I want him to look after my interests, too," Bobby said. "Grandma's estate ... I hate the way they're handling it. The lawyer, this man, Wentworth Fain, I break out in a rash when I have to talk to him. He's a dried-up old prune. He's like from outer space. It's like he went to law school in another galaxy."

"Actually, he went to Harvard," I said. "I think that's in our galaxy. I looked him up. And he has a terrific reputation in the field. I don't know him personally. But I know *of* him. As I said, he's got a good reputation."

"But will you do it?"

"Look, Bobby," I said, "you and Ashley, OK, you're a thing. That's beautiful, it really is. But I'll say it again: you're on opposite sides. Maybe you don't want to face up to that, but it's a fact. Bobby, sure, you can drop the lawsuit; but your brother won't. And if he wins, you get a lot of money. That's just the way it is. And Ashley—and she's my client, after all—she loses money."

"It's Christopher," he said. "I mean, he's the only one for sure who's doing this lawsuit. Cassie, she'll be OK, I promise. And I think I can work with Juno."

"Even so," I said. "Really, I can't take you on, Bobby. Trust me on this. But I do have to see what's going on with your grandmother's estate. What stage is it in? I assume she left some sort of will, that was filed and probated. You must have been told about this, Bobby."

But Bobby had no idea. I'm sure he had gotten notices from whoever was handling the estate but he either ignored them, or pretended to ignore them. He was on the verge of tears. He said, "I think I'd better go." At that point, he and Ashley got up and left. I sat there, puzzled. Ashley had wanted him to tell me "the truth," but all I got was a family history. As it turned out, I would eventually learn "the truth," but at that point, he wasn't ready to tell it.

I realized after they left that I would have to call Wentworth Fain, reaching across to that rarefied legal galaxy, the Harvard galaxy. I really needed to know what was happening to the Hortense Risley estate, that large and tangled estate. I had to know the facts.

So I made the call.

20

Wentworth Fain, despite his education in outer space and a rather dry personality, was considerably more polite and more forthcoming than Gideon. My conversation with him was pleasant enough, and his receptionist did not say he was in conference.

Fain said he had wanted to speak to me and would I come to a meeting at which he, Gideon, and myself would discuss the tangled affairs of the various estates, at least on a preliminary basis. Christopher Risley, representing the family, would also be there.

The meeting was in a conference room at the office of Fain and his partners. It was on the twentieth floor of a newish office building; the room had a staggering view of the Golden Gate Bridge and the Marin headlands. Everything about the office shouted "money," but more discreetly than Gideon's. Fain himself was a tall, thin man in his 60's, with a long nose and long, bony fingers. He was pleasant enough, though underneath no doubt he was as hard as steel. The meeting, which I won't bore you with, went well. It lasted about an hour. A young blonde woman entered soundlessly with coffee for everyone. A young associate, who said not a word, sat next to Fain and took notes. Fain did most of the talking. I was there as Ashley's lawyer; Fain as the lawyer for the Hortense Risley estate. Gideon was there as the lawyer for the Langley Savage estate, though he kept insisting he was just a placeholder, that he had bowed out of the picture. He would pass information on to his successor, whom he did not name.

When the meeting ended, I found myself in the elevator, standing next to Christopher Risley. It was an awkward moment. He stood there stiffly, without moving a muscle in his bland, expressionless face. He had blue eyes, but they were somehow faded, though I can't actually explain what I mean by that. He stared straight ahead, as if he was alone in the elevator car. But when we reached the bottom, he turned to me suddenly and said: "Do you have a moment? I would like to have a word with you, in private. It, uh, concerns your client Ashley Savage."

I was reluctant, for a reason I am almost ashamed to admit: parking fees. Parking is not only rare in San Francisco, it's extraordinarily expensive. I had parked my car in a convenient, but murderously expensive garage. But I felt I had to agree. We went to a coffee shop, where we each had another, and completely unnecessary, cup of coffee.

Christopher Risley, speaking in monotones, told me about his "extremely negative and painful meetings with Langley Savage. Even before my grandmother died, I was exploring possibilities of bringing a lawsuit against that man. I have to admit that I was dilatory.... I should have moved more quickly, and more firmly. Frankly, I hadn't seen my grandmother in years. I was living in Denver. I was engaged in business there, and it absorbed all my time and energy. My business was not, alas, successful. In the end I suffered severe financial reverses. And I went through a painful divorce. I had a trust fund, of course; which my grandmother had set up. But it was pretty much depleted: it was poorly drafted, and my ex-wives—there are two of them—got most of the rest of my assets. The child support.... I have three children, all in private schools. Two are in Denver, one is here. It's ferociously expensive. I came back here a few years ago, and of course at that point I decided to visit my grandmother."

I nodded. He at least had the decency not to pretend he had any deep affection for his grandmother. Clearly he was after her money—a loan, a gift, whatever. And of course he was deeply disappointed at her actual situation.

"I was shocked to learn," he said, "that she was completely

demented. Of course, I knew she was extremely old, but still, some people remain sharp even at advanced ages. I knew she was living in a hospital of all places, which I always thought peculiar. I went to see her. She was lying there in this hospital room, and she had no idea who I was. Imagine, a hospital room! This is a woman who had a huge estate in Santa Cruz, a woman who owned old master paintings, and had a condominium in New York and who knows what else. There she was, a kind of prisoner. Langley Savage was there of course, and the podiatrist, and some sort of nurse. I told them who I was and it seemed to make no impression on them whatsoever. I stayed exactly ten minutes. They were hovering about the whole time. To me, it was obvious that something was wrong with the whole setup. I began to make inquiries, and I discovered that they were systematically robbing her. You had to wonder if there would be anything left. I warned this Dr. Savage that I was not about to tolerate that kind of theft. He told me had a power of attorney, and it was perfectly legal and also that he was her agent, under an advanced health care directive. I told him that was all absolute rubbish, meaningless: I told him to expect a lawsuit."

I had to wonder: where was all this leading?

"You understand then, that in my view, your client, Ashley Savage, has absolutely no right to the money in her trust fund; or anything else, for that matter, which she might inherit from her late father. I want to make that crystal clear. I know the man is dead, and I don't ordinarily speak ill of the dead, but he was an absolute scoundrel, a man without the slightest conscience, a man who robbed and pillaged a helpless old lady. And he had the effrontery to offer me a deal. Can you imagine? This was right after my grandmother died. I had her buried in the family vault in Colma. He didn't have the decency to pay his last respects. But I suppose he was afraid I would throw him out or have him arrested on the spot."

"He offered you a deal? What sort of deal?"

"My attorneys have advised me not to speak of it. I turned it down, of course. It was a disgraceful proposition, in line with the character of that man. And then, more recently, when he was living in that hotel, he offered this deal to me again. Of course I turned it down again. I think it only fair to tell you, that I have every intention of continuing with my lawsuit—against his estate, and against your client, Ashley Savage. Of course, I am very well aware of her connection with my half-brother, Bobby. That makes no difference to me. Bobby is old enough to know better, but of course he doesn't. He's emotionally a child, and he's as gullible as the day is long. I suppose she entrapped him somehow, but that hardly matters. I know he won't join in the lawsuit; but it isn't necessary for him to be party to this matter. I'm perfectly capable of carrying on myself."

All this was spoken without making eye contact with me, and in a flat, matter-of-fact tone of voice. He was as cold as ice; and he spoke in complete sentences, unlike most of us. But you can't judge a book by its cover. Christopher Risley had been married twice. He had told at least two women that he loved them; he had kissed them, no doubt, hugged them, cuddled them even; and of course there was sex in the bargain. And three children came out of these marriages. No reason to think that they were the product of artificial insemination. And presumably he loved those children; most parents do. Did he take them piggyback riding? Did he squeeze their little feet, and kiss their toes? The inner life of Christopher Risley: what could that be? Everybody has an inner life. Surely the way he talked was no clue at all—the formal, bureaucratic language. And the three piece suit, the necktie, the starched shirt: those were disguises, perhaps, like a Halloween costume. I wondered: what was he really like underneath the disguise?

I had trouble imagining the real Christopher Risley. But then, maybe he had trouble imagining the real Frank May. Did he think of me as a human being? Or just as some sort of suburban small-time lawyer?

Well, I am a suburban lawyer. And small-time, I suppose. But I have my own inner life, thank you. Moreover, I have a lively curiosity. I had, of course, a pretty good idea what kind of deal Langley Savage had offered him. Christopher was tight-lipped about it; but his sister had told me all I needed to know.

It would have been nice to hear confirmation, but I could do without.

That was the end of our conversation. I watched him walk away, toward a nearby parking garage. I pictured him driving a black Mercedes; or something equivalent. I got my own car (a Toyota) out of the parking garage after paying the exorbitant fee. As I drove back to my office, I kept thinking about Christopher Risley. Did I misjudge him? He acted like an android, but nobody could be really like that. I had wondered whether, underneath, he had a warm, empathic side, a human side. But underneath, there could be the very opposite: something more sinister. A guy with whips and chains in his basement. A cold-blooded, calculating creature. He obviously hated Langley Savage. Was it possible he killed him?

21

I had lunch the very next day with Zelda Valdez. She was eager to talk to me, she said. About "our case." I felt guilty agreeing to meet her because of my promise or quasi-promise to Celia. I have to admit, though, that I liked Zelda. And I wanted to hear what she had to say. We met in a sushi restaurant, which helped my guilty feelings. Sushi is guilt-free food. Anything with that much seaweed has to be guilt-free.

Zelda was dressed entirely in black. Her skirt was ankle-length; this, together with her height and pointy nose, made her look even more like a Halloween witch. She only needed a broomstick and a pointy hat. I had to smile when I looked at her. With Zelda, unlike Christopher, what you saw was what you got. A woman without malice, for one thing. At least I thought so.

"I have to thank you, Frank," she said. "I haven't had such fun for years. I'm neglecting my work, I really am. I have writer's block, and I think it's all because of our case."

"Zelda, dear, for the hundredth time, it's not my case; it might be yours, but it isn't mine."

"Whatever. Frank, listen: Do you think Gideon Grambling could have something to do with this murder?"

"Gideon? Honestly, I don't think so, Zelda."

"Well, I can't say I disagree. But he was there that morning, at the hotel. You know that, don't you? So he has to be a suspect. I'm marking him down as a suspect, but you're right, it's very unlikely. Unless he's some sort of split personality, you know, like Dr. Jekyll and Mr. Hyde, he's this starchy lawyer, all buttoned up, by day, and at night, he's an entirely different person. A killer."

"You can't be serious, Zelda; next you'll be saying the same thing about me."

"Oh, no, not you, Frank. Well, not in the same way. But it's parallel, isn't it? The suburban lawyer by day, master detective by night?"

"Zelda, please!"

"I'm teasing you, Frank," she said, as she lifted a bit of yellowtail to her mouth. "This is so good, Frank. I love sushi. It reminds me of the sea. So many of my books take place on the sea. You know, pirates and all that. Anyway: You know, Gideon was supposed to have a breakfast meeting with Langley Savage, so I wondered where they were they going to meet. Possibly in his room, you know, room service, but more likely downstairs, in the hotel restaurant. They have this breakfast brunch, and lots of people eat there. It's expensive, but you can eat all sorts of things, fruit, pancakes, omelets. I had breakfast there myself. I considered it research. The hotel, that's the key, isn't it, Frank?"

"I suppose."

"Maybe after I do my hospital book, and I'm not sure I will, I'll do one on hotels. I'll put a lot of sex in it. People have sex in hotels, they go to hotels to have sex; they don't have sex in hospitals. Well, not usually. Langley, and that podiatrist, they were carrying on with women in the hospital, but that can't be normal. I mean, hospitals are full of sick people, dying people, people who have operations, old people: where's the sex? Anyway, my hotel book, I'm mapping it out in my head. I have this phrase I'll use: 'A thousand rooms, a thousand stories.' I'm not sure what angle to take. I could do something like those dreadful slasher movies, I don't know if you've seen any of them, they're low-grade horror movies. Let's say it's prom night, all the kids rent rooms, and there's a lot of sleeping around, and there's this horrible person, he comes into the room, and two girls are having sex, or should it be two boys? And he kills them. Or is that too disgusting? People buy disgusting, though, look at that book, the one about shades of gray, did you read that, Frank?"

"Why would I do that, Zelda?"

"It's trash, Frank, but there's money in trash. My detective, Max Drone, maybe he'll be the hotel house detective. Don't hotels have house detectives? I'll use him in this hotel book. I don't feel I've lived up to my potential yet. My romance novels, they were not exactly literature, and I wrote them so quickly. And now people want something else, I'm afraid. The competition is killing me. One of my best books has just gone out of print, the one about the Hindu princess and the young Christian slave, Spartacus, who was captured at sea, and sent in chains to the palace, the rajah's palace, and they fall in love. It was one of my favorites. Anyway, that's not the point. Hotels, they're the point. Especially now that I'm so friendly with Johnny. He's as sweet as sugar. And he wants to help. I told him everything I know, and he's on our side."

"Our side, Zelda? There are 'sides' here?"

"Well, we're on the side of justice, aren't we? Finding out who killed Langley Savage? Anyway: As you know, Johnny was there that day at the front desk. You know, at first, he didn't want to talk. He was interested in me, he likes tall women, he said, but he didn't feel he should 'spill the beans' as he put it. But I told him it was important, that you were working for the family, and that there's a substantial reward for information."

"Zelda, you didn't!"

"Don't be annoyed, Frank. Of course I did. Wouldn't Ashley Savage pay to find out who killed her father? I'm sure she would."

"And I'm sure she wouldn't. Zelda, she says she never met the man. Why should she care?"

"Well, he was her father, wasn't he? And she was there that day. At the hotel."

"I know that. But she didn't go to see her father. That's what she told me."

"And you believe her?"

"Why shouldn't I?"

"I think she's lying, Frank. Look: this is what Johnny told me. He was at the front desk. He got this call from somebody:

there's a dead body in Room so and so, I don't remember the number. It was already odd, because this was the same room where the guy said, no phone calls. It was Langley Savage's room."

"Did he know who called?"

"He didn't. He thought it was a woman, though. He's pretty sure it was a woman. I know, people can disguise their voices. But let's say it was a woman."

"You can't think it was Ashley."

"I agree, I don't think it was her. But who else?"

"It could be anybody," I said. "A maid, for instance. Came in to clean, and there he was, dead."

"Oh, Frank, no. Listen: all of the maids have accents, they hardly speak English, you know that. They all come from Mexico or Honduras or some place like that. Johnny says, they have very few American types. No, it wasn't a maid. There's one other possibility, though. I got Johnny to check, to see who had a reservation in the breakfast room that morning. Long shot. I mean, the guests don't need a reservation, they just come down and give their room number. But if somebody was coming in from outside. And it turned out, yes, there was a reservation. He told me, by the way, that the police were also checking on this angle."

"A reservation? Who from?"

"Well, there was no reservation for S. Langley; but there was a reservation for a Risley, and the initial was maybe B. Risley, or maybe not; it was hard to decipher; but suppose it's B. Risley, that has to be Bobby, no? Risley is not a particularly common name."

I had to agree, this was something that somebody should follow up on. Zelda was eager to do it, but I told her I would do it myself; I felt it was better if I deal with Bobby instead of turning him over to the tender mercies of Zelda Valdez. So I called Bobby the next day when I got to the office. I think I woke him up, although it was after nine o'clock; he sounded groggy. Of course, I had absolutely no right to ask him any questions about what he was doing the day Langley Savage was murdered; but I did this anyway. "You made a reservation for breakfast that morning at the hotel, Bobby? I'm checking up on a few things," I said.

I was banking on the fact that Bobby was naïve; someone more savvy would ask me why I was "checking up on a few things," and what business it was of mine.

"Oh, did I?"

"Apparently you did. Under the name of B. Risley."

He was quiet for a while. Then he said, "I didn't make a reservation. But I was invited to have breakfast at the hotel, so maybe somebody made the reservation in my name."

"Who invited you, Bobby?"

"That lawyer, Wentworth Fain. The one who, uh, is handling Grandma's estate. He called me earlier, maybe the day before. He said he invited all the grandchildren, he wanted to talk to them, before he talked to Dr. Savage; he said he had an appointment to see Dr. Savage. I got up early, because I couldn't sleep, I have trouble sleeping sometime. That's why I sleep late, sometimes I stay up for hours, and then I let myself sleep in. Ashley gets up early, she goes to work; I haven't got a job. I mean, I wish I had a job, but I don't know what I want to do, or what I'm qualified for. Anyway, I was up, I had been tossing and turning, and finally, I thought, this is not working, I can't sleep, well, I'll go to the hotel, and I'll take a walk around the block or something. But, you see, Fain canceled the appointment, for some reason, he called everybody, but I guess he didn't reach me, because I was gone already."

I didn't believe a word of this. Bobby was, as I said, a terrible liar, even over the phone, where I couldn't see his face. I'm not a good liar either, so I don't hold it against him. But I had to wonder: Why doesn't he want to tell me the truth? Why does he make up these stories?

"Frank," he said, "I need to talk to you. Can I come see you? Like now?"

"Why, Bobby? I'm kind of busy."

"Are you busy all day?"

"Pretty much, Bobby. Another time?"

He said OK. I spent the morning talking to clients. I had a lunch appointment with a new client, a middle-aged woman,

Mildred Burbank. Her husband had founded some high-tech company, and then gone off with his secretary. She got a divorce, and a rather good settlement, and we were in talks about setting up a trust for her daughter, Madison. Madison was a student at Berkeley, in feminist studies. "She's doing well," Mildred said, "and she likes it. I wish she wouldn't be so political, though. Always talking about something called patriarchy; and about heteronormativity: do you think there is such a word? Anyway, she's hopeless when it comes to money; and I don't like her current boyfriend, he's got a ring in his nose, I can barely stand looking at him." I was working on the document at 11:30 when Bobby burst in. "I had to see you," he said.

He was, as usual, on the verge of tears. I was irritated, but decided to swallow my irritation, which is usually the best thing to do.

"You have to help me, Frank, I'm at my wit's end," he said.

I had the feeling Bobby was usually at his wit's end. But I smiled and asked him what the trouble was. He burst into tears. "I love her so," he said, "Ashley. And we're ... together now, and that's so wonderful, and I think she loves me, she says she does, but I'm worried, worried sick, whether she'll stay with me. Because I don't know if she believes in me. Or trusts me. She says she does, but does she really? Can you help me, Frank? You're her lawyer, I think she listens to you, she's suspicious of people, she doesn't trust people, maybe it was her hard life, you know, I love her for being so careful, she says I'm naïve, I'm a baby, and I am; I need her. She protects me. She says she needs me, too, but I'm not sure. She's so strong. That's one of the reasons why I fell in love with her."

I felt I had to be a bit firm. "Bobby, I'm not a licensed marriage and family counselor. I'm not a counselor of any sort, except a legal one. I can't really help you. Maybe she doesn't trust you because you don't always tell her the truth. Is that the reason, Bobby? Is it because you haven't been honest with her?"

He was sobbing uncontrollably. "I'm so mixed up, I can't do anything right, I'm a worthless human being, everything I've done, I've screwed up...."

I said, "Bobby, get a grip on yourself. Stop feeling sorry for yourself. You know, in some ways, everybody's all mixed up, in one way or another. What's the issue here? Why did this come up? Here's my guess: you told her some sort of cock-and-bull story, and you think she doesn't think she's getting the true story, and she's right."

"Frank, I'm so confused. And I'm so terribly afraid...."

"Afraid, Bobby? Afraid of what?"

"Afraid she might think I killed her father."

"Bobby," I said, "I'm sure Ashley doesn't think anything of the sort. It's a ridiculous idea."

Big tears rolled down his cheek. "I know, I know. And I didn't kill him. Honestly, I didn't. How could I do such a thing? But she said, Bobby, I believe you never did such a thing; but, frankly, your story doesn't add up. She says she has total faith in me, but she says the police won't believe me. And she's right. She's always right. I don't know what to do."

"Then why don't you just tell the truth? You know, Bobby, you don't tell me the truth either. I'm well aware of that. Exactly what is it that people are questioning?"

"I mean, they want to know what I was doing in the hotel that day, anyway. I told people all different stories, and none of them were true, and Ashley knows it, and maybe the police know it too. Like, that story, the thing I said, how Wentworth Fain wanted to meet all of us, and Dr. Savage, and then it was cancelled, but he couldn't reach me. Cassie told me the police asked her about that, and she said nobody called her, she never heard from Fain. I guess I should have told Cassie, got her to back me up, but I'm too dumb to do things like that."

"Bobby," I said, "like I told you, I'm no expert on love affairs and relationships, but I don't think lying is the road to success with women. Especially a woman like Ashley. She's tough, she's intelligent, she's resourceful. And, by the way, what *were* you doing there? In the hotel?"

I had to wait out a few more sobs and fidgets. I really wanted to end this dramatic scene: Bobby is sweet, but he was beginning to get on my nerves. I had a wild sudden urge to get rid of him, and go to lunch. It was almost time for lunch, and I was feeling the pangs of midday hunger. Not to mention that I couldn't be late for Mildred Burbank.

But it was hard to be angry with Bobby. Irritation was possible, but not anger. He was just too vulnerable.

At last he sputtered out a name: "Hildegarde...."

"Hildegarde? Your ex-wife?"

"Yes."

"Well, what about her?"

"She was there."

"There? Where there?"

"In the hotel," he said. "She was in the room. With Langley Savage. She was sleeping with him."

"Bobby, I know that," I said.

I'm not sure he heard me, and he went right on: "It was going on for months, I think. Even before the divorce, I think she was cheating on me, with him, or somebody else. She told me it was his baby, Bobby Jr., but I don't believe it. Mostly, they kept the thing pretty quiet. I don't know why. Maybe because when she divorced me, she didn't want to seem like the bad guy, that was me, she said I abused her physically. I didn't. Once she got me so upset, I started smashing dishes, and she cut her finger picking up the pieces, it was pretty bad, it was bleeding and bleeding, and we had to go to the emergency room and get stitches, and she said later, when we were getting the divorce, she said I had attacked her with a knife and I cut her so bad we had to get stitches in the emergency room, and she was afraid of me, I needed anger management. She told so many lies. It broke my heart. Not that I loved her, no, that was over; but that she could be so mean, so awfully mean to me. I used to wonder, why did she marry me? I think she thought I was going to get millions of dollars from my grandmother, and when she decided that maybe that wasn't going to happen, or not soon, she got rid of me, and she switched to Langley Savage. Maybe she thought there might be more money there."

"OK, OK, Bobby, so she was sharing the room with him; but I still don't know why *you* were there; can you tell me that?"

"Because ... I thought maybe I could get somewhere with them, him and Hildegarde, about little Bobby. I know he was crooked, rotten to the core. I hate saying this, because he was my darling Ashley's father, but she wouldn't disagree, and anyway, she didn't know him. I was desperate. Maybe I could say to him, I know you've done terrible things with my grand-mother's money, and now you're with my ex-wife, she's not a fit mother, or something like that. I talked to him, and he said, oh all right, just come see me, I don't care, he sounded like, I don't know what, sort of weary of it all ... but he said, yes, we can talk about this in the morning, if you want."

"And you went to see him?"

"No.... I thought we were going to have breakfast, maybe I'm not remembering right, but I went to the breakfast room, yes, I made a reservation, if I said I didn't I was lying, and I sat down, and my cell phone rang, and it was Hildegarde, she said, just go up to the room, he's not coming down, it's Room 706, he wants you to do that, he told me that. I said, where are you? She said, I went home, I won't be there, just you go."

"And you went?"

"I did. I knocked on the door, nobody answered, and, I thought I heard a noise inside, so I knocked again, nothing; I tried the door, and it was open...."

"Was there one of those little signs, 'Do Not Disturb' on the door?"

"I don't remember. I don't think so."

"So you went in."

"I pushed open the door, and at first, I didn't see anybody, I said, Dr. Savage, are you there, and nobody answered. It was a big room, and there was this big double bed, and when I went a bit further in the room, oh my God, on the other side of the bed, I saw him lying there, I guess it was him, anyway, it was a man, and there was blood, and he looked dead, I mean, I couldn't be sure, but he looked dead to me, and then, every-thing was kind of a blur, I couldn't see straight, I freaked out, I was in a total panic, I don't know if I screamed or groaned or what I did, I couldn't have been there more than a minute, I ran out of there, I must have looked like a crazy person, I ran to the stairwell, and I sat down there, I couldn't even catch my breath, I know I was crying like a baby. God, it was the most awful experience of my life."

"Bobby: was there somebody else in that room? Did you see anybody?"

"I don't know. I didn't go into the bathroom. I had a feeling, just a feeling, maybe somebody was there, maybe in a closet, I can't be sure, I mean, it occurred to me, maybe the guy who killed him was still there, I wasn't thinking straight, I was so frightened, I was totally horrified.... The only thing I could think of: get the hell out of there."

"And you didn't call the police or anything?"

"Oh God, no. I didn't think of doing that, why would I do that, I was just scared, freaked out, I never saw a dead body before in my life, I never even go to funerals, I don't like dead people, my sister used to tease me, when my other grandma died, and they had an open coffin, they couldn't get me to look ... and this guy.... the blood—oh, Frank, it was awful."

"Did somebody see you?"

"No, I don't think so. The maids ... I didn't see them. It's a big hotel.... I just ran to the stairwell, like I told you, and I sat there, you know about that. Somebody came down the stairs and saw me, it was that lawyer, I didn't know it then, but I do now. Frank, am I in trouble?"

"How long were you sitting in the stairwell? How long was it before that guy came down the stairs? Can you remember, Bobby?"

"No, I can't remember. I wasn't thinking, like I told you, I sat there crying, and I was shaking like a leaf. I thought I was going to vomit, but I didn't. Maybe it was a minute later, maybe it was ten minutes, I just can't say."

"Gideon came down the stairs, he went past you, and he knocked on the door. He said it was locked. You said it was open."

"It was open, Frank. How else could I get in? Maybe I slammed it shut on the way out, I honestly can't remember. It was a total nightmare."

"Did you see a gun or anything?"

"Frank, there could have been six guns, machine guns, bazookas, I just took one look at that body and I was like a crazy person. I didn't see anything. Only that body there, legs were sort of twisted, and the blood. I hate blood, Frank, I can't stand blood. I have to take a pill when I get a blood test, when they stick a needle in me, Frank, I'm not meant for this sort of thing."

"Nobody is, Bobby. I might have the same reaction," I said.

"After a while, I sort of pulled myself together, and I went downstairs. I just had to get out of that hotel. I climbed down all seven floors, on the stairs. I couldn't face the elevator. I didn't want to see anybody. Then I went outside, I felt faint, and then I went home…. Do people think I killed him, is that the problem?"

"I honestly don't know, Bobby. Personally, I don't think you did. And I'm sure Ashley doesn't think so either."

"I hope so. I swore to her I didn't kill him, how could I kill your father, I said, well you didn't know me, she said. I said, I couldn't kill anybody, I'm not a killer, I broke down completely, and I held her close, and she said, Bobby, I believe you. But maybe somebody planted the seeds of doubt in her. I'll die if that happens."

"It won't happen, Bobby."

"Frank, I need your help. I saw Zelda the other day, she said you were working on the case. Oh, Frank, if you solved it, I'd be eternally grateful."

By now, I knew it was almost useless to protest, to tell people I'm not working on this case or any case; I guess somehow I'm wearing the crown of the great detective, and I'll never talk people like Zelda out of it. I did try, wearily, with Bobby, but I got nowhere. I told Bobby I was willing to help him, if I could; but I didn't think I could. "You don't think they're going to arrest you, Bobby? They don't have any evidence."

"They don't need evidence," he said, his voice showing a tinge of hysteria, "if they decide you're guilty, they just arrest you. I read about it in a book, how they frame people. Frank, what should I do?"

I told him to sit tight, not to worry; which was probably totally useless advice. When he had calmed down, at least slightly, I asked him the question that was really on my mind. "Bobby, let me get something straight. You went into the room, you saw a body, lying on the floor, on the side of the bed, isn't that what you said, with blood, and so on?"

"Yes, yes."

"Could you have made a mistake? They found the guy lying on the bed, with his hands crossed, and two big, antique dolls, one on either side. That's the story I got."

"I saw what I saw, Frank, and that's what I told the police. They thought I was lying. They said they had my fingerprints. I said, I told you, I was in the room, I touched stuff, that's why there's fingerprints. I got so nervous I thought I was going to throw up. This one guy, he said to me, you picked up the body, didn't you, you put it on the bed, isn't that right? I said, no, no, and I felt all dizzy, you know, like I was having some kind of anxiety attack, and they let me go, but they said they'd have more questions for me."

I said: "I'll give you the name of a criminal lawyer. Don't answer any more questions, Bobby. I think he'll tell you that."

He told me, over and over again, he didn't want to go to prison—no, he wouldn't survive it. And Hildegarde, she'd take his little son away, she already had him, she had custody, they always give it to the mother.... Bobby still had visiting rights, but if people think he's a killer, he'll never see his little boy again, and maybe Ashley would stop loving him, and on and on.

When he finally left, I breathed a sigh of relief.

22

Bobby was, I think, finally telling the truth. But something didn't add up. How did the dead body get from the floor to the bed? No wonder the police thought he was lying. But why would he tell that kind of lie?

Here's the conclusion I came to: somebody else was in the room. That somebody killed Langley Savage. Then, for whatever reason, that person moved the corpse to the bed. I couldn't for the life of me imagine why the killer would do that. But he—or she—did.

And who was that person? My current number one suspect was Hildegarde Risley. But I had no notion why she would kill Langley Savage, or what had gone on in that room.

I was getting somewhat reckless, at least as far as Celia's advice was concerned. I couldn't wait to make a move. I had trouble concentrating at lunch, and I don't think I heard half the things Mildred Burbank was telling me. She was afraid her daughter was on drugs, and she detested the boy with the nose ring—she was sure he was sleeping with her daughter, and she wanted me to make sure he could not get his hands on the money in the trust, and so on. I kept reassuring her, but in fact I barely listened.

As soon as the lunch was over, I called Zelda and told her I needed to talk to Hildegarde Risley, and could she arrange another meeting? I thought that Hildegarde was sure to refuse. But to my surprise, she told Zelda she was, in fact, eager to talk to me; she had something important to say....

She came to my office the next day, looking, as before, rather grim. "I know you have an important role in this affair," she said. "This woman, Zelda, she told me about it."

Coward that I am, I simply nodded.

"I have important information," she said. "And Zelda convinced me, you're the one to say it to. I definitely do not want to go to the police. I prefer to use an intermediary." That was me. The intermediary. I simply said, "Go on." She said, "As you know I was married to Bobby Risley. You know the whole story. It was never a happy marriage. It was a mistake from the start. I was considerably older than Bobby in years. Emotionally, we were even further apart. He was and is an infant. Immature. I taught high school English for twenty years, and believe me, my students, bad as they were, were more grown up than Bobby Risley. But that's not the point. You know, we're fighting over custody of our child. Bobby's not fit to be a father. He's emotionally unstable."

I said, "I can't comment on that. It's not my affair." She went on: "You know, too, that I had a relationship with Langley Savage. I was with him in his hotel room, the night before he died. But I left that very evening. I would rather not say why. I did agree to have breakfast with him, and with his lawyer, Gideon Grambling, the next morning. I had been at home. I waited in the breakfast room with Grambling. Savage never showed up. I tried to call his room, but they said he isn't taking any calls. After a while, Grambling said, I'm too busy for this, I can't sit here all day. So he left."

She continued, "I sat there for a while having coffee. Then I saw my ex-husband, Bobby; he came in the front door. I didn't want to see him. I went into the ladies' room to avoid him. When I came out, he was still there, looking around for somebody, I don't know who. I suppose he got fed up with waiting. He went out the door. I waited a bit, then I left myself, and I didn't come back to the hotel the rest of the day."

I guess I must have had a blank look on my face. I didn't know why she was telling this story, or what the point of it was. She said: "Don't you see? The police suspect Bobby. They've been questioning him. They think he might be the one who killed Langley Savage. But he didn't do it. I know that for a fact.

Yes, he came to the hotel, but that was it. I saw him come and go."

"But you were in the restroom, you said that, I mean, you didn't have your eyes on him the whole time."

"Yes, that's true. But I was only in there maybe five minutes. Ten at the most. Not long enough for him to go upstairs and do all that stuff. I want you to know that. And I know, you're asking yourself, why is she telling me this? Yes, I have a lot of resentment against this man. He treated me badly. He abused me psychologically. He's not a fit parent for my boy. I'll fight him tooth and nail over custody; I can't have my boy fall into his hands, he's too unstable. But he didn't kill Langley Savage. That's the gospel truth. I know that for a fact. I told you that: I saw him come, I saw him go. No way could he have killed that man. "

I listened carefully. Then I said: "But, Hildegarde, didn't you say that he attacked you physically, when you were married? Cut you with a knife? You had to go to the emergency room?"

She seemed startled. "Who told you that?"

I said: "Never mind. Is it true?"

She paused, and spoke in a low voice, looking down at the floor. She said: "I was lying.... I was so full of hate and resentment. He never attacked me with a knife. Never. I made that up. I did have to go to the emergency room, but it wasn't Bobby's doing. And of course he never laid a finger on little Bobby. I want you to know that. I told lies. I was desperate. I didn't want Bobby to get the child. I know, I was malicious, I was awful. But that child was my whole life. I have nothing else going for me. I've had a miserable existence.... My father was an abusive brute.... My mother was alcoholic. I never had a happy moment. I should never have married Bobby. It was a big mistake. But then there was the baby. I just can't give him up. Bobby... he's not good, but he didn't kill Langley Savage. I swear it. He didn't do it."

She said all this in a dull, monotonous tone. It was as if she was acting a part. "But who killed him, then?" I asked.

"I don't know," she said. "I have no idea. Maybe a burglar.

I think he had a lot of cash on him. Maybe a burglar came and took the money, and he made a fuss, and the burglar killed him."

"But why would a burglar arrange things, the dolls, you know, make the whole thing look like a kind of execution or whatever."

"How would I know? I never met a burglar in my life. Maybe this guy, he had some kind of quirk. I only know this: Bobby never went in that room. So he couldn't be the one."

"They say they have fingerprints."

"Who says that? The police? They're trying to frame him. They planted the fingerprints. Or they made it up. They have to arrest somebody, because of the publicity."

Was she lying? I thought so. I asked myself: should I challenge her, should I try to poke holes in her story? But I decided not to. Instead, I just thanked her profusely. "I'm glad you confided in me," I said. "This is important stuff."

"And you'll pass it along, won't you?"

"I'll do my best," I said. She seemed relieved, and she got up and left.

Leaving me completely puzzled and confused. Another person lying to me, lying through her teeth. The lies were so obvious, it was almost pathetic. I knew that Bobby *did* go upstairs. He went into the room, he saw a body, he ran out, and sat in the stairwell crying; Gideon saw him, Johnny the reception guy saw him come down, and Bobby admitted all this. Hildegarde apparently did not know about the stairwell, about Gideon, about Johnny.

But why did she make this up? We know she hates him, she's fighting him for custody. She admits she told a bunch of lies *against* him. Why is she lying now to protect him? It doesn't make sense. Could it be a guilty conscience? There are such things, after all. But in this case, I somehow doubted it. Of course, she was also absolving herself, along with Bobby: if *he* couldn't have killed Langley Savage, because she was watching him, then neither could she. Was that the point? Was she just covering herself?

More questions than answers, I'm afraid.

* * *

I got to the office early the next day. I worked for a while, had coffee, then looked at the mail, which usually came in mid-morning. Most of it, as usual, was junk mail, including a plea to help save various species of whale, and a brochure about a cruise in the Aegean, at discounted rates. But I also had a letter from Gideon Grambling. In it he informed me, in the most stilted language possible, that he had severed all connections with the affairs of the late Langley Savage, and with the estate of the late Langley Savage, and that there was to be no further communication on this matter. He had also resigned as trustee of the Ashley Savage trust, which the trust document gave him the right to do, in paragraph so and so, clause such and such. The estate will be represented by Philip Peabody, Esq. The Bank of San Jose will continue to act as trustee of the Ashley Savage trust, at least for the time being.

No interchange with Gideon Grambling could fail to be annoying, this one included. His withdrawal was, of course, no surprise; he had signaled this already. But Gideon owed me, as attorney for Ashley Savage, at least the courtesy of a phone call. I called Gideon's office. I was told, as usual, that he was in conference. I said I doubted that, and I told the receptionist that this was urgent, and would she please connect me with Mr. Grambling immediately if not sooner.

Of course, even Gideon had to tell the truth once in a while, and he might have actually been in a conference, but it turned out that I was right and he was in fact available. Maybe the tone of my voice—as severe and peremptory as I could manage—made a difference to Miss Murgatroyd. At any event, the next thing I heard was Gideon's voice.

"What do you want, Frank? I'm very busy. I haven't time for idle conversation."

"This isn't idle conversation, Gideon. It's about your client, I mean, your late client, Langley Savage. You were handling his estate."

"Didn't you receive my letter, Frank? I am not handling the estate. I have turned it over to another attorney, Philip

Peabody."

"Gideon, I have a few questions I want you to answer."

"What questions? And why should I answer? I explained to you, as explicitly as I could, that I am no longer concerned with this whole sordid affair."

I ignored this. "Gideon, I know that. Don't lecture me. I do need to know some things. I want to know something about Langley Savage's will."

"Well, what about it?"

"Has it been filed in probate court?"

"Frank, how often do I have to tell you: it's not my affair any longer. It's in Peabody's hands."

"Gideon, please don't play games. Has the will been filed?"

"Not by me. But I believe it has."

"And has it been proved? What's happening in this affair? Ashley is my client, and she's a beneficiary. And please don't say, 'ask Peabody.' I will of course, but why don't you just tell me and save me the bother. You can't just ran away from this thing."

"I can't? Try me."

"OK: and I will certainly speak to Phil Peabody. But look: you handled Ashley's trust. Gideon, we have a right to see the trust. The document. And a right to know about the settlor. You never said so, but of course we know it was her father. What did Langley Savage tell you about the trust? He must have explained something."

"I'm invoking the lawyer-client privilege," Gideon said.

"Gideon, the man is dead. Dead people don't have any privileges."

"I believe they do, as a matter of fact," he said. "But I will concede a small point. I will mail you a copy of the trust. It is going to be tied up in litigation, maybe for years. And, as I informed you, I am no longer the trustee."

Gideon was of course the classic rat leaving a sinking ship. But I needed his good will for at least long enough to find out something that was very much on my mind. I asked him, as subtly as I could, whether he knew about Langley Savage's dealings with the grandchildren. Langley Savage claimed he had in his possession a holographic will, Hortense Risley's will: he had threatened to use it, or destroy it, depending on how the grandchildren reacted to his offer. I wanted to know what Gideon knew, or didn't know about such a will. I tried to ask questions which might smoke him out. He was, as usual, evasive. So I asked him, quite bluntly, whether a document of a certain type, a holograph will of Hortense Risley, had turned up in the possession of Langley Savage. He hemmed and hawed again and refused to answer, but I got the distinct impression that he knew nothing about any such will; or even that Langley Savage *said* he had such a will. And now there was no trace of this alleged will. At least it was clear that Gideon and whoever had gone through Savage's papers had found nothing of the sort.

The will, in short, was gone—if there ever was such a will. Gideon admitted that he and a paralegal had gone through Langley's apartment, and so had the police, also the hotel room where he died. He refused to say explicitly that no such document had turned up. No matter. Clearly, it hadn't.

There was not much more that I could squeeze out of Gideon. I was tempted to remind him that he was, in a way, something of a suspect himself. After all, he had been at the hotel the day Langley Savage met his end. It would have been a real pleasure to make Gideon Grambling squirm, to remind him how badly his "old money" clients would react, if they knew their lawyer, the picture of elite respectability, was suspected of murdering a client. But I resisted that temptation.

I disliked Gideon; he was pompous, manipulative, snobbish. But he was not overtly dishonest. Or, to be more accurate, he was careful to stay on the legal side of the line between what was allowed and what was not. I called Wentworth Fain, just to make sure that I was right about the holograph. If Gideon had found such a document purporting to be Hortense Risley's will, he would have turned it over to Fain, the lawyer for Hortense's estate. Fain was dry as dust and formal, but more malleable. He said he knew nothing of any such will, had no evidence of any such will, and that he had long since filed what he believed to be the last will of Hortense Risley, executed some three years before her death.

"That's being contested, no?"

"It is. I'd rather not comment on details."

So much for Wentworth Fain. I picked up the phone and called Phil Peabody. Nobody answered the phone at his office. I left a message.

I knew him vaguely, at least by reputation. Hardly a good reputation. He was certainly not the sort of lawyer Gideon Grambling liked to deal with. I wondered where he got Phil's name; I wondered who had recommended him and why. He was definitely not chosen because of his lawyerly reputation.

Phil had an office in San Carlos, a suburb slightly south of San Mateo. The Bay Area is full of these old Spanish place names, besides the two big ones, San Francisco and San Jose. I had asked friends of mine what they knew about Phil Peabody. People thought he was smart and well-trained; but he also had a drinking problem, three divorces, and had once almost gotten himself disbarred. Something to do with mismanaging trust funds. Gambled a lot too, made at most a marginal living because he was chronically unreliable. But according to one of my friends, Phil was trying now to "turn the corner, make something of his life—cut out the booze."

"I screwed up," he had said to a friend, "but I'm trying to get my act together." At least this is what I was told.

I never found out who recommended Phil Peabody to Gideon. But it was obvious *why* Gideon went to Phil. The Langley Savage estate was risky business. Potentially, it was worth a lot of money. But every penny of that money was contested. Savage had plundered tens of millions from the late Hortense Risley. Savage claimed it was all legitimate; he held a power of attorney. Hortense, he had claimed, willingly gave money away out of gratitude for his services. Would this argument work? Probably not. Wentworth Fain and his fancy law firm would demand complete restitution. And they had a very strong case.

The next day, Phil Peabody called me and we arranged to have lunch in San Carlos. We ate at a small Italian restaurant near the Amtrak station.

Phil was about my age, but looked older. He was scrawny, had an unhealthy skin color, and a sort of sunken chest. He wore a suit and tie, but it was rumpled, as if he had slept in his clothes, and his shirt looked wilted. He had a bad case of five o'clock shadow, even though it was only half past twelve. His eyes were slightly bloodshot. His hands trembled slightly. "I've got Parkinson's," he said, "early stages." He didn't want me to think it was some kind of alcoholic tremor.

He was a wreck, clearly, but a wreck who was (he said) engaged in a salvage operation. He had a wicked, edgy sense of humor, even about himself, and I liked that. I did notice, though, that he had no appetite whatsoever. He ordered ravioli with tomato sauce and mushrooms, took a few bites, fiddled with his fork several times, piling pasta up on this side and that side of the plate, and ended up eating about 10% of the dish.

I had no trouble finishing my own pasta. But then, I'd never had Phil's problems.

I told him as much as he needed to know. He seemed to have a good grasp of the issues; and he knew about the (alleged) lost holograph. Of course, if it existed, if it was valid, and if it said what Savage said it did, then the Savage estate might be in for a huge amount of money. A big *if*.

"Let's be frank, Phil," I said. "This will, even if you find it, look, this was an old lady with Alzheimer's. She probably had no idea what the darn thing said. You know that. So what is the will worth anyway?"

"It's worth a lot," he said. "I mean, this is a huge estate, Hortense had zillions. Who even knows how much. I'm thinking, sure, the will may be, well, fragile, but I'm talking settlement here. It would be worth millions to them, millions, to get rid of the will. After all, the late Dr. Savage, that's what he was peddling: pay me off, and call off your lawsuit, and I'll get rid of the will."

This startled me. "How did you know about that business? I thought it was a secret. I mean, Langley Savage's offer or whatever you want to call it."

"Gideon told me. He knew all about it. That's one of the reasons he dropped the client, turned the whole mess over to me. Why me? I guess he thought, first of all, I was desperate, and secondly, I had no principles. He could be right. On both counts."

"And did somebody agree to Langley's offer? One of the grandchildren? And did he in fact destroy the will? If he did.... You know, that's against the law."

"Oh, dear me," he said sarcastically. "A crime! Dr. Savage, he might have to go to jail. He might lose his medical license. Oops, I forgot. He's dead. None of that matters."

"I repeat, Phil: did he?"

"I wouldn't tell you if I knew. But I don't know. Look: somebody came into his hotel room and shot him. Maybe that person took the will."

"You really think so? You think he had the will in the hotel room? Why would he be so stupid? I assume he hid it somewhere."

"Or maybe he didn't. Look: I've got a different scenario in mind. I think this is what happened: he did make a deal with one of the grandchildren. Maybe Bobby. They were supposed to meet in the hotel room. Savage would turn over the will, and Bobby would hand him cash, a check, who knows. Instead, Bobby took the will, put a bullet in the guy's brain, and walked out with the will. Which he later flushed down the toilet. End of story."

"Honestly, Phil: Have you met Bobby? If you had, you'd know that that story is ridiculous. And ... why would this murderer sit in the stairwell, sobbing his heart out. Did Gideon tell you about that?"

"Yes, he told me. But, hey, what does that mean? I don't trust anybody. I don't believe anybody. This Bobby, he's impulsive, let's say. He kills the guy, but then, look, this is something big, killing somebody, he's terrifically upset. It dawns on him he just murdered somebody. He could get the gas chamber, the little fool, and he goes to pieces. Happens. So, instead of running away, he's sobbing in the stairwell. But, look, I'm just guessing. What do I know? If you don't like Bobby as a killer, try one of the other three. I don't know them. I looked up the sister Cassandra, a woman who sits in museums stark naked, she's a mental case, obviously. She could have been the one. They all had a motive."

"OK, OK. But all this is a bunch of guesses. Let's get down to our real business, Phil. As you know, I'm Ashley Savage's lawyer. Far as I know, she was his only relative. Langley's will—I want to talk about that. You filed it, didn't you?"

"Yeah, I did. Anyway, he had a will, Gideon had it. The original, anyway. Gideon turned it over to me."

"What did it say?" Basically, I knew, but I wanted to hear it from Phil.

"It was weird. He was a mental case, too, if you ask me. Of course I never met the man. A crook and a mental case, but don't quote me. I'm trying to make a living here, and believe me, with this estate it won't be easy. It's like a lottery ticket. If I win, it's big money. If I lose, I get nothing, and maybe I'll have to pack it up. Anyway: he left half of the estate to his daughter, Ashley Savage; some money to the hospital, but only if the estate was worth more than a certain amount, I don't remember the details, and the rest of the estate, almost half, well, this is the crazy part, he left open, but then he had a codicil, and he left the money to Bobby Risley, in that codicil; and he also amended the trust. Why he did this stuff, God only knows. So you see, they all had motives, but Bobby, he had the biggest one."

I thought: a motive, yes—but only if they knew about these arrangements, which was extremely doubtful. I had to ask: "Did anybody know about this will? And by the way, I assume you filed it. Will and codicil."

"Who knew about it? Nobody, I guess. Maybe that broad he was sleeping with, Hildegarde. He only did it the day before he died. And yes, I filed the will. And the codicil."

"Do they know about it now?" Wills in California are public records. Anybody could go to probate court, and ask to see Langley's will. Most people don't know they can do this, I suppose; and I doubt that people make it a habit. But Christopher, perhaps, I suppose he could have gone and checked it out.

"Well, Ashley Savage knows about it," he said. "I called her yesterday. I'll send a letter to Bobby Risley, it's the thing to do, but he knows about it, he's sleeping with Ashley Savage. These people are all crazy. I've got to get in touch with somebody at the hospital. Who the hell knows if there's any money? He was either a very rich man or a bankrupt crook. Rich, if he gets to keep all the money he euchred out of Hortense Risley. But they're suing him up the kazoo. Especially Christopher Risley. And of course Wentworth Fain. Heavy artillery. They want every penny. My big hope is a settlement, of course. Maybe he wrote this will, giving them money, to keep them from suing him, maybe he wanted to give them a reason to let him get away with at least some of the loot."

"Not much of an incentive," I said. "For the grandchildren, anyway. If they break the will, Hortense's will, on the grounds that she was totally incompetent, she'd be intestate, they're the only relatives, and they'd get everything she had."

"Don't I know it," he said.

I said: "And they're also trying to get at Savage's money. You've got your work cut out for you, Phil."

"You said it."

"Meanwhile," I said, "I represent Ashley, and the whole thing is a mess. She's hooked up with Bobby Risley, I guess you know that. They say they're madly in love. His sister Juno, meanwhile, is mooning over the podiatrist. Crazy."

"They're all crazy," he said. "Yes, it's a mess. I just hope I can get some dough out of it. It's pretty iffy. I'm betting on a horse that's a real long shot. And I'm up against the big boys. I've got a whole army of lawyers against me. They all got lawyers, the hospital, the grandkids, or some of them, Hortense's estate. Hey, us lawyers, we're a bunch of vultures, picking over the corpse, if you'll pardon the expression. Well, Wentworth Fain and those fancy guys in San Francisco, the ones who are handling Hortense's estate, they'll make out like bandits; but me, I could end up with nothing. Story of my life. But it's worth a try. Your client, Ashley, maybe she's willing to settle. You know, give up some of the trust money, some of the stuff in her father's estate. Maybe the other side would be willing too."

I couldn't commit her, of course. Not without talking to her. And my duty was to protect her interests—in the trust, and in her father's estate. Nor did I have any idea whether the "big boys" were willing to compromise. Not at this point, of course.

I wasn't too optimistic. They had an excellent case. Langley Savage stole money from a demented old woman: that was their claim. Still, there were all sorts of legal and factual issues.

Plus the fact that somebody murdered him. Was it one of the grandkids? If it was Bobby, he couldn't get a share of Langley's estate. And then there was the missing holograph. If that ever turned up, and if it ever existed. Many questions, so far few answers.

I didn't know it, then, but the answers were soon going to come.

23

Zelda was in the habit of calling me every few days so I could "bring her up to date." Usually, I had nothing to tell her. But the next time she called, I filled her in on my conversation with Phil Peabody. I told her, among other things, about his suspicions of Bobby. "He never met Bobby," I said, "If he had, he'd forget about Bobby as a suspect."

"Frank," she said, "he's not the only one with that idea. I mean, Bobby is definitely a suspect. He was right there on the spot."

"Zelda," I said, "you know it's impossible. He's such a sweet, innocent guy. Mixed up, yes; but no way could he kill Langley Savage."

"But he's impulsive; you know that. He loses control, he told me that himself. I'm not sure what he meant. Maybe just that he can't help crying like a baby. Honest to God, I never met a man who cried so much. Milo, my ex-husband, he never cried. He was emotional, God bless him, but to burst into tears—no way. Hildegarde told me, though, that he had a violent side to him. I mean Bobby, not Milo."

"Zelda, I heard her, but I don't believe a word of what she says. She's lying, lying, lying. Why not? Everybody else is lying to me; or am I being paranoid?"

She said: "Well, I don't lie to you, Frank. You can trust me. Listen: I wanted to tell you this: the investigation is heating up, I think. The police have been around the hotel again, talking to Johnny; and of course he tells me everything. He's such a dear. He's so young, but.... He likes me. He said 'can we go out on a date?' Can you imagine, he actually said 'a date.' It made me think of my high school days. Not that I was popular, Frank; I wasn't. Too tall. All those short boys, I had to stoop if I wanted to kiss them. But anyway, Johnny is different. I love the way he looks, too. I'm putting him in my book; I'm going to make one of my characters look like him. He'll be in the hotel book. I told him about it, he got very excited. Oh, dear, I'm rambling, Frank; I'm boring you."

"Zelda, no way; you're not boring," I said.

"Frank, have we thought about the time of death? I mean, when was Langley Savage murdered? They found the body around 11 o'clock, I think. But he had been dead for at least a couple of hours, and maybe a bit more. Johnny found that out when they were questioning him, they were always asking, what happened at this time and that time; well, it was about figuring out who was where at the time of death."

"OK, then," I said. "I like that. Let's say he was killed at 8 or 9. That leaves Bobby out if he's telling the truth."

"A big if. I mean, he could have killed Langley, gone away, come back, and did that little act in the stairwell. Not that I believe that's what happened. But Bobby keeps changing his story. Why does he do that? There's something he's not telling you. You absolutely have to talk to Bobby again," she said. "Give him some excuse. He's the key to this whole thing. And all those lies!"

"Granted. Lies. But what do you think actually happened?"

"Think about it, Frank. He tells a story. He goes up to the room. Well, first of all, why? What was he after? Then he says the door was open. But that's strange. Why should the door be open? People don't leave hotel doors open. Especially if they just killed somebody there. I mean, if you're going to kill somebody in a hotel room, the least you could do would be to hang that thing on the door, you know, 'Do Not Disturb.'"

She was right. My little grey cells were not doing their job; but hers quite possibly were. I thought about an excuse to call Bobby. But as it turned out, I didn't need an excuse. He came to me on his own accord. It was in the middle of the afternoon. He looked even more distraught than usual.

"Frank, I'm desperate," he said. "I can't sleep at night. And in the daytime Ashley goes to work, and I lie there, tossing and turning. Last night, I had a dream that the police came and arrested me. Do you believe in dreams? I sort of do. I went to my psychic yesterday, she saw trouble ahead for me. I don't believe in it, but I go to her anyway. You know, it's like the horoscopes in the paper. I read them, I'm Pisces, and I know it's garbage, but sometimes it sends a chill up my spine. I've been so upset lately, I'm afraid Ashley will stop loving me. You have to help me, Frank. I don't see my therapist until next week, she's on vacation. I talk to Zelda sometimes, but it makes things worse. She doesn't trust me anymore. That's why I'm turning to you."

"Bobby," I said, "I'd like to help you; but I don't know what kind of help I can give you."

"You can find out who killed Ashley's father. I think sometimes his ghost is haunting us, you know what I mean? I mean, I know, there's no such thing, there's no ghosts, but I have this awful feeling, creepy feeling, I woke up, in the middle of the night, and I saw this shadow, it was a car passing by outside, but I was shaking like a leaf, I felt, it's Ashley's father! I know that's crazy, but I couldn't get that out of my head. I'm so upset that I can hardly move. This business, it's driving me crazy. It's even doing something to my body, I mean, it's embarrassing to talk about, but, you know what I mean, Ashley is so passionate, and I love her so much, and I want things to be good and sometimes they're not. If only this thing was over! If only they arrested somebody, anybody. Only not me. Zelda says you're working on the case. Do you think ... I mean, can you find out who did it, Frank?"

"It's not really my job, Bobby; and no, I'm not working on it. You know, even if I was, there's this problem: I talk to people, but they don't tell me the truth. And I can't figure out what's a lie, and what's not a lie."

"People lie to you, Frank? Like who?'

"Well, you Bobby, for example."

"Me?"

"First of all," I said, "you told me that you went in the

room, you found a dead body on the floor, it freaked you out, and you ran out of there. But the body was on the bed, not on the floor. Anyway, that's what we were told."

"I swear it! I'm not lying; that's what I saw. Maybe I was upset, but I'm not crazy, I'm not seeing things that aren't there. The man was on the floor. That's the God's truth, Frank. I don't know why they say he was on the bed."

"Well, OK, maybe. But there's a second problem. You said the door was open, which seems weird. Why would somebody leave the door open? Somebody who just put a bullet in the guy's brain, wouldn't that person lock the door? Why leave it so that anybody could get in? And why not put up that sign, Do Not Disturb. But you said it wasn't there. It just doesn't compute."

Bobby's response was immediate: He burst into hysterical tears. "Frank," he said, in between gusts of tears, "I'm a bad person, I don't know what comes over me, it's because I'm so upset, I do things I shouldn't do. I did tell you lies. I should have known you're too smart, I should have known I couldn't fool you." I handed him a tissue and he wiped his eyes.

"So the door wasn't open," I said.

"No, Frank," he said sheepishly. "The door wasn't open. I knocked and nobody answered, but I thought I heard a noise inside—and I wanted to get in. I saw a maid down the hall, around a corner, and I told her the room number, and I said it was my room, and I mislaid the key, could she open the door? She had a thick accent, I think she barely spoke English, she said, no, I should go downstairs, go to the front desk, she couldn't do it, it was against the rules. I said, it's really important, and I offered her money, $20, and she shook her head, no, and then I offered her $50, and she went with me, and opened the door a crack, and I waited until she disappeared around the corner, and then I went in. And that's the truth, Frank, I swear it."

"Can you prove this, Bobby? Can you get the maid to back you up?"

He shook his head sadly. "I wish I could. She was Mexican or something. I don't know her name. I told all this to the police, and they said they'd try to check it out, but then they told me they couldn't find her, and if I didn't have a name, they couldn't verify what I said; and there's high turnover at the place. There were at least six Hispanic women who were working there, that's what they said, women who could have been on that floor, and none of them said they saw me, of course, they could be lying because of the money, but three of them don't work there anymore, and two of them went back to El Salvador or some place. I don't think they believe me. I said he was dead when I went into the room, and I freaked out and just ran away.... And I lied to them, because they said where was this body, and I said on the floor, and they said, oh, really? I could see that was the wrong answer, and I said, look, I was all mixed up, maybe it wasn't the floor, maybe it was on the bed, and of course they didn't believe either story. They were really awful to me, too, and they scared me to death."

"Just stick to the truth, Bobby," I said. "There's no point lying. You're better off if you tell them the truth."

"And they say they have evidence, DNA they said. On a water glass or something. There were two water glasses, and they said, one of them had his DNA and one of them had mine, and they also have my fingerprints. And I said, well, sure, my fingerprints, I told you I was in the room, but then they said what about the DNA on the water glass."

"Did you drink water in the room?"

"Oh, Frank, not you too. I never drank anything. I was in that room for ten seconds, I saw a body and I ran out of there, I can't stand the sight of blood.... I'm a coward, Frank. When I was in grade school, they showed a film about Snow White and the seven dwarves, and there was a witch in the film—I got so frightened I was crying and I peed in my pants. I was totally humiliated."

"But Bobby, how do you explain the DNA?"

"I can't explain it. I think they're lying. They're just trying to trap me, get me all confused. And I *am* confused. I don't know whether I'm coming or going. Look, they just don't know me. Frank, believe me, I never shot a gun in my life. I'm afraid of guns. I was in the army for a few months, when I was 20. I joined the army, don't even ask me why, I didn't know what to do with my life, Cassandra said it might be good for me, but it wasn't, it was a terrible experience, all those guns, and people yelling at you all the time, I even had to fire a bazooka. I was terrible at everything and the other guys made fun of me, I couldn't stand it, I went away for a weekend and I came back late, and I did other things, I just didn't fit in, and then I ran away, and they gave me a dishonorable discharge. They said they could court-martial me, but maybe they thought I was a mental case. I just wasn't cut out for it."

"But Bobby, can I ask you, why was it so important for you to get in the room, most people would just go away if the door was locked and nobody answered; I think there's something you're leaving out here."

"I ... I just can't tell you."

"Bobby, you have to tell me. You absolutely have to. Please."

He was silent for a little while. Then he said: "I got a phone call. On my cell phone. Telling me I had to come, telling me it was important."

"When did you get that call? And who called you? Was it Langley Savage?"

"When? I don't remember exactly. Maybe an hour before. It took me time to get to the hotel. Maybe it was nine o'clock, maybe eight o'clock. I just don't remember."

"OK, and who was it who called you? I asked you that."

"It wasn't Langley Savage. It was ... a woman. Please. I can't tell you anything else." Big tears were rolling down his cheeks. "Please, Frank, please."

But I wasn't about to give up. "Ashley?" He shook his head, no. "Your ex-wife?" This time he hesitated, for some reason, but then he said no again.

"Then who?"

He hesitated, then he whispered, in a low voice: "Cassandra.... My sister...."

"Cassandra? What did she say?"

"She said it was important. Really important. She said

she'd seen Langley Savage and she wanted me to see him, to talk about the will. His offer, the custody. I always do what she says, she's been like a mother to me, even though she's only a few years older. When I was young, she looked after me. She's strong, Frank, and I'm weak. I'm bad, too, I'm a worm; please don't judge me."

"But why did you tell all those lies?"

"Frank, I don't really know. I just wanted not to get involved. Listen: I didn't kill him. You have to believe me. Why did I ever go into that damn room? I have nightmares, Frank, I wake up in a sweat, then I hug Ashley, she's the only thing that keeps me sane. Please, Frank, tell me you believe me."

"I believe you, Bobby. I believe you when you say you didn't kill Langley Savage. The rest of it, who knows? You seem to make things up as you go along."

"But I'm telling you the truth this time. Ask Cassandra; she'll back me up."

"I will," I said. Cassandra! Was she also the woman who called, and said there was a dead body in the room? I had assumed this was Hildegarde. What on earth did Cassandra have to do with all this? Could she be the one who killed Langley Savage?

I had the feeling something was coming to a head. That we were untangling the mystery, somehow. Was Cassandra the key?

24

I had absolutely no business calling Cassandra, but I did. My excuse was that Bobby asked me to do it. He had given me a number which he said was her cell phone. I called and left a message, since she didn't pick up. I said I would very much like to talk to her; that her brother Bobby wanted us to get together.

She never responded, but the next day in the morning she came storming into the office looking very angry. She plunked herself down in a seat across from my desk. As usual, her blouse was low-cut and her cleavage was plainly visible. She never seemed to wear a bra; maybe she thought a bra was too confining, or that it symbolized something, maybe the subjugation of women. In any event, bra or no bra, she was clearly very annoyed.

"Cassandra," I said, "thank you for coming."

"Spare me the thank you's. What is this all about? Why are you pestering me?"

"I'm ... trying to help out your brother Bobby. He thought you could help, too. Do you mind, Cassandra, if I asked you a few questions?"

"Do I mind? Of course I mind. What kind of questions?"

"It's ... on behalf of Bobby."

"Listen," she said, "what's in it for you? What's this quiz all about? Why are you meddling in?"

I said, rather meekly, "You do want to help him, don't you?"

She said: "Sure, but what's helping Bobby got to do with

you anyway? Why are you involved in this? Last I heard, you weren't a member of my family. You're a two-bit lawyer. And you're not his lawyer either. You're a lawyer for Ashley Savage, period. Maybe you should just leave my brother alone, huh?"

"But you got Bobby in trouble," I said, ignoring the insults. "You called him, and told him he had to go see Langley Savage, the day Langley Savage died. He did go, and it got him in trouble. Maybe Langley was already dead when you called. Where were you, and why did you do this?"

"How dare you ask me these questions! I absolutely will not answer them."

"But, I'll say it again, you say you love your brother, but you did something that got him involved in a murder case; and the police are asking him all sorts of questions, and the poor guy is a wreck. He came to me and begged me to help him. *That's* why I'm involved. And why I'm asking these questions. I'm trying to help him, and he wants me to talk to you, wants you to straighten things out. Look: not that *I'm* saying this, but somebody might even think *you* were the one who killed Dr. Savage and are trying to pin the blame on your brother."

I wish I were better at reading people's faces. She stared at me, with a cold, hard look—but whether it was anger, rage, embarrassment, or dismay, I simply could not tell. After a moment she said, "Are you quite finished?"

She had been right when she said it was none of my business. But I was doing it anyway. In for a penny, in for a pound. I plunged right ahead. "No, I'm not finished. OK, you won't answer my question about the phone call. I'll ask you another question. Langley Savage wanted to talk to all four of the grandchildren. You're one of them. Did you do it? Did you go to see Langley Savage? At least tell me that."

She paused for a moment, as if she was thinking this over. Then she said: "Sure. Why should I lie? Yes, I went to see him. The day before he died. I went to his hotel room. I had seen him before, naturally, in the hospital. I could see he was a crook. I mean, when I went to the hospital. A slick operator, a real devil. But in the hotel, he was a different person. The guy was a total disaster. He was all gray and he had some kind of tremor. I asked him, are you sick or what? Maybe he had Parkinson's disease, those people shake all over. Or maybe he was drunk, or high on something."

"What did you go to see him about?"

"None of your business."

I told her what I knew: Langley Savage claimed he had a will, her grandmother's will, and offered to tear it up, if the grandchildren would play ball with him. I asked her if she saw such a document. She snorted and said, no. Not that document.

"What document, then?"

"There was an envelope. He had been writing something when I came in and he stuck it in an envelope. When he went to the bathroom, which he did twice in a short time, I think his stomach was upset, or maybe it was the liquor, I smelled liquor on his breath. Anyway, I snuck it out of the envelope and read it. Or a bit of it. It was his own will, and that didn't interest me, so I put it back in the envelope. I mean, who cares. The bastard is dead."

I had one more question: "Was Hildegarde Risley there?"

"You *are* the nosy one. No, she wasn't there. They broke up, did you know that? Very noisily, too, I'm told. They were shouting and screaming at each other, people complained at the hotel. You know how I know this? I had breakfast in the hotel with Hildegarde. The next morning. The same day somebody put a bullet in his brain. Wait a minute: What are you getting at? You really think it's me? You think I killed the bastard?"

"I'm not saying anything of the kind. But you want to know what I *do* think, Cassandra? I think somebody talked you into calling Bobby, why and how, I don't know. It might have been Langley Savage, maybe he talked you into it. Or maybe it was somebody else. Maybe Hildegarde. You know the answer, I don't. I don't think you wanted to get Bobby in trouble, but that's exactly what you did."

"You think I don't know that?" she said. "You're so smart, right? You have things figured out. Mr. Great Detective. Mr. Lawyer. But you know what? You're not so smart. You're nothing. You're junk. You're shit."

I wilted under this storm. "Bobby told me...." I got no further.

"I'll handle this myself," she said. And she got up and swept out of the room.

* * *

I sat there thinking. Had I learned anything? Yes and no. I wish I knew exactly *when* she made this call. Why was she having breakfast with Hildegarde Risley? I had a vague idea, more than a vague idea. And I was convinced: it was Hildegarde who talked her into the phone call. But why?

Maybe I should unleash Zelda.

Cassandra hadn't really told me what I wanted to know. Not directly. But I had the feeling I had accomplished something. She knew she had to do something. For Bobby's sake. Cassandra, I felt, was not going to let the grass grow under her feet.

Something was happening. Something was moving. I felt vaguely excited. Maybe a solution was emerging. I had the feeling we were going to find out, soon enough, who actually killed Langley Savage.

I was right about that. The question was about to be answered. But not by me. Or Zelda. Believe it or not, Celia found the answer. Or what seemed to be the answer. And that happened quite soon.

25

I reported to Zelda about my encounter with Cassandra. She sat in my office—we were about to go out to lunch—and she listened intently. She seemed to be in a thoughtful mood. "You're doing a great job, Frank," she said.

I had to look carefully at Zelda to make sure she wasn't being sarcastic. She wasn't. To be honest, I had done a certain amount of sugar-coating with regard to my meeting with Cassandra. I left out the part where she told me I was shit.

"You're so great, Frank," she said. "I'm going to put you in my novel. But you won't be a lawyer. You'll be a hotel manager. Anyway, I have an idea what's going on here. Let me look into it, Frank. Did you ever read the Nero Wolfe mysteries?"

"I don't think so."

"He's this fabulous detective. He's enormously fat, and he spends most of his time raising orchids. He never leaves the house. He has a henchman who does all the running around. But Nero Wolfe, he sits in his house, he has a cook, he eats too much, he piddles around with his orchids, and he solves the mysteries without ever going outside the house."

"And that's me? OK, I'm a little bit overweight...."

"Oh, Frank," she said. "That's not the point. I'm just comparing the two of you. You just sit and think without running around and investigating; I do the running for you, and you're the one with the insights, the brain work."

"Zelda," I said, thinking of how to respond, but in the end, I gave up the attempt. We had a terrific lunch, at a Chinese restaurant; it boasted a top chef from Hong Kong, and I really enjoyed the meal. All in all, I had a pleasant day.

And other days went by; I was busy with actual work, for actual clients who actually paid their bills (well, most of the time). What Zelda was up to, I had no idea. Then she called me. I asked her how things were going.

"Not bad. You know what, Frank, your clients lie to you."

"Don't I know it," I said. I thought about Bobby, for example. He wasn't exactly a client, although in his own mind he was. In any event, he had lied and lied. Everything my actual clients say to me is confidential. I would never reveal a confidence. And the law protects this privilege; it's a sacred pillar of the legal order. Then why do they lie to me? Bobby must know that I would never betray a confidence, but he still tells all these lies. "You're thinking of Bobby?"

"No, not just Bobby. But first, I have to tell you, I've been doing research on Langley Savage. What a guy. I'm going to put him in a novel. The evil doctor. I wish I knew what he looked like. I need a prototype, Frank—but it can't be too obvious, you know, not a hunchback or somebody who looks like Dracula; no, it has to be more subtle than that. But anyway, he practiced medicine in Akron, Ohio, for a while, had a woman there he was living with, he was suspected of killing a patient, and he was on the wrong end of a malpractice case, but he always somehow squirmed out of trouble. I guess he has, I mean had, a lot of charm: he lied and forged documents, he fooled the hospital here, and God only knows how much money he stole from Hortense Risley. Millions and millions. The hospital is suing, of course. Along with the estate. But Hortense's lawyers are also suing the hospital. Hortense paid the hospital a whole lot of money, and she paid through the nose for the suite she was in."

"Poor Ashley," I said. "That guy was her father."

"It's Ashley I wanted to talk to you about," she said. "My friend, Johnny, the guy at the reception desk—he's so sweet, Frank: he's eating out of my hand. I told him I was a private investigator, and it got him all excited. I also told him I'm a novelist, and I'm going to put him in my novel. Johnny loved the idea. Anyway, the police have been talking to him all along.

And they've been very interested in Ashley Savage. They showed him her picture, and he said she was there, at the hotel, he recognized her."

"So? She told me, she talked to somebody at the reception desk about leaving a note, or something like that. Did he remember her? Leaving a note?"

"No, he didn't remember that. I know, I know, that doesn't mean anything. It's a big place, and people come and go. But she's been lying to you, Frank. He didn't remember anything about a note, and nobody left a note. But he distinctly saw her at the elevator. He's positive. Where was she going?"

"Maybe down to the parking garage; you have to take an elevator. That doesn't prove anything, Zelda."

"I know that, but I think you should talk to her."

"Zelda, sure: but she's my client, Zelda. I can't go around accusing her of things, or acting as if I think she's lying. I just can't do that."

But I didn't have to. Ashley came to see me herself. It was a somewhat unexpected visit. She called and said she wanted to see me; I wasn't sure why. When she came, we talked about the trust for a while and the trusteeship. Now that Gideon had backed out, the sole trustee was a bank and we talked about how to deal with them. I said I would get in touch with them, and find out what they intended to do. Banks, or rather the people who work for them, shy away from trouble as if they were exposed to the Ebola virus. I had a feeling the bank would bow out as soon as they realized how much trouble the trust was in. And then what? I told her Gideon was mailing me a copy of the trust, and I would study it and give her advice.

But this wasn't why she had come. Yes, we had business to talk about but it was hardly urgent, and she clearly had something else on her mind. So did I. I tried to be subtle. I mentioned Bobby and his story and asked her, weren't you there, too, that day, at the hotel? And I said, "Ashley, I'm anxious to help you and Bobby. But you absolutely have to be honest with me. I have the feeling sometimes that I'm not getting the full story."

I told her she was seen taking the elevator. "Were you going to the parking garage?" She said, "Yes, of course," but she answered a bit too eagerly. I should have followed up, but I didn't know how, so I switched to the guy at the reception desk, and did she leave a note for her father? He didn't remember that she did.

"Why would he remember?" she said. "It's a huge hotel."

I said nothing. Sometimes, silence is a tremendous weapon. And it worked its magic here. She began to talk. "Frank," she said, "I ... well, I haven't been telling you the whole truth. I'm not saying I lied, but ... I kept something back. I really shouldn't do that. I know Zelda is investigating, and she seems to have sources, I don't know how and why. Anyway, I have to tell you something. I don't want you to hear this from somebody else. The police have been talking to me; you know, they're suspicious of everything and everybody. And the fact that I'm living with Bobby.... That got them going, I guess."

"It's not a crime," I said.

"Oh, I know that. But they have records, phone records: who my father talked to before he died. And that's what they were asking me about. Because I talked to him, a long conversation. I should have told you about it, but I didn't."

"You talked to your father, on the phone? I'm sorry you didn't tell me, Ashley. I don't want to sound, well, harsh. But you have to be more honest with me. You can trust me, really; you don't have to hold anything back. Can I ask you what you and your father talked about?"

"It was a painful conversation. Very painful. Actually, after it was over, I felt guilty. About the way I talked to him. He wanted to be friends with me, he said, you're my daughter, he talked about the trust, he said, but that's only money, he wants more than that, he wants a relationship. He said he knows he was a bad father. I was pretty blunt. I said to him, a bad father? No, it's not like you've been a bad father. You haven't been any kind of father at all. Period. Full stop. And, I said, as far as the money is concerned, I don't need it or want it. You can't buy me with money after all these years. You can't suddenly appear, out of nowhere, and try to buy your way into my life. I was as cold as ice, Frank. And now I'm sorry. Sorry because ... he's dead."

"What did he say, when you told him those things?"

"Well, he sounded ... crushed. He said, can't we work something out? Like what, I asked him. And he said, can we meet, can we get to know each other, I don't ask you to love me, or even to forgive me, but I'd just like a chance to see you, talk to you. And I said no. I said I don't want to. I don't want anything to do with you. Was that wrong, Frank?"

"I'm not going to judge you. You didn't owe him anything."

"But now he's dead. And I wish I could turn the clock back, run it in reverse. I was pretty awful on the phone to him. He didn't give up, Frank. He wrote me a letter. I got it after he was dead. He mailed it to me."

"You never mentioned the letter."

"I didn't think it was relevant. No, that's a lie. Fact is I was ashamed of the way I treated him. He abandoned me when I was a child, just walked out of my life. True. But now I'm grown up, I'm supposed to be an adult. He reached out and.... I hurt him. I paid him back in kind. I shouldn't have done that. I go over and over in my mind.... I think about ... different things. I don't even want to talk about it. And then, this letter...."

"What happened to the letter?"

"A week before, I would have torn it up; I wouldn't have read it. But now he was dead and.... This letter, now, it's the only thing I have from him. Besides the money. I mean, the only personal thing."

"Can I see the letter?"

She handed me a sheet of note paper—a single sheet. The letter was handwritten, on both sides, in a tiny, somewhat nervous, spindly hand. There was no envelope, and it seemed to be torn at the top. I took it, and read it carefully.

"To my daughter.

"Ashley—can I call you that? You're my only child. You won't believe this, but I somehow feel close to you, closer than I've felt to anyone in a long time, and even closer recently, even though we had never met. I saw you once. You don't know that. You didn't realize it. I watched you across a room, how you walked, what you looked like. It was a meeting of donors to the University, I knew you'd be there, and I talked a friend of mine into letting me go in his place. I pretended to be a donor, in other words. Story of my life: one lie after another. I went because of you. You made a presentation. I was so excited when I saw you. But never mind.

"Our phone conversation was a huge disappointment to me, but I can't say that I blame you. I wish things could be different. My life is a misery, Ashley. Things are closing in on me. Look: I know I've made a ton of mistakes. I played a desperate game. It was great while it lasted. I was like Bernie Madoff, like men who run Ponzi schemes. I had a money scheme—not exactly the same, but you get the point. After a while, the music stops. Yes, I got a lot of things from Hortense Risley. Money, property, jewelry: everything she could give me, she gave me. I felt I deserved the money, why not? I was good to her, she loved me, in a way—this was the life she wanted to live. Who else cared about her, an old woman, sick and lonely? I know what I did was against the law, but I'm not sorry. Not about that. But nothing lasts forever. Ponzi schemes collapse in the end. Now I'm trying to make amends. With you, for example. I wanted you to have some of that money. It won't make up for the years I neglected you. But it's the only thing I can do.

"I've made many enemies, my darling. I'm a guy who could list a dozen people who want me to be dead. All of the Risleys—all four grandchildren. That's a start to the list. Maybe Peter Christoff. The people I've robbed and cheated. The people I've harmed. You, perhaps. In some ways, I don't care. I don't deserve to be forgiven by anybody. I'm not asking for forgiveness. But I want you to know: in some crazy way, you've meant something to me. I don't blame you for anything. I wish I could be your friend, if not your father; but that's not going to happen. And I'm deeply sorry about that."

That was it. There was no signature. There was no date. I asked Ashley, "Is this the whole letter? I don't see a signature. Or a date. And where's the envelope?"

"It's the whole letter. He didn't sign it. He didn't need to, Frank, it's obvious who wrote it. And I threw the envelope away."

I asked her if I could scan and copy the letter. She seemed reluctant, and asked me why I wanted it. I had no good answer, but I said something about the importance of the letter, because it showed his state of mind. She asked why that was important, and I said, well, probably it isn't, but if there's an argument about the validity of the trust, it might be useful. I think she realized how flimsy this argument was, but she let me do what I wanted. I'm not sure myself why I wanted a copy of the letter, but it did turn out to be important. We talked business for a while, and then Ashley went back to her office.

I took the copy of the letter with me in my briefcase when I went home that night.

26

Celia trusts me on most things, and I think I deserve her trust, for the most part. Anyway, she has a kind of radar, a way of reading me in certain regards. She sensed that I was playing detective again, and she wasn't entirely wrong. Mostly, of course, it was Zelda who was the detective, but I'm not entirely guiltless. Celia has warned me, again and again, to mind my own business; I don't tell her an outright lie, but I do say that I won't neglect my cash customers. And I remind her that Ashley is a client, and Bobby—he's not exactly a client, but he and Ashley are together, which makes his affairs in some ways my concern. He would be, of course, an extremely valuable client, at least potentially. He stands to inherit a lot of money from his grandmother's estate. Eventually, at any rate.

Was I doing detective work? I don't think so. Not really. Whatever it is that detectives do, I wasn't doing it. But I was mixing in, in ways that were not really relevant to my work as a lawyer for my clients. Zelda was my cover. I let Zelda do all the leg work. That preserved for me a certain amount of deniability.

And Zelda, of course, was both eager and active. I kept her informed of everything I was doing. I told her about my session with Cassandra, and what I thought it meant.

"She's definitely a suspect," Zelda said. "But I have a better one. Hildegarde Risley. She was living with Langley, you knew that, didn't you. Then they had some sort of argument, and she left the hotel. At any rate, she wasn't there when they found the body. Still, she made a reservation in the breakfast place; and she had breakfast there with Cassandra, and with Gideon Grambling, until he got up and left. I did some snooping around the breakfast place. It's very pretty, Frank, you should eat there some time. It has a nice view out the garden. I hope I don't have to go there too much, to investigate: I'd absolutely gain too much weight. They have a great buffet, Frank. There's a man there who makes wonderful omelets. He's good at it. Has a beautiful tattoo on his neck; I'm going to use that in my latest book. His name is Oswald. You don't meet many Oswalds these days."

"I don't know any Oswalds at all. Am I missing something?"

"Who knows? Names have meaning. My whole life has been different because I'm a Zelda. And you're a Frank; I think it has a real influence, it stamps you as a Frank instead of something else, say a Joshua or a Justin. You're definitely a Frank."

I wasn't sure my life had been molded by my Frank-ness. In English, Frank means honest, candid. Is that me? I guess so. Who knows what Frank might mean, say, in Chinese, if they have a Frank. I never heard a Chinese name that sounds the least bit like Frank, but my experience is limited.

"Anyway," Zelda said, "What do you think of Hildegarde as a suspect?"

"OK, she's Bobby's ex-wife, but why would she kill Langley Savage?"

"A crime of passion? They were lovers, and they had a quarrel. It's a genuine motive. She's a very angry woman: look how she's treating poor Bobby. I'm going to confront her, Frank. What have I got to lose?"

"A lot," I said. "Credibility. You can't go around accusing people of murder, without a shred of evidence."

"I'll be very discreet," she said.

27

But apparently Zelda wasn't discreet. She certainly did have a talk with Hildegarde. In any event, something inspired the woman to call me and say she had to see me, and when would I be available and so on. There had been, over the last weeks, a regular procession of people involved in the Langley Savage affair, dropping in on me for one reason or another. I didn't need to stir from my office. I was indeed growing into the role of Nero Wolfe, the way Zelda described it. All I needed was a cook, and a hothouse full of exotic orchids.

I'm fond of orchids. They're really beautiful. I was startled to find out that their name—orchid—comes from the Greek word for testicles. Makes you wonder about the ancient Greeks. They invented democracy, in a way, and they had great philosophers. But if they thought an orchid looks like a man's *cojones*, then I think there was something seriously wrong with their mental processes.

I've seen a Greek play or two. To be honest they bored me. In college, I had to read something by Aristotle. I remember almost nothing about it. But I wonder: did orchids remind Aristotle of his testicles?

As I said, I had a whole procession of visitors, people involved in the Langley Savage mess. The next one in the series was in fact not Hildegarde, but Cassandra. She dropped in totally unannounced. She was the kind of woman who simply assumed that I would push aside everything I was doing in order to accommodate her.

"Is that woman, Zelda, working for you?" she asked. "She

looks like something out of Grimm's fairy tales, some sort of a witch. She told me she's going to put me into her novel. Like hell you are, I said, I'll sue you if you do. She said oh, you'll like it, it takes place in a hotel, and you're going to be naked in the lobby, doing a performance thing. She must be stark raving mad."

"I like Zelda," I said meekly. "She's a good soul; and she's harmless."

"I'm not," she said. "Look: I had a conversation with that woman.... And, well, I came here to eat crow. That's not something I normally do. But in this case.... Anyway, I told you a pack of lies. Now I want to tell you the truth. Not that I give a rat's ass about you and your investigation; and as far as Langley Savage is concerned, the world is better off without him. But my brother Bobby: that's another story. He's my little brother. And he's helpless and naïve. And, you're right: I got him in a mess of trouble."

"It was that phone call," I said. "Why on earth did you call him? Why did you tell him he had to go see Langley Savage? And immediately?"

"It was that bitch Hildegarde. She told me a cock-and-bull story. Langley was screwing her, as you know, I guess he couldn't do any better: he wasn't as young as he used to be. These middle-aged guys get desperate, they think they're losing their juices, and guess what, they are. She said to me, Langley is cracking up; I broke up with him because I thought he might become violent. Then she gave me a graphic description of her sex life with Langley Savage and everything else, as if I gave a damn, and she said, he's vulnerable, now's the time, call Bobby, tell him to go see Langley, it's life and death, and Bobby will get the money, and Langley knows something that could help him. She said she needed money badly, and if Bobby could help her, she'd be more willing to share custody, but he had to go see Langley Savage: that was an absolute must.

"Well, it sounded awfully fishy to me, and I didn't really get the point: why she would want to help Bobby out? They hated each other, and she was absolutely vicious about him most of the time; why she ever married him, it makes me wonder. Well, I think Bobby loved her, at first anyway; he's so gullible, but she was just after him for money, which he didn't really have, so I was suspicious. But to tell the truth, she was putting on a terrific act. I said, why are you doing this, and she told me another cock-and-bull story, how she was sorry she had been so awful to Bobby, and she was trying to make amends. I don't believe people change: once they're rotten, they stay rotten; but she was so insistent, and in the end I agreed, and I called Bobby. And now I'm sorry. You know what? I think she killed Langley, and tried to frame Bobby. I really do. She told those stories, that Langley insisted on seeing Bobby in person, because he needed him to sign some papers. Only later did I realize it was all a bunch of lies. But then I thought, I can't say anything, because then they'll know Bobby was in the room, and they'll arrest him, and charge him with murder; and Bobby won't last a week in jail, they'll rape him and stick knives in him. But after I talked to Zelda, I realized, everybody knows he was there, he's blabbing to everybody under the sun about this and that. Anyway, if you're actually in charge of the investigation...."

"Honest to God, Cassandra, I'm not in charge of anything."

"Well, should I go to the police? Tell them what I know about that bitch, Hildegarde? Maybe they'll arrest her. I don't care if *she* gets raped in jail, the guards can rape her from here to Tuesday, she deserves it."

"You really think Hildegarde killed him?"

"I do. Look: She maybe had a key to the room, she was staying with him, wasn't she? She went up there, opened the door, and killed him. They had this huge fight. She was just plain mad. Then she thought, I'll make Bobby the fall guy. He'll come up, knock on the door, he won't get in. She couldn't know he *could* get in, but anyway he *did* get in, and he saw the body: she was hiding in a closet or something. Bobby said he thought somebody was in the room. It had to be Hildegarde. She killed Langley, and tried to frame Bobby: that's what she did. She dragged the body to the bed, and did that crap with the dolls."

"And the gun?"

"Threw it in the Bay, I suppose. OK, Mr. Lawyer, tell me

what to do? The police won't listen to me, I suppose. Maybe I should get undressed and walk into the station. That'll get their attention. I'd rather tell you, though: you can go to the police, I'm sure you have connections."

"Cassandra: I don't have any connections. None."

"Should I tell Zelda, then? She talks as if she has the whole police department and the detectives eating out of her hand. I know it's bullshit, but maybe there a kernel of truth to it."

I had no idea whether Zelda in fact did have some sort of way to get word to the police. I suppose it was possible. I thought about Cassandra's idea. Maybe in the end it was the right thing to do. Let Zelda handle it. I said so to Cassandra. When she left, I chewed these things over in my mind. I had to admit, Hildegarde was a likely candidate. There were gaps in the story, but at least it made sense on the whole.

28

The affair was still deeply puzzling. Even more so if Cassandra was right: if Hildegarde had killed Langley Savage herself. Her behavior seemed peculiar—at least her behavior now. Why was she protecting Bobby? What could she possibly gain by this? After all, she hated him.

Everybody seemed to want me to sink deeper and deeper into this hideous quagmire. They even seemed to think I had some sort of pipeline to police headquarters. Far from it. In my circle of friends and acquaintances, I have doctors and lawyers; I have dentists and accountants. I even have a carpenter and a plumber or two. But I don't know a single policeman. And whenever I see a patrol car on the road, I slow down, drive super-carefully, and break out in a sweat.

I was so engrossed in these thoughts that I totally forgot a domestic duty. I was supposed to stop by Draeger's, an extremely upscale food store, and bring home a chocolate cake with vanilla frosting which Celia had ordered. She needed to bring it to her school the next day. The occasion was a going-away party. Helena Bowman, who taught English literature, was leaving the school. No doubt she was a victim of burn-out. For twenty years, she had tried to teach Shakespeare to sullen adolescents, most of whom could not or would not pay attention to anything that was not on a screen, whether a large screen, or a small screen, or a middle-sized screen.

I expected a stern reprimand: I didn't get it. Celia was obviously in a forgiving mood. She said she'd pick up the cake in the morning, on her way to work. But Celia's annoyance was displaced onto something else. "Who is this Zelda person, Frank? She called just before you came. I mean, I've met her of course, but what on earth is she calling you about?"

"Oh, she's a friend, darling. Just a friend."

"A friend, Frank? She said she was working for you."

"Well, not exactly," I said.

"Frank, what's going on? She sounded downright conspiratorial, and said she was making progress. What sort of progress, Frank? What on earth are you up to?"

And then I had to admit that Zelda had gotten involved in the Langley Savage matter, and was doing "investigative work" on a purely voluntary basis, and that she had the bad habit of passing herself off as my assistant.

Celia put down her knitting needles. "Frank, really. You're at it again. Despite everything I told you. You're positively incorrigible. And you keep things from me. I want to know everything you're up to. And no tricks, no little white lies. I want to know the truth."

When all is said and done, I'm a good and a loyal husband. I hate the little deceptions that once in a while creep into my marriage. Deceptions like, for instance, what I actually ate for lunch, unhealthy things, deserts, fried food, instead of what Celia thought I ought to eat for lunch. And she loathed the idea of the Great Detective. I capitulated totally and told her everything, from the beginning to the end. Much of it, of course, she already knew. I ended up with Ashley's visit and the letter from her father.

"A letter from her father? Can I see it, Frank? Do you have it?"

I went to my desk, and brought out the copy. She read it carefully.

"You see, Celia," I said. "It's important, that letter. It says he had enemies. He knew he was in danger. He even lists the people who might want to kill him. And somebody did kill him."

Celia looked concerned. She picked up her knitting, and started working on it. I asked her what she was doing. "It's a sweater, for Martha's baby." She was silent for a bit. Then she turned to me, put down the knitting again, and said: "Frank, you might be a good lawyer; I'm sure you are. But when it comes to psychology, when it comes to *people,* in other words, you're hopeless. What did you get out of that letter?"

"I told you. He was upset, for one thing; he was sorry he hadn't gotten to know his daughter. And he was afraid, he thought he was in danger...."

"Afraid? In danger? That's what I mean about you, Frank. You missed the point entirely. This is practically a suicide note. The man was planning to kill himself."

"Oh, no darling, you must be wrong. He didn't kill himself. Somebody killed him. We know that."

"Do we, Frank? You say somebody killed him. But who? You don't know. Maybe it's because nobody killed him. He killed himself."

"But where's the gun? I mean, I see your point, Celia; but it can't be right. A dead person can't get up and dispose of a gun. And there was no gun there. It was gone."

"I don't know anything about guns or that sort of thing. I'm only telling you what that letter says. He knew he was in terrible trouble. Everything was closing in on him. I think he decided he had to end it all. And why not? He had nothing going for him. He was going to lose his medical license, he was going to lose all his money, he had no family, no friends, and he was probably going to jail. Life wasn't worth living any more. "

"I see your point, darling. I really do. But it doesn't make sense. It just doesn't compute."

"Listen, Frank. If your Bobby is telling the truth, Savage was dead, lying on the floor in a pool of blood. I tell you, he killed himself. Then somebody came in and moved the body around, and did things like that. Maybe that's what happened."

"But who would do that? And why? I just can't believe it."

"Who did it, you ask? Frank, I wouldn't know. You're the one who's knows all these people. I don't. Ask this Zelda woman. Maybe she knows."

She picked up her knitting needles again, and went back to work. And I sat there, in the living room, thinking. I had to digest what Celia said. Could it be true? Could she have hit on the truth?

I heard the click of the knitting needles. I sat there, for an hour or more, thinking and thinking, going over everything in my mind, the chronology, the people involved, everything. I ended up, mentally, with Zelda's idea about Hildegarde, her theory about Hildegarde. I interrupted Celia, and we talked over the Hildegarde theory. It made sense, I said, "But you think he committed suicide. That doesn't fit with the Hildegarde theory."

She put down her knitting. "Oh, but it does, Frank. In a way. He committed suicide, and Hildegarde came back to the room—you said she maybe had a key; anyway, she found him dead, lying on the floor. Then she got the bright idea of making it look like murder, and pinning it on Bobby. She got Cassandra to call him. She went back to the room, moved the body, arranged it on the bed with the dolls, took the note and the gun away. That way nobody could think he killed himself. Then Bobby came barging in, so she hid in a closet. He ran out of there, and when he was gone, she ran away herself. Nothing could be simpler. And there you have it, Frank."

I had to admit it sounded plausible. Everything fit: Bobby seeing the body on the floor, for example. The phone call.

"But wasn't she running a risk?" I asked.

"Of what? Of being accused of murder? Not much risk, Frank. The police would either stick it to Bobby, or do nothing—waste their time looking for a killer, and not finding one, because there wasn't any killer in the first place...."

I still had my doubts. "If that's what happened, Celia, OK, but since she wanted to frame Bobby, why would she come and tell me a bunch of lies about seeing Bobby coming and going downstairs and never going up to the room? Maybe she didn't know about Bobby on the stairwell. But she was in the room, she *saw* him; she knew he was there. Why was she suddenly protecting him? That doesn't make sense."

"Well, she changed her mind. She realized she'd made a big mistake, she had done something terrible, and she had to save Bobby if she could."

"But why would she do that? She hated him enough to want to frame him for murder."

"I don't know, Frank. And I'm tired now; I'm going to bed. You figure it out."

I thought and thought. I turned everything over in my mind. I felt a little sheepish: I'm supposed to be the Great Detective, but it was Celia who hit on a story that finally made sense. Made sense except for one detail: why Hildegarde changed her mind. But then—and it sort of redeemed me—the answer came to me in a flash. Langley Savage's will. It was right there, in an envelope. Maybe she read it. Not then, but later. She took the envelope with her. That will, for all she knew, disposed of a giant pile of money. And Langley Savage, strangely enough, left a great deal of that money to Bobby Risley.

Why would he do that? Guilt. He was overwhelmed with guilt. He was killing himself because of guilt. And he wanted to make things up—to Ashley, his daughter, and to the Risleys. But he couldn't stand the Risleys, except for Bobby. Sweet, harmless Bobby.

And Hildegarde was a mother. A loving mother. When she saw the will, she realized something: if Bobby was convicted of murder, he wouldn't get a penny from Langley Savage's estate, and that would mean her little boy would be left totally penniless. By framing Bobby, she was running the risk of stealing her little boy's inheritance.

Maybe she also thought Bobby would be cut out of Hortense Risley's estate. In fact, he wouldn't be: he didn't kill her, and he was one of the heirs, even if he was a murderer. I know that, it's the law; but maybe Hildegarde didn't know it. Maybe she thought murderers don't inherit from anybody. Or maybe she thought lawyer fees would eat up all his money. You wouldn't believe what people think about lawyers: they think we're bloodsuckers, parasites. They have fantasies about how much money lawyers take from estates. Maybe this problem preyed on her mind and she decided, suddenly, to switch gears; she decided to try to protect Bobby, for the sake of her son. She did it pretty badly; but at least she tried.

But if she did this, that is, if she arranged everything to look like murder; and if she regrets this now and might want to undo it, why not go to the police?

The minute I asked myself this question, I knew the answer. Go to the police? Admit she tried to frame somebody, and that she moved the body, destroyed evidence, and messed around with a crime scene? No, this would mean confessing to a serious crime. She might lose everything: her freedom, and custody of little Bobby, too. Hildegarde had baited a trap, and fell into it herself.

What was to be done? I didn't know for sure. It was by now late at night, but Zelda was, as I knew, a night owl; she stayed up late, and slept in the next morning. I picked up the phone and called her. I told her what Celia had said—and what I knew and what I thought I knew.

29

Zelda came through. I'm not sure exactly how she did it. But she did have contacts in the police force—maybe she knew a detective or two. Maybe she promised to put them in her novel. Whatever she did, it was successful. She convinced the right people. Hildegarde was taken in for questioning, and she broke down completely. In between hysterical sobs, she admitted everything.

She and Langley had had a terrible fight. He had threatened to kill himself, but she didn't take it seriously. After breakfast, she went back up to the room, to pick up some of her belongings, and she found him dead. She put a Do Not Disturb sign on the door, called Cassandra, and got her to call Bobby and make him come to the hotel. She waited for Bobby; she took the sign down; she listened for his knock on the door. Instead he burst in, she hid in the closet, and when he left, she dragged the body to the bed, wiped up the blood on the floor, took the suicide note and the gun, arranged the body with the dolls; and slipped out of the room. Then, from a public phone, she called the front desk and reported a body in the room. She had also taken the envelope with a copy of Langley Savage's will. But she didn't read it until later. So it was only later that she realized her mistake. Bobby stood to gain a great deal of money from Langley Savage's estate. By then it was too late to undo what she did. But she tried. She tried to give him an alibi. Of course, it didn't work.

And what about the holograph—Hortense's holograph—the one that Langley Savage used as bait, as a way to induce the grandkids to come to some agreement? It never showed up. I think it never existed. I think this was just one more Langley Savage scheme. Either way, the scheme was an utter failure.

* * *

So: as far as everyone was concerned, the case was solved. Of course, that's not the end of the story. The two estates were, of course, a horrendous tangle: Hortense's estate, and Langley Savage's. Hortense had left a great deal of money behind. Of course, a very large sum had passed into the greedy hands of Langley Savage, Peter Christoff, Nurse Barbash, not to mention lavish gifts to the hospital. But many millions were left: stocks and bonds, real estate, works of art.

There were lawsuits galore, enough to make lawyers rich; Wentworth Fain, of course, was already rich. In the end, as is usually the case, a settlement was reached. Christopher held out for a while, insisting on unconditional surrender. But in the end, he realized that the war could last for years and cost a fortune. Wentworth Fain and his firm were tough bargainers, but they well knew the value of compromise. In the end, everyone concerned, including me, recognized that fact. It was the best way, indeed the only way, to end the war.

I don't need to give you the precise details. Ashley kept her trust. Langley Savage's estate was, however, stripped of the rest of its assets, which went back into Hortense's estate. Peter Christoff and Nurse Barbash escaped extradition; the estate recovered some of their ill-gotten gains, but apparently enough remained for them to live nicely in Brazil. The hospital kept its money and a share of Hortense's estate. Enough was left over to make all four grandchildren quite comfortably rich. The settlement was good news for Phil Peabody; he earned a generous fee. (The bad news was: he started drinking again.) Oh yes, I too profited, and rather handsomely.

And my prospects were also quite good. I was getting Bobby as a client. He came to see me the day the settlement was reached. I had phoned Ashley with the news. She seemed strangely distant, but I ignored her manner; I was too happy about the outcome. Anyway, there was Bobby, in person. I had never seen him look so happy. He had a broad grin on his face. He was crying, of course; but these were tears of joy. He hugged me, and thanked me again and again.

"I'm so happy," he said. "I'm so grateful to you, Frank. You and Zelda. She was great. And Hildegarde, she's willing to share custody, and forget all the lies. I've got a great lawyer, Jenny Forest, she's helping me with the custody thing. And ... Frank, things are so wonderful for Ashley and me, it's like a honeymoon every day, I swear."

"That's terrific, Bobby."

"I said, honey, I want to get married. I want us to drive to Las Vegas, and get married in one of those chapels, or maybe go to Hawaii, I don't care. I went to a wedding once, it was so beautiful, because of the butterflies...."

"Butterflies?"

"It was by the ocean in Mendecino. It was so beautiful. The water and everything. And the sun was going down, but they had all these lights, colored lights. And every guest got a little box, with a blue ribbon, and inside the box was a butterfly, all blue and white, and the idea was, we would all let them go, so there's be a cloud of beautiful butterflies, well, actually, the one in my own box was dead, and it just fell to the ground, and I was so embarrassed, but I loved the idea. I want something sentimental, Ashley all dressed in white, and me in a tuxedo, and I want rings and bridesmaids. Ashley, she doesn't want it, she's so sensible, she says that's old fashioned, she loves me, but she doesn't want to get married, marriage is so yesterday, she says, and of course I'll do what she wants. But I said, Ashley, I want to say to people, this is my wife, not just partner or something, as if we were running a store; and I want her to have all the money, every last penny. I want to be like a monk, no money, I'll take a vow like the monks do, I'll sign it over, it'll all be hers; Frank, I love her so much."

I told him he could love Ashley as much as he wanted, without giving all his money away. That certainly wasn't necessary, and she probably wouldn't agree to any such thing in the first place. I thought marriage was a good idea. After all, I'm married, and if he has a wedding, he should please be sure to invite me—but if Ashley says no, that's all right too. Queen Victoria has been dead a long time. Today, people live together without getting married, it's almost normal—and they can be happy either way.

What I didn't say, but which was very much on my mind, was that Bobby and Ashley were going to have all that lovely money; they would be terrific clients for me. I could handle their estate plans, I could draft wills and trusts for them, I could even give them tax advice. Of course, at that particular moment I didn't press that point.

* * *

So that was that. Case ended. But ... you know, even though it tied together so neatly, I had a funny feeling about the case. Something didn't smell right to me. I think I had guessed correctly why Langley Savage tried to leave money to Bobby. Of course, he couldn't know that Bobby and his daughter would get together; that hadn't happened yet. But the man was plagued with guilt. Guilt about everything, including the Risley family. He had met all four, and Bobby was the only one he liked. Not a big surprise. And Langley had had an affair with Hildegarde Risley: Was that another motive? Did he leave money to Bobby to spite her? Or to benefit her? Either one was possible.

But there was something else. I couldn't quite put my finger on what that was. I decided to ignore this small and shadowy doubt. Zelda, who had lunch with me, and begged me for "another case" (I had none to give her, thank God), was completely satisfied. Langley Savage had come to the end of his rope; he could see nothing ahead but gloom and trouble and disgrace; and he took the only way out he could see. Hildegarde came along and mucked things up, but that too was over. The state, in the end, decided not to prosecute Hildegarde, and she could go on with her life. She and Bobby could share Bobby, Jr. That had been all worked out, I guess.

Zelda and Johnny had broken up. "Well, Frank, actually, there was nothing to break up. We never went very far. I kept hinting and hinting. I think maybe he's gay."

"You'll find somebody else," I said.

"I'm going online," she said. "There are all these sites. You can look for people in all sorts of categories. A friend of mine went on this particular site—it's for Jewish people—and she found the loveliest man."

"You're not Jewish, Zelda."

"Doesn't matter, does it? They don't give you a test. There are sites for Christian singles, I'm Christian, and I'm single, but the men on that site, they probably have all kinds of hangups about sex, and they're looking for somebody religious. No thank you."

"Good luck, Zelda," I said.

"I'll find someone," she said. "And I'll meet people. I can put them in my novels."

She promised to keep in touch. I think she was hoping I would give her "another case," as she put it. For now, the story seemed to have ended.

But it hadn't. Not quite.

30

As I said, I had high hopes of representing Bobby and Ashley, especially now that Bobby was so rich. I sent him a letter, suggesting that we get together to talk about trusts and other financial arrangements: how to handle the money, and whether he should set up a trust for Ashley. I pointed out that California was a community property state, but that applied to married people. Maybe they needed some kind of contract, some sort of agreement, since they didn't plan to get married, at least for now; I said I'd be happy to help out.

Strangely enough, he never replied. I tried again: nothing. I heard later, through the lawyer grapevine, that he and Ashley had hired another lawyer, a man named Simon Bendix, one of Wentworth Fain's partners. I was disappointed, a bit hurt, and puzzled, too. Why had they dropped me? Had I done something wrong? Or something to offend them? Or did they just think I was too small potatoes, too suburban?

Months went by, and I more or less forgot the whole affair. I had other clients to worry about. But then one day, I bumped into Ashley. She and Bobby, I had heard, had bought themselves a house in Atherton—one of the wealthiest suburbs, and not far from San Mateo. I saw her shopping in Whole Foods in Palo Alto. Celia had sent me there for olive oil, warning me not to get the kind with garlic (which I had once done, with unfortunate consequences). I walked past the aisles with things like bee pollen and various other sorts of new-age concoctions, to the part of the store where they sold actual food (strictly organic, of course). There was Ashley, carefully examining the tomatoes, picking them up one by one and examining them. She was quite obviously pregnant. I was sure she had seen me but was avoiding me, pretending to be so deeply engrossed in the tomato issue that she took no notice of anything else on the planet. But I was not about to let her get away with this. I said hello, and she blushed. She seemed embarrassed—something I never associated with Ashley.

I decided to be up front with her. I asked her, what the problem was. She said what problem. I said, you and Bobby dropped me, you got yourself another lawyer. Of course, you have a perfect right to do that. But, still, was it something I did that dissatisfied you? Or did you feel you needed a big San Francisco firm? I said I really wanted to know.

She said, "Frank, it's water under the bridge."

"And I have another question, Ashley, since you won't answer that one. Why did you bring me your father's letter? Why did you want me to see it?"

"Well, you were our lawyer. I guess that's why."

"It wasn't really relevant, Ashley. You were trying to tell me something. But you didn't come out with it. And I've been wondering ever since."

She said: "Frank, really, this is not the time or the place. I have to get home, and I've got shopping to do. And later I've got an appointment with my obstetrician. I'm due in two months, Frank; it's a little girl, by the way."

She began fingering the tomatoes again; her face was turned away. Then she moved down the aisle, picked up a rutabaga and put it in her cart. Clearly, she didn't want to talk any more. But I said, "Ashley, I know I shouldn't say this, but really, I'm disappointed. You and Bobby.... I'd really like to know what went wrong. Can we talk some time?"

I could see the reluctance written all over her face. But she decided, I suppose, to humor me.

"OK, Frank, sure. Only not now."

"Can you come to my office? Or have lunch with me? Are you still working at Stanford?"

"I'm not working right now. I took a leave. The pregnancy.... It was pretty rough for a while, I had nausea, bleeding, I needed bedrest for some weeks. That's why I took a leave. Things are better now, by the way. Right now I feel fine, and the baby seems fine too."

"Lunch tomorrow, then?"

She hesitated. I could almost see the wheels turning in her brain. Of course, she could just say no. And without giving any reason. But maybe she felt she owed me at least the courtesy of a conversation.

We met at an Italian restaurant at noon. She ordered a Caesar salad. I ordered lasagna. I asked her about Bobby, how he was doing, and we made small talk. She said they were so happy together, and I believed her, but there was something on her mind. She was clearly ill at ease.

What the hell. I had nothing to lose. "Ashley," I said, "maybe I'm crazy, but something about that business just doesn't compute."

"What business?"

"You know. Your father's death."

"What about it? It's all over and done with. Bobby and I, we're starting a new life. Why are you asking these questions?"

"Well, it's the letter your father wrote," I said. "I just can't understand it. He wrote you that letter, my wife took one look at it, she said, it's a suicide note, no, not a note, but it's a letter explaining why he's going to kill himself, and then he does. He kills himself. Shoots himself. And then Hildegarde comes in and makes it look like murder. But there's no suicide note, there's only that letter, and it doesn't really qualify. I don't know when you got that letter. Did you get it after he died? The date was missing. Did you tear it off the letter? Why? And you're my client; but you lied to me, you were there that morning, you talked to him, and you told me you didn't. And I don't know why. I guess I shouldn't ask, but I'm asking anyway."

She was quiet for a while. She looked around, as if she wanted to get up and run away. Which she probably did want to do. I said: "Maybe I'm just getting worked up over nothing. I mean, the suicide note. I guess Hildegarde took it, just picked it up and took it, when she was arranging the scene."

She looked up at me. "You're right, Frank. He ... did have a suicide note. It was right there, beside him, next to the body. But Hildegarde took it. You're absolutely right."

I stared at her, with my mouth open, and a forkful of lasagna in midair. She looked at me, and then suddenly turned beet red. "I mean...." she started to say; and then she closed her mouth, and looked down at her plate. She realized what she had said. And what it meant.

"There was a note? You *saw* it, Ashley? Where did you see it? Did Hildegarde tell you? No, she wouldn't. Did Bobby see it? But no, he ran out of there as quick as he could. But you said you saw it, you actually saw it. Ashley, it's none of my business. But I'd like you to tell me ... what happened? What are you telling me? He did commit suicide, didn't he? I mean, that's what happened, isn't it? He killed himself, no? But you were there? You were in the room?"

You're not supposed to ask clients questions like this. Criminal lawyers never ask their clients: Did you actually do it? But I was not her lawyer any more, and this was not a criminal case, as far as I knew. And I was overwhelmed with curiosity. What was Ashley hiding?

She could have kept silent. But suddenly, I guess, the urge came over her—the urge to talk, to divulge, to tell me, or at least tell *someone*, the truth about what happened that day. She was crying, now, overcome with emotion.

"Ashley.... I don't mean to upset you...."

She took a tissue out of her purse and wiped her eyes. "Frank," she said, "you've been good to me. Really good. I don't want to lie any more. I've been hiding something important. And also, I know we treated you badly. We dropped you. We didn't use you as a lawyer. It was because of me. I felt ... guilty and embarrassed. Can I tell you what happened in strict confidence?"

"Yes, absolutely."

"My father ... everybody believes he killed himself. Shot himself. Then Hildegarde made it look like murder. That's the story. He committed suicide. But is it true?"

"It isn't?"

"Well, yes and no."

"Yes and no? What does that mean, Ashley?"

"Look: I lied when I said I never talked to him. I lied about the phone call. And I lied about seeing him. I got the letter *before* he died. I tore up the envelope, and I tore off the part with the date. I told you I got it after he died. But that was a lie. I got the letter the day before, and I knew what it meant. So I went to see him. The day he died. I was in the room. Why did I go? I don't even know. I felt I had to. He wanted me to. It was because of the letter. Anyway, I went. I was there. He was there too, of course, this stranger, this man who was my father, this man who had in many ways ruined my life. Damaged me. And there he was. A wreck. A pathetic wreck. He was a loser now. Everything was in ruins. He started talking, sentimental stuff, about me, his daughter, and how he had made a mess of everything, and now it was time to pay the bill. He said he wanted to die, he had written me that letter, and he also wrote out a suicide note, he had pills, he had a gun, but he just couldn't bring himself to do it. He wanted to do it the night before, but he just couldn't. He was shaking like a leaf. He said he was a coward…. And he begged me to do it. Kill him. I said, you're crazy. He handed me the gun, he said, I don't deserve to live, I want you to pull the trigger…. This is what I deserve, it's the only thing I'll ever ask of you, but you're my daughter, and I am asking you to do it…. He said, I want this, I want to die, I'm trembling all over, I won't be able to do this myself, but you can, you're strong, do it, do it for your father, it's the only way. He said, nobody will know it's you, they'll read the note, it's right here, on the desk, they'll know I killed myself…. I said no, no, this is insane, I can't do it; the gun was in my hand, and he was begging and begging, and, Frank, don't ask me what came over me, maybe a lifetime of hatred and resentment…. All of sudden, somehow, something snapped, and I pulled the trigger. And he was dead. He fell to the floor. There was blood and … other stuff, I couldn't stand it. Immediately I thought, what have I done, I've killed him, and I was horrified, sick to my stomach, I wanted to vomit…. I wiped off the gun, I had enough sense to do that, and I wrapped it in a handkerchief, and then I took off the handkerchief, and put the gun in his hand, and I got out of there somehow, fast, nobody saw me, and I went home and was sick, sick, sick. But I wasn't worried about getting arrested. Everybody will think it's suicide, I thought. There's a note and all that. How was I to know about Hildegarde, that she would come by, would come in the room, she'd see he was dead, and she'd try to arrange it so that it looked like murder. Or that she'd talk Cassandra into calling Bobby and getting him to come. She wanted him to be accused of killing my father. Oh, it was a stupid idea, and it didn't work.... But I couldn't know she would do those awful things."

I stared at her in amazement. Then she said: "Really, it *was* suicide, wasn't it, Frank? He killed himself, he really did. Only.... It wasn't his finger on the trigger; but that hardly matters, does it?"

I didn't have the heart to tell her, yes, it matters. Legally speaking, she was a murderer. Asking to die doesn't make any difference in the law: if you kill somebody, it's murder. True, there are these mercy killing cases, you know, an old person, say an old lady, dying of cancer in excruciating pain, she begs her husband, do it, do it out of love, and he does it. Technically, he's a murderer. But juries don't want to convict. That wasn't exactly this case. This was ... different. But who could predict how a jury would react?

But there was never going to be a jury. The case, after all, was closed.

And I was certainly not about to open it. If the word got out, there would be all sorts of consequences. She would lose her inheritance from her father. She might be ostracized. She might even face trial. But nobody had to know.

I dodged the question she asked, which she must have noticed. I couldn't help wondering though, whether Bobby knew; and I asked her that.

She began to sob. She dropped her protective skin, her curtain of iron dignity and solitude. "He doesn't know. I can't really tell him. Do you think I have to? Is that what you're saying?"

I shook my head, no. "Maybe some day. Maybe years from

now. It won't matter then. You two have a life together now, a relationship. You've got to work on it. Relationships are hard. And there's a baby on the way."

Maybe pregnancy was making her sentimental; maybe the life inside of her was melting the ice. Or maybe it was Bobby's influence. She came over to me, hugged me and held me tight for what seemed like ages. Then she let go, and said: "Thank you, Frank. I needed to talk. Thank you for listening."

"It's OK, Ashley," I said.

She hugged me again, on her way out. When I got back to the office, I sat at my desk for a while, thinking. A former client had just confessed to murder. Well, sort-of murder. But, legally, murder.

It was one of the strangest episodes in my career. And, as it turned out, one of the most lucrative. A few days later, Bobby called me on the phone. He sounded embarrassed. He told me, he and Ashley, they were so happy together, he would always love her, but they weren't actually married, she didn't like the idea of marriage, and he could see her point, and meanwhile, they were having a baby, it was going to be a little girl, a sister for little Bobby.

They were thinking about the future, he said: she had her trust fund, you know, the money from her father, and Bobby was already getting money from the Risley estate, and they had had this lawyer, Wentworth Fain's partner, and, well, Bobby had been satisfied with him, and he thought Ashley was too, but then, just the other day, Ashley said to him, she had no faith in this guy, maybe he knew a lot of law, but as a human being, he fell short of what was needed. So Ashley said, why don't we go back to Frank, we know him and we trust him, and I guess she had bumped into you, and that's what brought all this up.

"And of course," he said, "whatever Ashley wants, I mean, don't get me wrong, Frank, you know I love you, and Ashley loves you too, so, we'd like you to represent us, I don't know why we weren't using you all along. I just do what Ashley says, what I mean is, I'm asking, we need advice, estate planning, that's your thing, so, well, if you're not too busy...."

Too busy? Of course not. Two rich clients? And soon I had a third one. Juno Risley. Bobby and Ashley must have talked to her. Would I help her set up her foundation, the one she told me about, money to teach algebra or whatever to little African children. Of course I would. I would be glad to. So it all had a happy ending for me. And when I told Celia the news, about these events, these clients and the potential business they would bring, she put down her knitting, and said: "Now, at last, Frank, can we please remodel the kitchen?"

"It's as good as done," I said.

About the author

LAWRENCE FRIEDMAN is a professor of law at Stanford University. He teaches courses in American legal history and law and society. He is the author of *A History of American Law*, *Crime and Punishment in American History*, *The Human Rights Culture*, and *Total Justice*, among other works. Professor Friedman has also published *The Big Trial: Law as Public Spectacle* and, most recently, *Impact: How Law Affects Behavior*. His book *Dead Hands: A Social History of Wills, Trusts, and Inheritances* deals with a subject that is the backbone of Frank May's (fictional) practice.

Visit us at *www.qpbooks.com*.